UNWANTED FAMILY

Book Four of
The Unwanted Series

Books by Sandra Denbo and Tamarine Vilar:

The Unwanted Series:

Unwanted Discovery – Book One
Unwanted House Guest – Book Two
Unwanted Agenda – Book Three
Unwanted Family – Book Four

UNWANTED
FAMILY

Book Four of
The Unwanted Series

by

Sandra Denbo
& Tamarine Vilar

Book Lamp and Chair, LLC
Portland, Oregon

Scan this QR code
to learn more about
this series or visit our website at:
www.theunwantedseries.net

Cover art by Diane Avenoso

Editing by Adele Brinkley

Photography by A C Denbo

PUBLISHER'S NOTE: This is a work of fiction. Names, characters, places and events have been created from the imagination of the authors. The heroine and her daughter are loosely fashioned after the authors but no other person is depicted in this work. Any character's resemblance to a real person is strictly coincidental.

ISBN- 978-0-9967895-4-7

Published in 2017 by Book Lamp and Chair LLC
Printed in the U.S.A.

Acknowledgements

Personal thanks to Emery Denbo who inspired the subplot and provided many suggestions and much encouragement.

Thanks to Adele Brinkley for her superb editing which made this work a much better read.

Preface

Two paramedics rushed the young, black-haired woman in through the emergency room doors.

"We have an unconscious, 20-year-old female, shotgun wound to the abdomen and head trauma!"

"Get the trauma team!" Doctor Callahan called to the intern on duty as he directed them into emergency room number two.

After a quick analysis of her condition, he ordered, "Prep her for surgery – STAT!"

Chapter 1

Although Rudy Burke was in his sixties, he was fit. He had to be to continue working safely as a private investigator. His wife, Georgia, had convinced him to dye his graying black hair last year, but he grew it out again, deciding it was too much trouble to keep it up. Although the returning gray temples were back, that was less important than ease of maintenance. Thus, he kept it short, in a butch cut. Most people never guessed his mixed racial background, and he called himself a mutt. He dressed casually most of the time, preferring blue jeans and a polo shirt and, of course, quiet shoes.

Clutching his briefcase, he walked in through the side door of the old warehouse as instructed. Coming in from the bright sunlight, it took a moment for his eyes to adjust to the dark expanse. A black man in faded coveralls and several days of stubble shut the door he'd just entered and frisked him. After he checked Rudy's ID and examined the contents of his briefcase, he led him through several rooms. Rudy saw several other men in the room, and Roy Jackson stood to the right. Rudy nodded, wondering what had caused the anxious look on Roy's face. Since Rudy had done some less than legal actions in his past, he became worried that the Feds found out.

Rudy had been working with Roy for some time now. With Roy being a detective, Rudy thought their arrangement had been perfect. But when Rudy discovered Roy's involvement in a corrupt incident from over three years ago, things changed. At first, Rudy had trusted Roy with his life. But now, after learning what Roy did – even though Rudy knew Roy had a good heart – he would always have nagging doubts about his choices. Rudy had insisted that Roy go to the Feds, confess, and make a deal for the two of them to work at bringing down the powerful syndicate that had infected the city of Portland. Rudy hoped the deal would get Roy a lighter sentence out of it. They both knew there was no guarantee, but working with the Feds would certainly have a better outcome than getting caught.

Of course, Rudy's grandniece, Callie Cooper, broke off her engagement with Roy when he finally told her what he did. As she put it, "It's bad enough that he was dishonest, but I can't be with someone I can't trust." For Roy, that was the hardest part of this whole mess.

So here Roy stood wearing civilian clothes, short sleeved shirt, blue jeans, and running shoes in the warehouse. Since he had arranged this meeting between Rudy and the Feds, his demeanor didn't fit. His green eyes seemed distraught, and he ran his fingers through his dark brown hair. His six-foot frame seemed weak and unsteady as he shifted his weight from one foot to the other. Something was wrong, and Rudy wondered if their "deal" had fallen through.

A bearded man with a ruddy complexion, cautious brown eyes, and bushy eyebrows stood up to shake hands. "Rudy Burke?"

"Yeah, that's me." Rudy shook his hand and looked him over. He figured the man was wearing a disguise. As he headed towards the back of the warehouse with Burke, another man joined them. Rudy got another glimpse of Roy. Something wasn't right.

"Special Agent Brooks here. Let's talk as we walk." He headed for the back end of the warehouse.

"Isn't Roy going too?"

"No ..."

Since Roy was so crucial in getting everything started, Rudy wondered why he wouldn't be included. The thought that Roy might be charged and go to prison after all made Rudy's stomach churn. Poor Roy, he had worked so hard to try to make up for what he did, and now this. When he thought about how he had convinced Roy to work with the Feds, he felt nauseated that he would be responsible for Roy being put away.

Brooks added quietly, " ... he's our bait."

"What do you mean?"

"The mob thinks he wasn't discovered in the clean-up of the police station. So, we're going to be ready when they contact him for more bribes ... the bait."

Rudy nodded solemnly. *No wonder he's nervous.* "So, what do we do now?"

"First, we want to thank you for that collection of new evidence. We're working to overturn all the cases where wrongly convicted people were sentenced to prison. And we're working on the evidence to arrest the actual guilty parties in all those cases."

On impulse, Rudy laughed aloud and raised his hand for a high five.

Brooks responded enthusiastically.

"You moved pretty fast. What happened?"

"The tech guy at the station, Maxwell – you called him Todd?"

"Yeah. What about him?"

"Sang like a canary. We convinced him that his slight build and pretty-boy looks would make him a target for predators in prison. He showed us money trails and ratted out the captain, confirming the captain's connections. Then, when the captain realized there was no escape, he asked for protective custody and relocation in exchange for what he knows about his contacts with the syndicate and his testimony against the Governor." Brooks turned left and started up the stairs.

"What about the Governor?"

"He isn't cooperating – won't say a thing."

"I'd say it's probably because he's family."

Brooks paused at a landing, apparently to digest that information. "Well, with all the evidence that came out against him at the trial, his permanent residence will be federal prison. And he'll still go to trial for the murder of the man he stole the identity from twenty years ago. Remember that box of evidence you gave us? One of the pieces of evidence turned out to be the murder weapon – even had the governor's prints on it. So, I'd say he'll be locked away for a long time. The DA is pushing for life on that one." He patted Rudy's shoulder as he shook his hand. "Thanks for getting that to us. We were suspicious of several of his crimes for a long time, but the murder was a total surprise and the tie-in."

"So, do you want me to tell you the rest of what I know?"

Brooks reached the third floor and opened the door to a hallway, which apparently held offices. "We'll get to that. We'd like you to work with a stool pigeon that has inside information. We've already interrogated him, but we'll record as you two collaborate. With his information and yours, we've already been able to arrest those four dirty cops at the precinct."

"The captain, Novak, Harrison, and Maxwell, right?"

He nodded.

"I don't know how much this stool pigeon told you, but what Detective Jackson and I told you should be plenty to get them put away for a long time."

"True, but our stool pigeon had details that glued everything together."

Rudy really wanted to know who this informant was and what other information he told them. "Just for my own curiosity, and if you can tell me, I'd like to know what charges and evidence you've got on them."

"So far, it's tampering with evidence, interfering with a police investigation, aiding and abetting a felony, and obstruction of justice – several counts each. And we aren't even done yet."

Rudy smiled.

Brooks opened the last door on the left where Roy and two other men were inside. He acknowledged them with a slight nod. "As Detective Jackson told you, since you were so critical in our investigation, we'd like your assistance in going after the crime syndicate that's behind all of it. Since you have a history investigating them, you may know something else."

"Okay." Rudy assumed he'd be working with an undercover Fed that was part of the investigation.

The bearded man led Rudy out of the room and handed him an FBI vest so he would look like he was part of the team.

Brooks led Rudy into a darkened room, stood in front of a one-way mirror, and pointed to the thin man sitting at a table on the other side of the mirror. "This is the man you'll work with. You may already know him."

When Rudy looked at him, his mouth dropped open. The thin man's brown dye job was nearly grown out, including the sideburns, revealing graying black hair. And he'd regrown the notorious pencil mustache. "Pierre?! He's supposed to be dead!"

Rudy Burke's steely poker face had failed him, revealing shock and confusion. Although he recouped quickly, he was irritated with himself at this momentary loss of control. In his wildest dreams, he never imagined that he'd see this man again.

His thoughts flashed back to the very beginning of this whole mess. Early in his career as a private investigator in the early 1970's, Rudy worked as a file boy in a lawyer's office. One of the lawyers hired him to follow his second wife, Alice – long story. It turned out to be his longest assignment ever, lasting more than two decades. Near the end of the assignment, Rudy assumed she was merely having an affair with Pierre. It wasn't until a couple of years ago that he found out Alice was also working with Pierre in various criminal activities.

Alice's daughter, Sharon Cooper, found out about the affair when inventorying her mother's mansion and found Rudy's reports to her father. Rudy's assignment had been to follow Alice; thus, he had foolishly neglected to do a complete workup on Pierre. Now, he blamed himself for not catching Pierre's connections with the mob. Because the syndicate connection wasn't discovered and subsequently not in the report he gave to her father, Sharon never learned about it. Rudy had made a pact with Sharon's husband, Jack, never to let her find out about Alice's connections He figured Sharon had already suffered enough. So, when Rudy thought Pierre had died, he was actually relieved; he assumed the secret was safe. Now that Pierre was alive, the threat of Sharon finding out reemerged with a vengeance.

"So, you've met." Brooks observed dryly.

When Rudy heard the suspicion in his voice, he vowed to himself that he wouldn't betray himself again. He couldn't allow another lapse in control. Although he had only been married for a short time, he suspected Georgia was learning his unconscious, but subtle, signals even when he thought he had total control. Professionally, however, a lapse could be deadly. He turned to face Brooks. "Not technically. But I have to know. How'd this happen when all the news reports said he was dead?"

Brooks nodded. "He was afraid for his life, and apparently he was right. When he was let out of prison almost a year ago, the syndicate put him back in charge of their books. Then, somehow, two million bucks disappeared from their off-shore account, and they decided it was him who took the money." Rudy's heart skipped a beat, but he maintained his cool façade. "That's why they wanted to ice him. So, he called us to make a deal. We save his life, and he gets revenge for the betrayal. We had an ambulance ready because we wanted to make sure that no news reporters got wind of it from actual paramedics. Of course, we put him in a secured medical facility and arranged for the fake news reports of his death. In exchange for his cooperation to get hard evidence on the syndicate, we'll give him a new identity; and when all is done, everyone will still believe he's dead."

Still in disbelief, Rudy sat down carefully in a chair next to a small table. *No wonder Roy looked so nervous!*

Brooks eyed him. "What's this hesitation all about? You know something?"

"Before I go in there, you have to tell me everything he's told you."

Brooks folded his arms. "That's not how it works."

"I'm not going in there without knowing what he said."

"This is highly irregular." He glared at Rudy for a few seconds, sat down across the table from him, and eyed him. "Look, we've been investigating this syndicate for three years now. With what we've already discovered from Pierre's statements, Roy's information, your contributions, and statements from the dirty cops, we have a good picture of what's going on, but not enough to prosecute yet, and we still need to get the kingpin."

"And?"

"There were five divisions to the syndicate. Two have been busted – the gambling ring last year and the police infiltration that we busted last week. That leaves art smuggling and forgery, drugs, and protection. Each division has a handler; Pierre handled art before he went to prison, but someone else is running it now, and Pierre's given us all the names involved. The handlers are the only ones that report to the kingpin, Andre."

Rudy's heartbeat quickened. He forced himself to breathe naturally. *Just listen*, he told himself.

"That way, the muscle doesn't know Andre from Adam. Now, he told us about a big yearly mandatory meeting. It's disguised as a week-long family reunion, and the next one is in just a few weeks. So, we're arranging to take them down when they meet. Here's the place, date, and time for it."

Brooks wrote down the information, handed the piece of paper to Rudy, and continued, "He's also given us the locations of the hubs for each division. Since you already know so much, we want to bring you in on the plans to take them down."

Rudy studied the paper for a moment and nodded. "Was there ever a mention of me or suspicion of someone following him?"

Brooks eyed him. "Do you think he knows you?"

"Unlikely. I supplied a lot of information to you, and I had to follow him in order to get it, so I don't want to go in there if he might recognize me."

Brooks nodded. "He never mentioned anything."

Rudy swallowed hard. Although he always wore a disguise when following Pierre, there was the possibility that Pierre might recognize his face from any one of several close calls. It was a gamble, but he followed Brooks and another agent into the room where Pierre was waiting.

Pierre watched him carefully from his seat at the small table. Somewhat reassuring, Pierre's body language didn't reveal any signs of recognition. However, Rudy had learned that wasn't always foolproof, so he kept his guard up.

Brooks pointed to Rudy. "Pierre Martine, this is Rudy Burke ...." Rudy cringed inside. Too late, he realized they should have used an alias. "... you'll be working together. Everything said here will be recorded."

Rudy was careful to conceal his disdain for Pierre when he reached out to shake his hand. He would never forget how much pain this man caused as a result of his connection with Sharon's mother. He was just thankful that Sharon never found out the extent of Alice's indiscretions.

Brooks directed Rudy to sit down opposite Pierre. "So, Pierre, fill Rudy in on what you know."

"Everything? Again?"

Brooks nodded slowly. "That's what I said."

When Pierre was finished listing names, nicknames, descriptions, addresses, operations, and contacts, Brooks asked, "So, that's everything?"

"Why would I withhold anything after what they did to me? Besides, I've told you this stuff five times already."

"Just making sure."

As they discussed the details, Rudy contained his impatience and nodded.

When they finished with the details for the takedown, Brooks walked Rudy out of the small room. During his escorted departure, Rudy was troubled.

On the way home, Rudy wondered, *Pierre has to be protecting Frankie by giving them a fake name. I wonder why Roy didn't speak up about who the kingpin really is? Maybe he did and Brooks is testing me to see if I'll say something. 'Cause if Roy told them, they'll get suspicious if I don't. But if Roy didn't say anything, and I say something – that'll ruin his deal.* He decided to stop making his head spin and call Roy later.

Chapter 2

Although Sharon Cooper was nearing fifty, she looked much younger and was still in good shape. Her strawberry blonde hair was light enough that the growing gray hairs weren't really noticeable. She loved to laugh, so a few laugh lines had recently shown up on her fair skin.

She finished filling the dishwasher, poured two tall lemonades with ice, and joined Jack on the patio. Jack was her devoted husband and the love of her life. Yes, he was wiry for a man of his age and decent looking, but his ethics and sense of humor were what had won her heart. She never made an issue of it when his mustache tickled, for without it, he wouldn't be Jack. When they were first married, she had asked him to grow out his sandy colored hair, but when it became apparent how unruly it became, she agreed that he should keep it cropped short. Her heart was always drawn to him when he laughed in his special way, which was often. But more importantly, he was a firm protector and provider, and she felt safe and content by his side.

Life wasn't always kind or fair, but they worked together to make their marriage work. Although they had a few rough spots financially when the kids were growing up, the last few years had been especially trying. Almost three years ago, her estranged mother broke her hip, and Sharon had to inventory her mansion. That chore was difficult enough, but it initiated a succession of crises. She struggled to work through reopened unresolved emotional wounds and suffered new shocks as she discovered previously-unknown extended family members, Alice's affair, and then having to deal with the circumstances around Alice's death shortly after. When that crisis was over, they were plunged into a series of emergencies connected with Jack's dad and his addictions. Then, last year, she and Jack helped her newly found half-sister deal with an abusive ex. Sharon was still building relationships with two of the three half-sisters, Bonnie and Charlotte. However, Arlene was unable to accept her, and stopped all communication last year. With all those issues behind them now, life was finally starting to look up.

They sat in the shade, and the light breeze was just right. The back yard was starting to look pretty good. They had recently put in a lot of new plants and a pond – in imitation of her Aunt Georgia and Uncle Rudy's back yard. From the day she first saw it, she admired their Eden-like landscaping. Just last week, Georgia had again commented on being flattered that they considered their yard worthy of copying.

Sharon's mind drifted back to when she first laid eyes on Georgia. It happened shortly after Sharon had started the inventory process and discovered Alice's diaries with Georgia's name in them. Until then, she didn't even know she had an aunt. The diaries prompted her and Callie to find her. Sharon recalled how worried she was that Georgia might be like Alice. Then, she smiled thinking about how relieved she was when they got to know each other. Thankfully, Georgia was nothing like Alice. Now they couldn't stand it if they let more than a few days pass by without contact. Georgia quickly became the mother figure that Alice never provided, and Sharon relished it.

It was almost prophetic how easy it was for Callie to find Georgia from an Internet search. Now, at a mere twenty years of age, Callie's research skills were helping her in her new career. Never in a million years would Sharon have guessed that their baby girl would want to be a private investigator under Rudy's guidance. After the stress of dealing with Jack's parents last year, Callie moved in with them to help them out and to keep an eye on them. Sharon missed having her at home, but she had to accept that Callie was growing up.

Then when Callie broke up with Roy, the breakup was especially difficult. Callie still hadn't told her why, and Sharon wondered about the reason. Callie's silence was puzzling, for they previously had talked about everything. Although she was curious, she decided that when the kids grow up, you have to let go.

When Sharon got her inheritance last year, she and Jack decided that he should take early retirement so he could pursue his long-delayed hobby of restoring old cars. This topic, however, would not be the subject of tonight's discussion.

When Jack looked at her from his lounge chair, she was reminded again that – other than his hair – he resembled the comedian, Jeff Foxworthy. He grinned. "Everything ready?"

Their son, Mark, would be arriving from college tomorrow. During those four years, the time had seemed to pass so slowly. Yes, they'd been busy with all the family drama and they enjoyed visits during school breaks, but they never seemed enough. Although she yearned for things to go back to normal, she knew Mark would be changed; even they were changed. But he would always be their precious son. She wondered if he'd grown any more since he'd had been there on spring break. She thought about how surprised she was when she saw that he'd grown so much taller and filled out.

At first, Mark took out student loans and worked to pay for college expenses. Then, when Sharon's inheritance hit, she paid everything for him, enabling him to quit his part-time job. He was able to put all his energies into studying and earned a 4.0 GPA in his classes from then on.

It would be good to see Gary again, too. He had grown up next door, practically living here and becoming part of their family. Gary even called Sharon and Jack "Mom "and "Dad.". Gary's dad was a widower who never recovered from losing his wife. As a result, he was uninvolved in his son's life and unconcerned about anything except liquor to shut out the world, so there was no money for college. Thankfully, with Jack's and Sharon's encouragement, he worked hard in high school and earned a full scholarship. When the boys decided to go to college together, it made the transition easier for everyone, knowing they would have each other's backs while they were away from home.

Now, the boys had graduated and were finally coming home. Sharon and Jack had just come back from watching them walk across the stage and receive their diplomas, their parental faces bursting with pride.

She smiled. "Of course, everything's ready! We've been preparing for over a month. What time do you think they'll arrive?" she asked anxiously, twisting the end of her ponytail.

"They'll get here when they get here." He winked at her.

"Do you think they'll trade off with the driving?"

Jack reached over and put his hand on hers. "They're smart kids. You know they'll do the right thing."

"Do I worry too much?"

He chuckled. "I want them to be here just as much as you do, but if you fuss like this until they get here, you're going to be a wreck. Why don't we call Rudy and Georgia to come over for cards? That should keep you busy for a while."

"How'd you get so smart?"

"I just know you." He winked again.

"I'm sorry I'm such a worrywart."

He got up, bent over to her, and put a hand on her cheek. "Pookie, it's a good thing." He pulled her up from the patio chair and hugged her.

She pressed her cheek against his shoulder. "How'd I deserve such a good match?"

"I ask myself the same thing every day about you."

Rudy held the door open as Georgia came in with a covered tray. She wore a sleeveless, yellow buttoned shirt, tan Bermuda shorts, and sandals. Like Sharon and Alice, she didn't look her age. At almost seventy, her figure had filled out a little, with her curves still in just the right places. Her happy blue eyes always cheered up everyone she met. When Sharon first met her, Georgia's gray hair was down to her waist, usually pinned up in a bun. At first, Sharon was surprised at seeing her tattoos, but now they were just part of her. Less than two years ago, just after marrying Rudy, Georgia cut her hair to shoulder-length and dyed it auburn, her original color. Being a newlywed again, she was eager to please her new husband. She didn't need to worry; Rudy would have been pleased no matter how she wore her hair.

"We're here," she called out.

Sharon laughed. "We didn't call you just so you'd bring dessert."

Rudy closed the door. "Hey, you should know by now that's what she does." He wore the usual polo shirt and jeans, this time with sandals.

Jack pulled up one edge of the foil. "Ooh, fudge!" He grabbed a piece and popped it into his mouth. "Mmm." He raised his hand and gave her an okay.

Georgia playfully slapped his hand. "Hey! Not all at once! So, why the invitation for tonight? We're still coming tomorrow, aren't we?"

"Sharon was stressing about Mark and Gary driving all the way from Southern California. I thought we'd distract her for a while, so I used you guys, sorry."

Rudy laughed, and Georgia put the tray down and hugged Sharon. "Oh, you poor thing. I can only imagine your excitement." She held her friend at arm's length. "I'm excited too!"

Jack put paper and pencil on the table. "Canasta or Pinochle?"

Rudy shrugged. "Better make it Canasta; we won't have to think as much. Let's mix it up a little, men against women."

"Oh? A glutton for punishment, huh?" Georgia cooed.

"We'll see about that."

They all sat down, and Jack dealt the cards. "I figure they'll be here sometime tomorrow afternoon … if they don't break the speed limit."

Sharon put her cards down. "Why'd you say that? Now I'm worried."

Rudy chuckled. "Isn't that why you bought that compact for him, so he wouldn't be tempted?"

"So he'd get good mileage," Jack stated firmly. "We wanted to make it easier for him to visit on breaks."

"Oh. *Right*," Rudy agreed sarcastically.

Georgia smacked his arm. "If you talk like that, Sharon's going to burst. So, cut it out and behave."

He shrugged. "If you say so."

She put her fists on her hips. "In this case, I do say so." She picked up her cards. "Be nice."

Rudy smiled devilishly.

"I'm going to ignore that." She looked across the table at her partner. "So, Sharon, have you planned the welcome home party yet?"

"Sort of. We want to have it for both Mark and Gary."

"Is that because Gary's dad won't?" Georgia interrupted.

"Yeah – well, sort of. Billy's in the hospital right now."

"Hospital? What happened?"

"He's got a broken hip."

"Ouch." Georgia grimaced.

"But even if he were fine, I'm pretty sure he wouldn't do anything special."

"I know you said he wasn't involved as a parent. Why is that?"

Sharon took in a deep breath and let it out with a puff. "Just after his wife died – Gary was only twelve – he started to drink pretty much all the time. He lost interest in just about everything and his health went downhill. Jack's gone over there a few times for some emergency fixes on the house, and I talk to him occasionally." She paused. "Gary decided he didn't want anything to do with him because of his drinking. But he quit a few months ago and Gary doesn't know."

"Well, tell him!"

"We can't. Billy made us promise not to say anything. He wants to tell Gary when he sees him."

"Oh, what a shame. But wouldn't that make Gary more likely to want to see him?"

"You'd think so, but like I said, he made us promise."

"So, about the party. Mark and Gary gave me a list of people to invite, but I don't want to have the party right away. I want them to settle down for a bit first."

"If you haven't rented a place yet, just use our back yard. It's big enough, and we've got the barbeque and smoker. We could rent chairs if there are a lot of people," Georgia offered.

"With friends and family, it looks like we'll have about 50 people. Do you think your backyard is big enough?"

"Of course, we'll just open up the house too. I'll take care of the chairs, and Rudy can smoke a pork loin, a prime rib roast, and a turkey. Or maybe just barbeque a lot of hamburgers and hot dogs."

Rudy chuckled. "Looks like I'm on the hook."

"I'd really appreciate it," Sharon begged.

"Pssh. You know I love it."

By the end of the evening, Sharon was a little less anxious.

When Rudy and Georgia got home that night, they talked for an hour, happy that Mark and Gary would be returning home even though they had met them only briefly last year. Since the boys had to work during summers, they couldn't come home for visits until last year when Mark was able to quit his job. Now they were excited to be able to get to know the boys better.

Georgia was in the other room, and Rudy was brushing his teeth when his phone rang. He quickly rinsed and looked at who was calling. "Hey Roy, I was going to call you."

"About what?"

"If your deal is good. But mostly, I wanted to ask, didn't you tell the Feds Frankie was the kingpin?"

"Why do you ask?"

"Because Special Agent Brooks said his name was Andre."

"No, that's what Pierre told them."

"And did you correct him?"

Hearing silence, Rudy felt suspicious, but he decided to give Roy the benefit of the doubt and wait for his response.

"Pierre's deal is based on him telling everything. When it's found out he's lying, his deal will be worthless, and he'll go to jail. So, it'll work out."

Rudy held the phone away from his ear and looked at it as if he had Roy in front of him. He wondered, *What are you thinking?* Instead, he asked, "So, what were you so nervous about in the warehouse?"

A slight pause concerned Rudy.

"I knew you wouldn't be expecting Pierre. I know I wasn't."

Rudy shook his head. *You had plenty of time to adjust before I got there, so that doesn't quite ring true.* He decided to see how this played out. "So, why'd you call me?"

"I'll be calling my contact soon."

"Okay. You know how to play it. Just keep me in the loop."

"Yeah, they said it'd be okay to let you know when anything happens. I just have to be careful not to let anyone be within hearing range."

"Hey, I know you've got this."

"I'm not too sure about being a guinea pig though."

"Probably a lot better than prison."

"I suppose. How's everyone?"

"Mark and Gary have graduated and are moving home. Everyone's all excited about that. And Jack's retiring at the end of the month." There was silence on the other end." Look, I'm sorry about you not being included anymore, but you can't break someone's trust and not expect consequences."

"I get it. She doesn't trust me. Well, I'd better sign off for now."

Rudy heard bitterness in Roy's tone, but he acted as if he missed it. "Keep me posted."

They said their goodbyes, and Rudy shook his head. "Poor kid. He's probably just stressing about this charade he's about to do." Although Rudy felt sorry for Roy, he of all people should know what the consequences are when you break the law.

Then he thought about himself and what he had done in the last couple of years. He shook his head. *That sure was stupid. And now that I've got Georgia … what was I thinking?* Now, the guilt and the danger he'd put them into loomed nearer.

Chapter 3

Gary Rawlins relaxed in the dining room chair as Callie Cooper massaged his shoulders and neck. Instead of releasing tension, he became more alert and conscious of her body heat. He felt her soft breath as she bent forward to whisper into his ear. That and the warmth from her cheek made the hair on his arms stand up and his face flush. She nibbled his neck, and he turned to give her a kiss.

"Hey, wake up! We're almost there."

Disoriented, Gary moaned, "Huh?"

"Time to wake up, man." Mark repeated. "I know how long it takes you to function. Here, drink some coffee," He handed Gary a steaming to-go cup.

Gary blinked. He let out a sigh of disappointment. "Thanks. But you could've waited for a couple minutes," he mumbled.

Mark laughed and pushed a disk into the CD player. He skipped to "School's Out" by Alice Cooper.

Gary yawned and stretched his six-foot frame as far as the passenger seat would allow. He rubbed his eyes and looked out at the passing scenery. Still groggy, Gary ruffled his blonde hair and sipped from his cup. "What time is it?"

"Almost eleven."

"Hey, we made good time. Thanks for the nap." He looked at Mark, "Need a break?"

"Nah, I'm good. Besides, we're almost there, and you're not quite awake."

"I can't believe it's actually over now."

"Yeah, I thought those four years would never end."

Deep in thought, Gary frowned.

Mark noticed. "Hey, I thought you'd be happy."

"Did you notice that it seemed more difficult being able to visit last summer than the previous years when we couldn't come home?"

"That's because we didn't want to leave home to go back to school."

"I guess. It just seems weird, is all." Gary hung his head.

Mark glanced at him. "I understand; you had more reasons to want to stay."

"Do you think there's any hope for me?"

"I don't know. But if you don't try, then no."

Gary shook his head. "But she's planning her wedding."

"And if you do nothing, then you'll always wonder, what if? If it were me, I'd fight for it. So, be a man and go for it."

"That's easy for you to say."

"Well, that's because I haven't spent half my life pining over her."

Gary gave him a sour look. "That's because she's your sister."

"You know what I mean."

"Do you think she knows?"

"I know for sure she doesn't. It's not like you've ever told her."

"Yeah, I guess I blew it."

"It's not over until she says, 'I do,' so let her know *before* the big day. Okay?"

"But she thinks of me like a brother."

"Does that mean you aren't going to try?"

Gary threw his hands up in surrender. "Okay! I'll look for the first opportunity!"

"Well, you'd better make it sooner rather than later."

Sharon stirred the large batch of potato salad as she looked out the kitchen window. Jack was tending the ribs and chicken on the barbecue, and Callie was setting up the patio for Mark and Gary's arrival.

She beamed, knowing that soon her family would be whole again. As she thought about the kids, she mindlessly stopped stirring. Callie had become a woman before her eyes. With Georgia's tutelage, her self-confidence had grown immensely in just the last few months. How thankful she was that they had found Georgia, and she was part of their lives now.

Callie's features were the same as before, large green eyes, long wavy red hair, and a curvy figure. But her newly-developed confidence made her seem different and almost taller than the inch she had on Sharon. Even Callie's usual green tank top and favorite white shorts seemed to fit differently. *It must be all that working out and running she's been doing.*

When Sharon heard the voices filter in through the front screen door, she snapped to attention, hastily set the potato salad on the counter and ran to the back door. "They're here! I hear them!"

"I hear them too." Jack waved as he trotted towards the front of the house. "I'll see you out front."

"I'm going with Dad," Callie called out as she started running.

Jack was already hugging Mark when Sharon ran out the front door. "Jack! I wanted the first one!"

Jack looked back, "That's why I ran." He winked at her.

"But I got here first," Callie announced proudly as she did a victory dance. She turned to give Gary a hug, too.

When Sharon sprinted up to Mark, she gave Jack a playful slap on his shoulder. "You putz." She gave Mark a mighty hug. "I'm so glad you're here!" She turned to Gary and gave him a big hug, too. "Both of you!"

Gary grinned as he hugged her back. "I'd almost forgotten how much this family loves to hug." His blonde hair had turned almost platinum in the California sun, making a strong contrast to his deep tan and brown eyes. He had grown too, both in height and in bulk, making him look like a surfer.

She started to cry.

Mark put his arm around her. "What's wrong, Mom?"

She wiped the tears away. "I'm just so happy." She hugged him again. "You're both so grown up. And I missed some of it happening." She slapped his arm. "Don't you *ever* do that again! You hear?"

When he laughed, his tired eyes sparkled. "What, grow up?"

"No! Leave me like that!"

"Well, I'm all done with college, so I don't think I'll be going anywhere for a while. I don't plan on moving out of here right away, not when you're going to spoil me rotten." He winked.

He had grown a little, adding a couple of inches which brought him up to almost six feet tall. He had tanned more than she remembered, but then he had been in California for four years. He had lost the gangly teen image and looked so mature. Yes, he looked tired, but somehow his hazel eyes seemed to have more color and his brown hair seemed lighter. Sharon suddenly felt old.

After everyone unloaded the car, they helped with preparations. As they were carrying food to the patio from the kitchen, Rudy and Georgia arrived with dessert. Another round of hugs and handshakes took up the next few minutes.

Everyone filled their plates and sat down to talk.

"When you called to say you were almost here, I had to scramble to get things ready. You guys must've driven awfully fast." Sharon shook her finger at Mark. "You could've fallen asleep at the wheel."

"It's okay, Mom. Gary and I took turns driving. We only stopped for food and bathroom breaks." He chuckled. "We're fine. Just a little tired is all."

"We figured you might be, that's why we're going to wait for a while for the graduation party. Mom's almost done with the plan."

Mark rolled his eyes. "You don't have to do that."

She swatted his shoulder. "Hey, you earned it. Besides, we want to celebrate your accomplishments."

Jack shook his head. "You know better than to argue with your mother."

Sharon gave him the evil eye as she shook her finger at him.

"You won't believe what I saw when we got into Portland. We were stopped at a red light and this woman in a short white dress was singing and pole dancing around a street-light pole ...."

Jack laughed out loud.

"... all made up with heavy makeup, earrings, and high heels. Then I realized it was a *man!* I know our city has the motto, *Keep Portland Weird* – but really?"

"You just wait," Rudy mumbled. "You'll see plenty more."

"Why didn't you wake me for that?" Gary blurted out.

Mark stared incredulously. "Because by the time you actually woke up, we'd be a mile down the road."

Gary rolled his eyes.

Mark kept looking at his sister. "Something else has changed; you look different."

Callie rolled her eyes. "Well, of course. I'm grown up now."

"I don't know how to say it. You look the same – but different …."

"It's because she's been working out," Sharon explained proudly.

"Really?! What brought that on? You weren't interested in it the last time we were here."

Georgia giggled. "It was me."

Gary's mouth sagged open. "Don't tell me you're working out with her?" He turned red as he stammered, "Not that I'm saying it isn't possible … I just …."

Georgia laughed. "It's okay. I'm not offended. I've been tutoring her."

"What do you mean, tutoring?"

"Well, now that she's working with Rudy, I offered to teach her self-defense."

Mark's eyes popped. "Wait, what?" He turned to Callie, "Does that mean you're a P.I.?"

"Well, for now I'm learning how to do research. I guess eventually I'll do more when Rudy decides to teach me."

"Whoa! I'm impressed! What brought that on?"

Callie turned red and bit her lip.

Sharon spoke softly as she explained, "She was mugged. And with Roy out of the picture …."

"Wait, what do you mean he's out of the picture?" Mark blurted out.

"They split up …."

Mark dropped his fork. "What? When did that happen?"

Gary sat speechless.

"Just a few months ago."

Mark and Gary looked at each other with wide eyes and open mouths, but Gary's eyes changed, energized.

"Sis, you told us about the mugging, but why didn't you say something about Roy?" Mark asked with genuine concern.

"I didn't want you to feel sorry for me."

"Hey, you know I wouldn't feel sorry for you – well, I would. But how can I support you if you don't let me know? Do I need to beat him up for hurting you?"

"No, I can handle my own problems, but thanks. I didn't say anything because … I guess I wasn't handling it well. Anyway, when Rudy asked me to do some research, I figured, why not – it was something to keep my mind off him. But when I discovered some pretty unnerving information, I kinda got scared."

Gary leaned forward. "What research? What made you scared? Or can you tell us?"

Rudy laughed. "She's the one that discovered the scandal about the governor, who he really is, the murder, everything. Her research is the reason he's on trial."

Mark let out an incredulous laugh. "*You* did *that*? That story was on *all* the channels! Even down in California!"

She shined her nails on her shoulder. "Yup. It was me. But I let Rudy take the credit. He's the one that told me what to look for. Besides, I didn't want anyone to know I was involved, just in case someone might want to know – you know – for revenge." She grimaced.

"So, all this cloak and dagger stuff is why you look so confident?"

"Well, Georgia had a lot to do with it."

Mark eyed Georgia. "Is that why you taught her self-defense?" He looked at Georgia suspiciously and then jerked forward. "Wait a minute, *you* taught her? Seriously?"

She gave him a stern glare. "Look, mister, I've taken classes. I'm not someone you should mess with."

He still looked doubtful.

Georgia stared him down, "You think just because I'm a woman …."

"No! Not that!"

She put her hands on her hips, "And don't you dare say it's because I'm old!"

He put his hands up in surrender. "I'm not saying another word. Really."

She nodded emphatically. "Good."

Rudy chuckled. "Believe her. It's true."

"Can I see you in action sometime?" Gary cautiously suggested.

"Still don't believe me, huh?"

"I didn't say that," he stammered.

Georgia patted Callie's hand. "How about we give a demonstration tomorrow?"

Callie squinted at her. "Am I the perp again?"

Georgia giggled. "Well, I'm the one they don't believe. So – yes."

"Can't Mark do it? I'd love to see that!" Callie grumbled.

"No, he hasn't been trained on how to fall safely."

"So?"

Gary laughed, and Mark punched his shoulder.

"Hey, cut it out. That hurt."

Mark glared at him. "Good."

Sharon and Callie piped up at the same moment, "Maybe later."

Mark scratched his head. "Are you two doing that stereo thing again?"

In unison, they chimed, "Never stopped."

Mark shook his head.

After a high-five with Callie, Sharon picked up a couple of deviled eggs. "Have you got your grades yet?"

Mark shook his head. "We won't know for at least another week, but we'll be able to go online to find out. Don't worry; you'll be the first to know."

"Have you decided what you're going to do with your fancy business administration degree?"

"Well, I could do just about anything. But if you don't mind, I'd like to chill out for a while before looking for a job."

"Take all the time you need, but I'll probably be retired by the time you find a job."

"When's your last day at work, Dad?"

"Last day of June. I've already put down the first and last month's rent on a garage."

"Oh, right! So is the Mustang your first project?"

"Well, the Mustang is running, so I thought I'd work on the truck that Don left for me."

"Are you going to make a business out of it? You know, restoring cars?"

"Naw, just a hobby for now. But I want to do it right."

"Is it still okay that I help out now and then?" Mark's eyes brightened when he asked, "Especially when you work on the Mustang?"

"Of course. I'm counting on it."

Mark's arms shot up in victory, and he hooted excitedly.

Gary leaned in hopefully. "I don't suppose I can help?"

"Of course. You're always welcome."

He leaned back and pumped his fist into the air. "Yes!"

"Hey, Dad?"

"What's up, Mark?"

"Gary's been wondering. Would it be okay for him to stay with us? He'd rather not stay with his dad while he's been drinking."

"Certainly." Jack put his hand on Gary's shoulder. "You know it's a standing invitation. You're always welcome to stay here, especially now."

"What do you mean, especially now?"

Jack's demeanor deflated as he continued, "Your dad's in the hospital."

Gary's face darkened. "Why? Did he give himself alcohol poisoning? Or did his liver finally give out?"

"There was an accident. He's got a broken hip."

"Please tell me he wasn't drinking and driving."

"He wanted to tell you, but I think you need to know. He's been clean for three months."

Gary pulled back and squinted with disbelief.

"The accident wasn't his fault, – and he wasn't driving. A board on the front porch gave way."

"He never did do any repairs on that old house, so I guess it's no surprise there." Gary folded his arms and looked warily at him, "So how can you be sure he's been sober?"

"I've been keeping an eye on him and taking him to his AA meetings. There really is a difference in him."

Sharon reached across the picnic table to pat Gary's hand. "I think you should go see him."

His face tightened. "Why should I? He was never interested in *me*."

"I've been thinking a lot about that. I wonder if he has some kind of condition that makes it impossible for him to relate to others emotionally. But, the fact that he stopped drinking says a lot," Sharon pointed out.

"I can't. There's just too much history."

"I understand how you feel, but I think you need to go. For your sake as well as his."

Gary frowned.

Callie cleared her throat. "I'll go along for moral support if you want."

Gary inhaled deeply and blew the air out through his nose.

Sharon nodded. "You should go. In a couple days, he'll be transferred to a nursing home to recover and get therapy. He'll need some personal belongings when he gets there, so you can take them when you go."

Obviously trying to change the subject, Gary looked over his shoulder. "I see you've been working on the back yard."

"Gary, we'll support you in whatever you decide. But please, I urge you to see for yourself. If you want, we can all go with you," Jack added.

Gary closed his eyes and huffed, finally putting his hands up in surrender. "Okay. I guess. But you don't *all* have to go with me." He turned to Callie, "I'll take you up on your offer."

Callie smiled weakly and put her hand on his shoulder. "Tomorrow then?"

"Let's make it the day he's transferred. I don't want to have to go twice." Gary cleared his throat. "So hey, where will I be sleeping? 'Cause as good a friend that Mark is, I can't sleep in the same room with his loud snoring. That time we visited and we had to sleep in the basement together – *that* was torture."

Jack laughed. "Mark can have his old room, and we'll set up a bed for you in the basement."

"Thanks."

Mark grinned. "So, not to change the subject or anything; but when do we get to see Georgia's demonstration?"

Callie glared at him.

Georgia laughed. "I'm ready if you are, Callie."

She huffed. "I guess." Then she scowled at Mark as she shook her finger at him, "You're going to get it, mister."

After several throws to the ground, Callie surrendered. "That's enough, I give up." She got up slowly and brushed off the grass and dirt. "Oh, great – grass stains." She glared at Mark again.

Rudy laughed. "Well, Georgia. I think it's time for us to go home. Nothing can top that." He leaned over to whisper into her ear, and she beamed.

After Rudy and Georgia left for the evening, Sharon brought out another pitcher of iced lemonade to the patio. As she walked past Mark, she tousled his hair. Then she did the same for Gary. "You don't know how glad I am that you're back."

Mark chuckled. "It's been a long time since you've done that, Mom. I missed it."

She did it again, kissed him on the forehead, and sat down.

Jack smiled at the sight. "Brings back memories."

As dusk set in, they went inside to continue talking.

Chapter 4

Mark relaxed for the first time in a long while, especially after the long drive home. He lingered at the breakfast table talking with his mom after everyone else left for the morning. He finished his last bite and said, "I'm surprised Gary went to see his dad. Don't get me wrong, I'm glad he went, but I know he didn't want to."

"Yeah, we did push, didn't we?"

"I was getting a little nervous when it was going down the other night. While we were at college, Gary told me over and over how much his dad's lack of interest hurt him. During the whole first year, he repeatedly vented about how much he felt abandoned. I was relieved when it became less often, at least until we started thinking about graduation. Then, the grousing started up again. He wondered if his dad would go to the graduation, maybe send a card, or even think about him. Then when he didn't show up and nothing came in the mail, it was back to the same thing, only worse. I couldn't get him to let it go, so I know there's a lot of hurt and anger boiling inside him."

"I hope our pushing doesn't make things worse."

"I'm just glad Callie went with him. I hope she can diffuse any conflicts that are bound to happen."

"She's pretty good at that until she gets emotionally involved. Then she can be a tiger."

He paused and a knowing grimace spread over his face. "So, she hasn't changed there, huh?"

"Sorry to say, but no. We *are* working on it. Even Georgia, in their training sessions, has told her that she has to learn how to master the poker face and not react impulsively."

Mark was silent for the next few minutes wondering how the visit between Gary and his dad would go. He thought, *I sure hope he can come to some kind of truce with Billy. At least, he won't be pining over Callie while he's fuming over his dad.*

Callie turned to look at Gary. "It's the same nursing home where Alice was, so I know a few of the people that work there. They're nice people; they'll take good care of your dad."

There was no change in Gary's expression, as if he didn't hear her. He looked out the passenger window as they drove past a shopping complex.

"Thanks for picking out his clothes for him. I'm sure he'll appreciate it."

"He never appreciated anything before!" he snapped. "Why should he now?"

Callie turned red. "Well, maybe he won't know how to express it, but I'm sure he'll think it."

Gary huffed. "You don't know that. You didn't grow up with him." Then he took a breath and paused. "I'm sorry. I didn't mean to snap at you. I know you're just trying to help, but you just don't understand."

Saddened, Callie refrained from saying anything until they got there, which turned into several uncomfortable minutes of silence.

"We're here." She pulled into the parking lot near the front door to make it easier to transport Billy's belongings. They carried two boxes to the receptionist's desk.

Since Gary wasn't talking, Callie took over. "Can you tell me which room Billy Rawlins is in? We've brought his personal things."

"21A. Down that hall on the right." She pointed the way.

A small, elderly woman with thinning hair and large ears came up to them. "Have we had lunch?" she said with a tremor in her voice.

Gary squinted as Callie smiled and said, "I'll bet this nice lady here would know that." She led the old woman to an aide who was walking by. When Callie turned around, she was just able to avoid bumping into a motorized scooter that stopped between her and Gary. The silver-haired woman with a short perm sat in the seat and looked up at her. Deep wrinkles lined her inquisitive face, and when she smiled at Callie, the wrinkles deepened. Her drooping gray eyes took on a happy demeanor as she said, "If you need to know anything, I'm your gal. I know everyone here and everything about them." She cupped her hand to her mouth and whispered, "Nothing gets by me."

As she pointed down the hallway to her left, Callie noticed her arthritic knuckles and the wrinkled skin that sagged on her thin arms, like crepe fabric sleeves. She continued, "Mr. Townsend in 18B is going to be moved to the dementia unit. He always goes into someone else's room and takes things. He thinks he's shopping." Then she covered her mouth. "Oh, I'm sorry. I should've introduced myself." She held out her hand, "I'm Bertie."

Callie smiled. "What a nice name. I'm Callie. Nice to meet you." She was careful not to squeeze the old woman's hand.

Bertie nodded with another smile, but then she guarded her mouth again. "Make sure you don't go to 6C." She pointed her shaky finger to her right. "Inez is crazy. She'll accuse you of stealing her underwear."

Callie's eyebrows shot up. "Really?!"

"She's done it to several people. She even accused me of selling them to my friends."

Callie snorted. "Oh, I'm sorry." She put her hand on Bertie's shoulder. "I just didn't expect that."

"I didn't either when she accused me. But the *real* scandal is in 2D. Poor Vera. Such a sad case. The police are involved, you know."

"The police!"

"Oh, yes. Her sister actually shot her with a shotgun – right in the gut. I heard through the grapevine that she was high on drugs when she did it – her sister, that is. I couldn't believe it. Her own sister! What's this world coming to?"

"Wow! That *is* terrible."

"I feel so sorry for her. She doesn't remember a thing, lost her memory. Still thinks her sister is an angel. Such a pity. You might want to visit her, to cheer her up. I tried, but ...." She shook her head and then looked up again. "If you need to know anything, just ask. And I can show you where you need to go if you tell me who you're here to visit."

Callie smiled. She was about to pat her hand, but thought better of it, thinking that might hurt her swollen knuckles.

Gary held his hand up. "Thanks for the offer, but we'll find it okay," he blurted out.

As they walked away from her, Callie elbowed him. "That wasn't very nice. She was just trying to help."

"We can find it ourselves. Besides, she sounds pretty nosey. She'd probably spread rumors about us, too."

"That's not the point. I've learned that these poor people get lonely, and it doesn't hurt to be nice to them. Besides, they love to talk."

Gary rolled his eyes. "Okay. I'm sorry," he said reluctantly. "But you have to admit, she's pretty nosey."

"I guess. Oh, apology accepted." As they entered the hallway, Callie looked over at Gary. "You'll feel better after seeing your dad."

"I doubt it."

"I remember when I went with mom to visit Alice after the accident. Mom was so wound up, and even though it didn't go well, she felt better for trying. She would've felt really guilty if she didn't, especially when Alice died so suddenly.

He glanced at her and shrugged. When they got to the door, Gary stopped at the doorway as Callie entered the room. When she realized he hadn't come in, she stopped, turned around, gave him a stern glare, and made a quick motion with her hand so that Billy wouldn't see. Gary hesitated, took a deep breath, and took a step inside.

Billy had a single-bed room, and they could see the sunlit courtyard outside. The overall feel of the room was cheerful, and Billy smiled slightly when he saw his son. Even from across the room, Gary saw that the usual redness that he remembered in his dad's gray eyes had dissipated, and the yellowish hue was now apparent. His gray skin had a little more color, but he still looked older than his age, with prematurely wrinkled skin, the pitted bulbous nose, gnarly teeth, and thinning, disheveled hair. In the last ten years of drinking, he had neglected his personal hygiene and damaged his health. Gary wondered if the damage was irreparable.

Callie put her box down onto a chair and walked over to his bed. "Hiya, Mr. Rawlins. How've you been holding up in here? Are you breaking all the caregivers' hearts?"

Billy chuckled and looked over at Gary who had put his box down and stood between the closet and the door, staring at his hands. Apparently uncomfortable, Gary looked aside as he picked up his box again and headed for the closet. He swung the closet door open so that it blocked the line of sight to the bed and started hanging up his dad's clothes.

Callie swallowed hard and whispered to Billy, "I'll talk to him." She picked up her box again and walked over next to Gary. She put the box down on top of Gary's and whispered to him, "I'll do this. You go talk to your father."

He glared at her. "Fine!" he whispered back.

She started organizing the closet after he walked towards his father, but she made sure to be quiet so she could listen in.

"So, how long are you gonna be here?"

"I don't know. I had to quit smoking so the bones would heal. Even at that, Doc doesn't know how long it'll take, even with the pins in me. It'll take longer to heal 'cause I was smoking before."

"So, you actually quit?" Gary stammered.

"Had to."

"How long's it been now?"

"Since I fell. That's been about two weeks."

Gary's voice seemed a little less aggravated. "Sorry it happened."

"Yeah, me too. Ain't been no picnic." He grimaced as he pushed himself up higher on his pillow.

Callie leaned out to peek at them. Gary's back was to her, and his dad was on the other side of him.

Billy's face was nondescript. "I heard you graduated."

"Yeah. I get my grades next week."

Billy nodded. "I never got to go. Just high school for me."

Gary seemed impatient, repeatedly shifting his weight from one foot to the other.

Callie finished hanging the clothes and then took the box of toiletries to the bathroom. She left the door open so she could hear.

"I had to work hard for that scholarship." The tone of Gary's voice seemed impatient and irritated. "And I worked hard for my grades." Gary seemed to wait for the acknowledgement that never came. After a pregnant moment, he said, "I'd better help Callie unpack." When he joined her in the bathroom, his face was red. "Well, I'm not feeling any better," he whispered firmly.

When they finished putting everything away, Callie went over to Billy's bed. "So, how's the recovery going?"

"Okay I guess, other than the pain, of course. Then the therapy hurts too. No fun, I tell you."

"Well, at least you're going to get better. Just look forward to getting back home."

"I s'pose. But it doesn't look like that'll happen for a while."

"Well, you take care and do what the doctor says, and you'll be fine." She turned around. With her back to Billy, she raised an eyebrow at Gary, motioned with her eyes, pointed to Billy's bed, and mouthed, "Go."

Gary sighed and stepped forward. "See you later. Bye." He reluctantly shook hands and left quickly. Callie ran out to catch up.

On the way to the lobby, Callie punched him in the shoulder. "You were downright depressing! That was no support at all. What's the matter with you? Couldn't you at least fake it?"

He rubbed his shoulder and glared at her. "It was the best I could do under the circumstances, okay? He never, *ever* showed me any support! So bug off!"

"You've got to let go of that anger, Gary. It'll hurt you more than it hurts your dad."

"Oh, and you're miss psychobabble? Where do you get off telling me anything?" He rubbed his shoulder again. "And that hurt!" He gave her a little shove which knocked her off her stride.

She stopped to look at him straight on with a challenge in her eyes. "Look, you don't want to take me on, mister. Don't you remember Georgia's demonstration?" She put her fists to her hips and set her jaw.

"Yeah, I saw what she did. All *you* did was fall to the ground though. Real impressive," he mocked.

She poked him in the chest and then put up her fists. "Come on. Put up your dukes."

"Yeah, right! At least we're in the right place. They'll be able to take care of you after *I* take care of you!"

"In your dreams!"

"Oh, knock it off. Let's get outta here. You're making a scene." Lengthening his stride, he headed towards the lobby.

Callie scowled after him but was approached by the woman on the scooter again. The woman held out a shaky hand and said, "I see you came to visit Billy. I'm glad you did. He seems so sad. And remember, if you want to know anything, you come to me."

Callie took her hand gently and smiled. "Thank you, Bertie. I'll be sure to ask you if I have any questions."

Bertie beamed, and her chest seemed to burst with pride when she took in a deep breath. "You're so sweet, dear. You come back soon, now."

Callie waved as she turned to leave. She jogged a few steps to catch up with Gary. When she got into the lobby, she saw a help-wanted sign looking for a part-time physical therapist, and she stopped to read it.

Gary stopped at the front door and turned around. "Well, are you coming?"

"Hold on." She waved him over.

He rolled his eyes and came up next to her. "No way! That's not going to happen," he announced with waving hands when he saw the poster.

"But you need a job, and this is what you went to school to do. Why not?"

"You've got to be kidding, right?" He let out a pathetic laugh. "Why would I want to spend more time with *him*? It would be torture."

"It wouldn't be *that* bad. And how much time would you actually have to spend with him?"

"Too much!"

"What's wrong with that? It's not like you have to be there 24/7. Besides, you might find out more about him – like what he's like when he's sober. My grandpa turned out to be totally different when he quit drinking. I actually like him now. I don't even call him Grumpa anymore."

"That's different." Pointing down the hall, he said, "I had to grow up with that pathetic excuse of a father. Living with him was no picnic. You know what it was like."

"Well, he's sober now. Even I can see a difference in him. You'll be surprised."

Turning around to leave, he waved his hand over his shoulder, to dismiss her. "No, I won't 'cause it won't happen."

She let out an exasperated breath and followed him out the door.

They climbed into her VW bug and slammed the doors. She glared at him. "Don't slam the door. It isn't even a year old."

"And what's your excuse?"

"You make me mad! You know that? You are *so frustrating*! How are you going to get along in the world if you won't bend?"

"You sound like your mother."

"Good! She's got a good head on her. Not like *you*!" She started the engine. "Put on your seatbelt," she snapped.

He saluted. "Yes ma'am, miss know-it-all." After clicking it, he crossed his arms and stared out the passenger window.

The tension grew as she drove to Rudy and Georgia's house.

Chapter 5

They arrived about ten minutes before the graduation party was scheduled to start. Several guests had already arrived and were mingling in the back yard where Rudy and Jack tended the barbecue and smoker. Georgia and Sharon were in the kitchen with last minute preparations.

"Well, we're here," Callie grumbled. She was still fuming about Gary's stubbornness.

When Gary unsnapped his seatbelt, he taunted, "See, if we'd stayed any later, we'd be late." He got out and shut the door before she could reply.

She jumped out. "We still had a few minutes. You could've been civil. But no! You were just being *you*!"

He sighed. "Look, this is supposed to be a party. Can you dial it down a little?" He walked off towards the back yard.

"Right," Callie growled. She took some cleansing breaths, put on a pleasant face, and tried to pretend everything was fine. When she rounded the back corner, she saw Gary engaged in a cheerful conversation with some old buddies. She went through the patio door and into the kitchen. "Hey, you guys need any help in here?"

Georgia waved her in. "Yeah, the paper plates, cups, napkins, and plastic ware are in that tub over there. Will you take them to the picnic table? The drinks and ice are already in the cooler, but we'll need all the cold food brought out too."

Callie noticed that Lucky, their dog, was underfoot, and Georgia nearly tripped over him several times. "You want me to put Lucky outside? He seems to be getting in the way."

"Already tried that. He just whines and scratches at the door. Much more annoying than him being underfoot. He's become such a momma's boy lately."

"You just be careful." Callie picked up the tub and headed outside. She couldn't help noticing Gary having a great time. After cooling down a bit, she started to feel guilty. *I shouldn't have started that argument, especially today. I was really stupid, and I overreacted. I'll have to apologize later.* By the time she went back inside for another load, her anger had evaporated.

The food was ready, everyone had arrived. Jack stood on a stool, put two fingers into his mouth, and whistled loudly. It was the only way he knew to get everyone's attention. He made a flattering speech, acknowledging Mark's and Gary's achievements, how proud he was of them, and how sorry he was that Gary's dad was unable to attend. Soft murmurs and whispers could be heard among several of their friends when he said that. Jack pretended not to notice and let everyone know that they could start eating. He was glad he wasn't between the food and the crowd; he could've been knocked down in the rush.

Forty-three guests milled around the barbecue, pond, waterfall, and mini-forest. Several groupings of chairs populated the yard, most of them looking like they were part of the game of musical chairs. Music, multiple conversations, and bouts of laughter blended into a low roar, forcing many to raise their voices, which increased the volume even more. But everyone was having fun.

Just before three, Jack hopped onto the stool and whistled for their attention again. "Mark and Gary want everyone to participate in the games. The first game is a scavenger hunt that starts after this announcement. Do not run off until I blow the whistle though, or you'll be disqualified. You'll go in teams of two each, and since there are an odd number of you young folks, Callie is going to join you. Everyone's name is written on a piece of paper and is in this bowl." He held it up. "Rudy will draw the names. As two names are drawn, that is the pairing. No trading partners. You will receive a bag containing a disposable camera to take pictures, a map, and a list of sites. You'll have two hours to take as many pictures as you can, but make sure one of you is in every picture. We don't want anyone cheating by getting pictures off the Internet. Be back here by five. If you don't make it back before the timer goes off, it won't matter if you got all ten photos, you'll be eliminated. The winning team will be the pair with the most photos. If there is a tie, then the team that returns in the least amount of time will win. After the winners are announced, we'll eat again!"

That announcement was met with a loud, unanimous cheer.

Finished with the instruction for the hunt, he got down, and Rudy started pulling names. About halfway through, Mark's name was called right after Heidi, the girl he took to the senior prom in high school.

Mark grinned, "Hey, was this a setup?"

Heidi laughed, and a slight blush covered her freckles. "Couldn't be better if it was. I'm driving."

After a couple more pairs were called, Rudy called Callie's name. Eager to find out who she'd be matched with, she held her breath. She let it out audibly when Gary's name was called.

Gary looked to the ground, shaking his head.

As Rudy read off more pairs, Gary leaned over to Callie and said, "You'd better let me drive."

"You? Drive *my* car? I don't *think* so!"

"You know where everything is located. It's been a long time since I've been here."

"Exactly. Since it's been so long since you've been here, you won't remember the roads."

"But you'll be the navigator; you'll just tell me where to go."

She crossed her arms as she glared at him. "It's not happening. And don't tempt me with telling you where to go."

"So, you want to lose?"

"The only way we'll lose is if you drive. You just tell me address, what the item is, and I'll find it. Okay?" It was a stretch, but she managed to avoid yelling.

His frown lines formed a pitchfork at the bridge of his nose as he squinted at her. "Fine! Have it your way."

She nodded firmly.

After everyone else was paired, Jack blew the whistle, and the crowd took off.

Gary got into the passenger seat and clicked his seatbelt. "See, I remembered," he growled sarcastically.

She started the engine. "What's the first site?"

He opened the folded paper. "What's a free little library?"

She sighed. "Just tell me the location."

"Southeast Portland, 31st and Knapp. What's a free little library?"

She explained as she drove, "They're made by homeowners usually. It looks kind of like a large bird house with a latched door where people take their used books and leave with others. It's a library, but little – a free little library."

"Huh. Pretty cool. What will people think of next?" He shook his head.

"Wait a minute. 31st and Knapp, right?"

"Yeah. Why?"

"Is there anything closer?"

He looked over the list. "The Willamette National Cemetery sign is the closest."

She pulled over. "Let's put them in order so we won't have to cross paths. We'll get a lot more pictures that way."

He gave her a thumbs up. "Great idea." He got a pen out, and they marked them in geographical order. "Let's eliminate the St. John's Bridge, it's too far away. We won't get as many pictures, and we might not get back in time."

"Agreed."

"Okay, the cemetery's first." As she took off, he added, "How about I jump out, and you take the picture while the car's running? It should shave a few seconds off each stop if you don't have to turn off and restart the car every time."

She grinned. "Good idea! We make a pretty good team." They gave each other a high five.

They took the picture as planned. "Now the mini library."

"I know the shortest way to get there. Hang on."

"You're not going to speed, are you?"

"No, but this baby turns corners really well. Besides, Rudy made me take a defensive driving course, so I've got it." After a couple of minutes, she asked cautiously, "Gary?"

He squinted at her. "What?"

"I'm sorry I was so gruff with you earlier. I realize you're under a lot of stress, just finishing finals, your dad, and not having a job. I just want you to know I was out of line. I'm sorry."

"Thanks. And it's okay. But *him,* I just don't know if I'll ever forgive him." He sighed. "He was always so absent, I felt like an outsider. Jack and Sharon, they pretty much saved me, you know."

She nodded.

"If not for them, I don't know what would've happened to me. They had their work cut out for them when they took me on."

"I know."

He whipped his head around. "And *what* is that supposed to mean?"

"I'm just agreeing with you."

"Mmm-hmm. So, you're saying I was a troublemaker?"

"At first ...."

"I hear a *but* in there."

She shrugged. "But you turned out okay. I'll give you that." Her face softened. "I know it was hard for you. I felt sorry for you so many times, especially when your dad wouldn't go to your games or parent-teacher conferences."

"Yeah. Well that's because he was stinking drunk most of the time."

"But remember, he quit."

"Well, it would've been better if he never started."

"He's sober now. *That's* what's important."

"I'm not putting any stock in it until I see if it sticks. And then it's a pretty big maybe."

"He's going to need your support to make it. If you hold back, he'll think being sober is not worth it. He could have a relapse."

He looked at her with a frown. "Are you sure you're working to be a P.I.?"

"What do you mean?"

"You sound like you could be a pretty good lawyer with the way you argue a point."

"Does that mean you'll think about it?"

He inhaled deeply and blew the air out his nose. "We'll see."

"So, when will you see your dad next time?"

"You're not going to let it go, are you?"

"Nope."

"Fine!" He let out a big sigh. "Tomorrow."

"I'll take you to make sure you go."

He shook his head.

"You really should look into that job opening at the nursing home."

Jaw set and eyes afire, he whipped his head to glare at her. "*I told you,*" he stated emphatically, "*it's not going to happen!*"

"You need the job and it's close by. Besides, it'll be a good way to reconnect with your dad."

"You don't seem to realize, I tried that. For years. It doesn't work."

"Remember, Mom said he has some kind of emotional disconnect. He doesn't seem to be able to understand how to express feelings. So, when normal people like us look at him, we see distance, lack of concern, sometimes even hostility."

"So, you want me to try to get close to someone that ... that can't be close? That makes a *whole* lot of sense!"

"But Mom says that he does love you. He just doesn't know how to express it."

"Well, I need that like I need a hole in the head."

"Gary, he's your father. Are you going to abandon him?"

"I don't need to. He already took care of that by abandoning me."

"Actually, he didn't. He could've let everything go, lose the house and go homeless, commit suicide, or maybe just pine away and die. But no, he stuck it out trying to support you. He did what he was able to do. Don't diminish that."

Gary worked his jaw as he stared out the window.

She slowed down. "We're almost there. Keep your eyes open."

"I really don't know what we're looking for."

"I see it." She pulled over across the street and pointed to the free mini-library.

Gary jumped out, and she took the picture. He ran back to the car and pointed north. "Reed College, main entrance next." They were there in three minutes and hardly took another few seconds getting the photo.

"The Rhododendron Gardens are next. Uh-oh, we have to get out of the car, the picture has to be of the lake from the bridge."

She sighed. "We'll have to run. It's quite a distance from the entrance."

"I know." He smiled. "Remember that picnic your parents took us on? I must've been ... what, fourteen? I still have the pictures Jack took."

"I remember. That was a fun day." She did a quick turn into the parking lot and parked. "Come on. We've got to hurry. There are already two other couples here."

"But that means we're ahead of them. Since we rearranged the order, this is our fourth site and only the second for them."

"If they didn't rearrange them too," she called out running down the path. One couple passed them running towards the exit.

"But we didn't see them at any of the other places, so they couldn't have rearranged them."

Panting, they stopped on the bridge and she took his picture with the sun to her back. She noticed he was looking over her shoulder and she turned around. Someone was running a remote-controlled, toy speed boat across the lake. An older couple was throwing bread crumbs to the ducks, geese, and two swans that were spread out among the reeds and lily pads. They took a few moments to watch the scene and a sense of peace came over her. She snapped out of the reverie when she realized a second couple ran running their way with their camera.

"Whoa! We've got to go!" She grabbed his hand and ran, almost yanking him off balance.

"You could've given me a warning!" He quickly outpaced her, almost dragging her behind him. They jumped into the car and took off.

"What's next?"

"Skidmore Fountain and the sky bridge at Portland State University."

She groaned. "I hate driving downtown."

"At least it's Saturday."

"I know, but I still hate it."

As they headed north, Gary was quiet as he stared out the passenger window.

"Don't be mad at me," Callie implored.

"I'm not mad."

"You kind of look mad."

He turned to her. His eyes seemed red and downcast. "Do you think he'd go back to drinking?"

"You mean if you avoided him?"

"Yeah."

"He might. And I'm not just trying to coerce you into it. I really believe it's a possibility."

He blew a quick breath out his nostrils. He seemed deflated and morose. He was quiet until they arrived at the fountain.

Callie pulled up and announced, "I'll stop and take your picture. Let the other drivers honk if they want."

Gary gave her another thumbs up. "Gotcha."

She got his picture, and they did the same thing at the sky bridge.

"What is this 'ugly sculpture' near McLoughlin and Tacoma?" He frowned.

"I know what it refers to." Callie headed for the Ross Island Bridge. "The city's been putting up a lot of artwork. If you ask me, it's just a waste of money; they're ugly, rusty and – well, you'll see."

Gary had been glancing at the speedometer on the straightaways, and this time he cringed. "I thought you weren't going to speed."

"Keeping tabs on me?"

"If you get pulled over, we'll lose."

She huffed and slowed down to the speed limit just before taking the McLoughlin Boulevard exit.

"Thanks. Besides, I'd like to live a little longer, too."

"I'm a good driver!"

"Just saying."

In a few minutes, she called out, "There it is. I'll pull over here." She pulled over and pointed, "Stand right there. Even though it's across the street, it's big enough that it'll show just fine."

"Yuck. I see why you call it ugly. It looks like a giant, rusted bike chain." He jumped out, and Callie took the picture from the driver's seat. He jumped back in and looked at the list. "Next is the top of the Oregon City elevator. Do you think we have enough time?"

"I'll make time."

On the way, Callie took a deep breath and exhaled through pursed lips. "I think you should see your dad at least once a day."

"Don't you think you're pushing this?"

"No. I wouldn't suggest it if I did." She shrugged. "Well, maybe."

He chuckled. "You're never going to change, are you?"

"What do you mean?"

"Being so pushy. You're like a bulldog on a bone."

"Do you remember what it was like growing up? I had to learn how to stand up for myself with you and Mark always picking on me."

He smiled slyly, and the grin grew as he thought about it. "Yeah. I'll give you that one." He looked over at her. "But it was fun, wasn't it?"

"For *you* maybe. Not so much for me." She smiled imperceptibly.

After a few minutes, she announced, "We're almost there."

She stopped, Gary jumped out, and she snapped the picture.

"Next is the waterfall at the bottom of the hill."

"Got it. See this works pretty well."

"Yeah, I guess so."

She pulled into the sightseer's pullout just a few minutes later. "We'll have to get out; you can't see the waterfall from here. Let's go."

"Right."

When they got to the stone wall, they looked over the edge. Since the spring runoff was just past its crest, it was more of a turbulent down-current than a waterfall. She sat on the stone wall and posed. Gary had to lean slightly over the edge to make sure the waterfall was captured behind her. He pretended to lose his balance and almost pushed her over the wall. She screamed as she grabbed his arm, and he pulled her back.

"Don't ever do that again! I almost went over!"

"I got you." His eyes had the look of a cat playing with a mouse when he added, "I knew what I was doing."

She scowled at him. "See! That's the kind of thing I had to put up with all those years!"

"Hey, there's someone pulling in. We'd better run."

They dashed for the car and fumbled for the seatbelts. Gary looked at his watch. "We've got less than twenty minutes left. We have to head back now to get back in time."

On the way, Callie took a few chances that made Gary grip the panic bar with white knuckles. "Are you nuts?! You realize we have to get back in one piece, don't you?"

"Be quiet and hang on." She got on the freeway and gunned it.

"You're going to get a ticket! Or get us killed!"

"Maybe – maybe not."

Still hanging on tightly, Gary gasped as she repeatedly switched lanes with just inches to spare. He closed his eyes and held his breath when she aimed for another spot. He bounced sideways several times in the race back to Georgia's house, once bumping his head on the door frame.

She skidded into the driveway and shouted, "Come on. We can make it!"

Shaking, he fumbled to undo his seatbelt.

Seeing that he couldn't open it, she reached over and popped it open. "Hurry!"

They ran to the back yard. "Gary, where's the camera?"

Flushing, he stammered, "It's in the car."

She raced back, grabbed it, and ran back to the finish line holding the camera over her head.

Jack shook his head. "You just made it." He took her camera and gave it to Rudy. "He'll count your pictures." When his timer went off, he shouted, "Time's up! We'll tally how many photos each team got and announce the winner when we're done."

Callie was still breathing hard when she turned around to give Gary a high-five. She looked around and saw that there were six other couples that arrived ahead of them. She leaned over to him, "I think we've got it. We had to have gotten more pictures."

"I'm going to sit down. My heart is still racing."

"Did I scare you?"

He looked at her incredulously. "Duh!"

"I'll get you a soda. You still drink cola?"

"Yeah."

She returned with drinks, handed him the cola with ice, and sat down next to him. "We did okay."

He chugged it down. "So, this training you've been getting. Is that why you're such a maniac behind the wheel now? 'Cause I don't remember you being like that at all!"

"I don't think so. Well, maybe Georgia *has* been helping me be more assertive."

"Assertive? I'd say you're downright aggressive!"

"Really?"

He rolled his eyes.

During the next twenty minutes, the remaining couples straggled in.

The rest of the evening was a casual mix of conversations, eating, music, hanging out, and laughing.

Callie was right. They had gotten more pictures and won.

Chapter 6

The large conference room was filled to capacity. Rudy, Roy, and Pierre were among the men and women who were fine-tuning the details of the largest sting operation ever planned in the state of Oregon. The syndicate was finally going to be taken down and brought to justice. Special Agent Brooks was going over the time line of the operation and assigning different phases of the plan to specific agents' teams, other agencies, and SWAT teams. Since the criminals were meeting in such a large mansion, the team had blueprints of the floor plans of each floor so each crew member would be as prepared as possible so this takedown would run like a well-oiled machine. By the end of the meeting, everyone was confident in their assigned tasks.

After the meeting was over, everyone filed out of the room abuzz with the upcoming operation. In the disorganized chaos, Pierre palmed a phone from an equipment table, pulled away from the crowd, and slipped into an empty office. When the call went through, he whispered, "Plans are set. One in the afternoon, week from tomorrow. They don't have a clue." After the call was complete, Pierre deleted his call and turned off the phone. When he came out of the room, Rudy appeared from around a corner looking for him. Thankful that Rudy hadn't seen where he'd just come from, he calmly asked, "What's next?"

"I'm sorry, but we have to keep you in isolation until this is done. We can't have any possibility of this going south. Please follow me." As they walked past the equipment table, Pierre slipped the phone back where it belonged.

Pierre was searched and taken to a small room where there was a cot, water fountain, and a small fridge with enough food to last until the takedown was over.

"If you need to use the bathroom, just knock on the door, and the guard will escort you. Seems like you kept your end of the bargain, but we can't take any chances. To be honest, I was skeptical about you helping but you really came through. I don't think this could have been planned so well without your help. Once it's done, I'm sure they'll let you go soon after."

As Rudy left the room, Pierre showed the flicker of a sinister grin.

Roy carefully followed directions to a remote area below highway 43, about halfway between Portland and Lake Oswego. He parked his car behind some bushes and walked to the river's edge. It was almost dark, and the stars were just starting to wink at him. Crickets started to communicate behind him. The sound of water lapping at the rocky shoreline gave him a deceptive sense of serenity. The lights across the river reflected onto the water like fireflies dancing before him.

A fleeting smile skirted across his face as he remembered the last time he took the time to gaze over the river. That was the night he proposed to Callie. An abrupt return to the present burst his bubble as he remembered she was gone, no longer part of his life. The joy of that night seemed like a distant dream, being eclipsed by the stark contrast of despair that engulfed him now. He tried to shake off the strange chill as the sparkling flashes of light taunted him.

Thinking back to that bribe he had accepted, he wondered whether he'd make a different choice if given a second chance. Probably not, his grandfather's life was in the balance. So, he fretted over his sins, that awful decision that led him to this point. The worst consequence was losing Callie.

He shuddered as he told himself to stop rehashing the past. He looked at his watch; his contact was ten minutes late and still no sign of him. He just wanted to get this done.

A twig snapped behind him, initiating an adrenalin rush. It must be him. He waited as instructed.

A disguised voice asked, "Jackson?"

Without turning around, Roy responded, "You bring the money?"

"Tell me what you got."

"Pierre told us about a meeting you're having. The Feds are planning a raid."

"Give me the specifics."

Roy explained exactly what Pierre had said and then outlined the Feds' plan of action. The contact paused. Just as Roy began to wonder if something was wrong, the contact asked suspiciously, "How do I know you're legit?"

"Look, I lost my girlfriend. We were going to get married, but that's not going to happen now. My friend at the station was arrested. And if anyone finds out about that bribe, I'm a goner. There's no future for me. So, I might as well rack up some money and disappear. And like I said in my call to you, when this is over, I want some fake ID, too. I'll do whatever else needs to be done until it's over."

The voice told him to replace a piece of evidence from the evidence locker at the station. As the voice told him the details, Roy was handed a gun in a zippered bag from behind.

Roy noticed the man's hand was wearing a glove.

"Have it done by tomorrow night."

"What do you want me to do with the other gun?"

"I'll call. And here's the money for it. Half now, half when it's done. Wait for ten minutes and don't turn around until you leave."

After a moment, he heard tires driving over gravel and then the receding hum of tires on pavement until all he could hear were crickets and the rhythmic lap of water along the bank.

Chapter 7

The pounding in Gary's ears made him wonder how high his blood pressure had gone. His breathing was shallow and rapid, and his hands trembled. He pulled at his collar to get more air and wiped a few beads of sweat from his brow. It was bad enough that he had to see his dad again, but right now, he couldn't help thinking, *how do I work up the nerve to tell her?* He glanced over at Callie, who was driving. *What if she just laughs at me?* He closed his eyes, but being without sight didn't make things any better. He jumped when Callie chirped, "We're here." He swallowed hard. *Ok, after we get out of here, I'll tell her.*

"Well, are you going to take off your seat belt?"

His lips became a tight line, and he reluctantly unlatched the seat belt. Then, he followed her into the nursing home carrying the few things they had forgot last time.

Callie brightened and waved at an aide who was walking towards them. "Hi, Marci."

Gary looked at Marci. She was medium height, slim, and had bronze skin, black eyes, and short curly black hair. He assumed that she and Callie had known each other for a while.

"I was hoping I'd see you," Callie said cheerfully.

Marci walked up with a happy smile. "Oh, hi! Callie, is it? What brings you here? You haven't been here since …" Her face fell. "Uh, since Alice passed." She became apologetic when she added, "Sorry."

"No problem. Gary, this is Marci Collins. And this is Gary Rawlins. Ha! Collins, Rawlins, I just realized that you guys rhyme! Anyhow, we're coming to visit his dad, Billy."

Marci shook his hand. "Glad to meet you, Rawlins." She had warm hands and her smile was inviting and interested.

"Nice to meet you, Collins."

She lingered in the handshake. "Your dad is Billy? He's got a broken hip, right?"

Callie smiled. "You know everyone, don't you?"

"It kinda comes with the job." Her pager went off, and she checked to see which room required assistance. "Sorry, gotta go. A new resident needs me." As she hustled down the hall, her hips seemed to sway a little more than necessary.

Callie leaned over to Gary to whisper, "She's one of the good ones. I met her when Mom and I came to visit Alice two years ago. Marci works part-time so she can go to school to be a nurse. If I remember right, she'll graduate this year. Mom made sure to tell her that she always appreciated the concern she had for all the residents." As they started towards Billy's room, she looked at Gary as if she had a question.

"What?" he asked suspiciously.

"Didn't you see it?"

"See what?"

"I think she likes you."

"Go on. She did not."

Callie put her hands on her hips. "I can tell. I am a girl, you know." She tilted her head as she put her hand on his shoulder. "She was flirting with you. You should ask her out."

"Yeah, right." He waved her off.

"It'd make coming to work a lot nicer." She grinned.

"Oh, I get it. You're still trying to get me to take that job."

"Come on. They need help, and you need a job. It's simple. And you could use a friend."

He tried to breathe normally, but he couldn't. "I can't handle that right now. Okay?"

"You are so stubborn!"

"You ought to know! You're the queen of stubborn!"

She stopped short and glared at him. Then just as quickly, she shook her head and took a cleansing breath. "Wait. I'm not going to ruin this visit with your dad, okay? We're going in there, and we're going to be pleasant." She tipped her chin down, opened her eyes wider, and held out her hand. "Truce?"

He rolled his eyes. "Right."

"You should still ask her out."

"Oh, brother," he mumbled.

Like the last visit, he waited at the doorway when Callie walked into Billy's room. She turned around with her back to Billy, her eyes glowering, and mouthed, "Come on! Now!"

He stepped in. Without thinking, he crossed his arms.

She picked up Billy's water pitcher. "Let me get some fresh water for you." She turned around, got Gary's attention, and pointed for him to approach the bed as she left the room.

Gary's ears pounded again. He swallowed again, but his voice didn't seem to work and his mouth was dry.

Billy looked up at him. "Hi, Gary."

Gary cleared his throat, took a deep breath, and said, "Hi."

Callie rushed in. "Here you go, Billy. I even put in some ice for you."

"Thanks."

Callie put her hand on Gary's shoulder. "You'll never believe this, Billy. Gary's thinking about applying for that physical therapy position that's open here."

Billy's eyes lit up. "Really?"

The color drained from Gary's face, and he stopped breathing. He didn't hear anything except for the intense pounding in his ears. He reached out with a shaky hand to pour some water for himself and drank it quickly.

Callie looked at him strangely. "Gary. What's wrong? You don't look well."

Billy's mouth opened halfway, and he tried to sit up. But the pain made him stop, and he lay back down.

Gary wanted so badly to strangle her. He turned to stare her down with restrained rage.

She turned red and quickly added, "Well, I told him to think about it anyways."

"Ahh, I see. Well, son, I hope you do. I'd like to see more of you."

Gary found his voice, and it was loud and agitated. "So then how come you didn't even send me a card when I graduated?"

Billy's face fell. "Well, I couldn't exactly pick out a card from the emergency room."

"What do you mean?"

"I didn't think I'd need one if I was going to be there. But then I went and fell through the porch when I was on my way to the airport."

"What?" Gary was stymied by a jumble of shock, disbelief, and confusion. "You were going to get on a plane?"

"Yeah."

"But you hate flying."

"Well, I had to ... the car broke down, and that was the only way I could get there in time to see you walk across that stage. Then, I had to go to the hospital instead."

Except for his mouth opening slightly and eyes blinking slowly, Gary stood frozen. Although Callie was next to him, she seemed miles away. A hazy nonexistence seemed to cloud his mind as a thought formed, *He was actually going to fly. I can't believe it! This doesn't make sense.* He returned to the present when he realized his shoulder was jiggling.

"Gary?" Callie had a grip on his shoulder and was shaking it repeatedly. "Gary, are you okay?"

He shook his head. "What?" He turned to look at her and saw that she seemed worried about something. "Are you okay?" he asked.

She squinted at him. "That's what I asked you." She waved her hand in front of his face.

He brushed her hand aside. "What makes you think I'm not okay?"

"Hello! You were spaced out. What happened?"

"I was?"

"Yes. Your dad saw it too. Didn't you, Billy?"

With his eyebrows raised, Billy nodded.

Gary turned pale when he recalled what they had been discussing. He turned to his dad, "You were actually going to fly to my graduation?"

"Yeah. What's wrong with that?"

"Uh ... nothing. But, why didn't you tell me?"

"I wanted to surprise you."

"Well, you accomplished that." He scratched his head. "How would you have found me after you got there?"

"I was gonna just ask around after I got there."

Gary closed his eyes and shook his head. "It's not that easy, Dad."

Callie squeezed his arm and whispered, "Let it go."

Confused by his sudden drain of energy, Gary opened his eyes again to really look at his dad. *This is not what I expected – totally out of character. Could this really be him? After all, he did stop drinking. Maybe during all those years, I had seen only the ghost of a man that was obscured by liquor.* Deciding to figure it out – with caution – he braced himself, took a cleansing breath, and asked his dad about the nursing home. As his dad talked about his daily routine, Gary listened and became engaged in the conversation.

Billy stopped in mid-sentence, "Oh, get my bag over there, would you?"

Gary pulled it out of the closet. "What do you need?"

"I want to give you the keys to the car. The clutch needs fixin'. I don't suppose you'd mind?"

Gary's breath escaped like a ruptured balloon. *I should've known. He needs something, again.* He rummaged through the bag and pulled them out. "I'll take care of it," he said quietly.

"When you're done, the car's yours."

Gary stared at him blankly.

Callie nudged him and whispered, "Say thank you."

Gary nodded. "Thanks." He turned to Callie. "It's time to go." He put the keys into his pocket.

When they got to the hallway, Callie elbowed him. "That was really nice of him, Gary. He gave you his car."

He stopped in his tracks. "Nice? Seriously? Have you seen it? It's just a pile of rusty junk! Now, he's going to expect me to drive it. Five years ago, it was always breaking down. How reliable do you think it is now?!"

"He gave you what he could. That means something."

"Yeah. It means I'm worthless to him!"

Callie scowled at him. "You really are ungrateful ...."

"Yeah? Well, of course *you're* grateful – miss 'has everything and a new car!' I'd be grateful with that, too!"

"He doesn't have much, but he gave you the most valuable thing he has. The least you can do is appreciate the gesture."

"Fine. I'll appreciate it all the way to the mechanic and then I'll have to pay the bill." He walked briskly to the lobby but was cut off by Bertie on her scooter. She held out her hand.

Gary stopped, put on a polite smile, and shook her hand. "Good afternoon. Bertie, is it?"

"Oh, you remembered! You're so sweet." She looked around to see if anyone could hear. "I should warn you though, stay away from Roger. I think he could be an alien."

Gary's mouth dropped open. "Huh?"

"His ears wiggle like antennas when he smiles." She leaned forward to whisper, "He could be sending signals to his mother planet."

Gary chuckled.

She wheeled alongside as he and Callie walked past some comfy chairs in the great room when they were again stopped by the old lady from the last visit.

"Have we had lunch?" she asked with a shaky voice.

"Yes, Elaine," replied Bertie, "about twenty minutes ago."

"Thank you, dear." Elaine smiled and walked away.

"So, I see you came out of Billy's room again," Bertie continued as if there had been no interruption, and Callie followed them slowly through the lobby.

Expecting to hear gossip about his dad, Gary waited to find out what she would say.

Her face dropped. "He's been so sad."

"Sad?"

"Yes. His son ..." Her face lit up when she continued, "... Oh, you're his son, aren't you?"

He nodded.

"I'm so glad you're here. I can tell he misses you. But now that you're visiting, he seems a little happier ... he told me he's hoping you'll stay. But I know this – he loves you very much."

Gary frowned incredulously. "And you know this because ...?"

"Because you're all he talks about. You *do* know that people talk about the things they love, don't you?"

He arched an eyebrow.

"You're a very lucky young man. I lost my dad when I was only ten."

"Oh, I'm sorry."

"Well, that was a long time ago. But I'm telling you this so you don't squander your time with him. Make every minute count."

"Thanks. Nice talking with you."

She waved as he turned to leave. Callie hurried to his side and whispered, "I couldn't help but hear. What she said is something to think about." After a moment of silence, Callie cocked an eyebrow. "Did she really say Roger was an alien?"

"Yeah. I wonder about her."

"Well, with everyone here, you have to take everything with a grain of salt."

"Would that include her assessment of my dad?"

She sighed as they walked out the front door.

Gary didn't say much on the way home; too many thoughts were spinning in his mind. The conversation with Callie would have to wait for another time.

Chapter 8

At midnight, large groups of law enforcement officers, FBI agents, a SWAT team and others gathered in an empty building near the house. A large monitor displayed a live infrared feed of the building showing not only where the mob's men were stationed inside, but also the invading teams waiting outside a block away. Most of the ones inside appeared to be asleep, with a few of them standing guard outside. A last minute change in the time of the operation had been carefully relayed to those who had a part in this to make sure there were no leaks. A lot was riding on this operation going off without a hitch.

As one o'clock drew closer, the teams moved out to their assigned positions around the house. At the radio signal, the teams silently took down the outside guards, and the remaining teams went in through their assigned entry points. Each one was quickly bound, gagged, and removed so he couldn't call out or signal the others.

Eventually, only three moving bodies showed on the infrared monitors, and the teams were directed to each one. The man monitoring the infrared feed alerted the teams, "The last three men are running for the exits."

As the SWAT team swept the basement, the lead man called into his mike, "This place is wired, and it looks like it's ready to go! We've got to get out of here, *now!*" In the scramble to get out of the building, one of the last to reach the door brushed against a hidden trigger that set off a series of explosions.

Roy didn't care much for this meeting place. From his experience, the homeless tended to congregate here, so he was concerned about privacy.

Yes, he'd scouted the place before parking his car, but there was always an off chance that something unexpected could happen.

As usual, it was dark, just different from the last place they had met. The moon was new and the trees made a thick canopy, so he couldn't see squat – eyes open or closed. With this kind of darkness, he just assumed his contact would be wearing night goggles.

Although he was expecting it, the disguised voice startled him.

"The evidence?"

Roy handed him the gun in a plastic bag.

Here's the rest of your pay for the evidence switch. Now, give me a full report on what happened at the house on 183rd."

"How much do I get?"

"Ten thousand. The report?" This time the voice sounded irritated.

"A snitch leaked information that there was a mob meeting there today, so the FBI has been working with the police department to get them. I don't know why, but the swat teams went in early. But it turned out to be a trap, because the place was rigged with explosives. When they realized it, they tried to run, but the place went up too quick. Everyone died, the swat team and your guys. The Feds are feeding a different story to the media, something about a gas leak. There's a big investigation going on right now."

"I'll call you when we have your next assignment," the voice hissed. "And if you have additional information, it may be valuable to us. Here's a number to call if you do." He handed Roy a card. "Like last time, wait ten minutes before you leave."

The next afternoon, Agent Brooks walked in, his face showing no expression. He stood in front of Pierre and handed him a large envelope. "The ambush went as planned. Per our agreement, here is your new identity, cash, a plane ticket, and the information you'll need when you deplane. We'll escort you to the airport."

"I won't need it. You took care of them, so what's the point? I really don't have anywhere to go, no job, and I don't know anyone." He looked glum. "I'll take the cash though. I'll need something to go on until I get my feet on the ground again." He looked up. "Thanks for saving my life; I really appreciate it."

"Just one more thing. There's something else we need to talk about before you can leave."

Pierre eyed him.

Brooks waved for Agent Riley to bring the "something else" in.

Recognition flickered in Pierre's eyes as Riley wheeled in a rolling cart with an old wooden box with worn rope handles at each end on it. The box had a hinged lid and was approximately two feet long, eighteen inches wide, and a foot tall.

Brooks stared at Pierre, finally saying, "You know what's in here since this came from your basement less than a year ago. You're going to tell us how you got all this evidence from the police evidence locker. You're also going to tell us why you had it. Obviously, we know what cases are involved. You've probably heard on the news about several cases being overturned. That all happened because of what we found in this box."

From behind the one-way mirror, Rudy nodded with pleasure to see Pierre waver.

Pierre would never find a way to bluff his way out of having that box. He heaved a large breath and started, "You probably already know how I got all of it." He looked down and shook his head.

"Why do you have this?"

"Look. I already told you, I had suspicions – for a long time. I was just trying to get some leverage. I figured that if I had all that evidence, well, maybe they'd think twice about doing me in."

"We haven't been able to determine two of the cases since you didn't write the case numbers and only wrote down the initials of the culprits. Give us the names and cases."

"Look, all that stuff was from the nineties. Most of those guys are dead already."

"Who are AR and VP?"

Pierre shrugged. "It doesn't matter, they're dead."

It was dark by the time Pierre was finally released.

Chapter 9

Pierre walked into Frankie's office with a swagger. "That went better than I expected."

Even sitting behind his desk, Frankie commanded respect. Although his salt-and-pepper hair lent a distinguished air, his square jaw, large hands, and 6'1" robust frame emanated power. Few dared to challenge him, but not for long. Thus, many of his men cringed when Frankie fixed those hooded, almost-black eyes at them, for they never knew what he was thinking.

Frankie nodded. "Ah, my favorite cousin, welcome home. Are we free to proceed with our next job?"

"Of course. I had the Feds eating up everything I gave them, including that fake meeting. I convinced them that I had no idea the place was rigged. Our plan worked so well, they couldn't thank me enough before they let me go. As expected, they went in early, and I understand it went off as expected."

Frankie offered Pierre to sit down in the chair in front of his desk. "It's all over the news. We know it went our way; our mole gave us a report. Good job. So, how did they react when you called the Feds with that story about us trying to eliminate you?"

Pierre grinned. "I had them eating out of my hand. "They really thought they were saving me and getting rid of you, too." Pierre chuckled. "Putting the grunts in that house worked perfectly! Not only did the Feds think you and your men were blown to smithereens, but we got rid of the grunts too. Now, we're left with a tight and loyal brotherhood. Couldn't be better."

"Just as planned."

"I wish you could have seen me. I was a very convincing victim," Pierre moaned dramatically.

"I heard Brick almost missed the vest you were wearing. I'm glad you're okay."

"Me, too! Even with the vest, I still got a couple of broken ribs out of it." He lightly rubbed his side. "It's still a little sore."

"As we discussed, everyone knows you're second only to me now. Congratulations on a job well done."

"So, what's our next score? And what's the fake story we feed the Feds?" Pierre watched for the telltale crooked smile on Frankie's face. Having grown up together, he knew it would be the sign that Frankie was self-satisfied and feeling in control. He didn't know of anyone else who had picked up on it – even Frankie was unaware of it. Knowing about this quirk meant he had knowledge beyond anyone else. When Pierre saw it, he relaxed. This plan was going to work.

"I'll tell you later. And then we let the Feds hear about the fake one on your bugged phone."

"Sure. But let's clear up everything else first." Pierre leaned back and stared at him for a moment. "Just wondering. Any idea how the police payoffs were discovered?"

Frankie's nose flared. "No idea. I was hoping you knew."

Pierre cocked an eyebrow. "I hope you don't mean you think *I* told them?"

"Of course not! I just thought you might have heard something when the Feds had you in custody."

Pierre breathed a little easier, but not much. Other than his satisfied crooked smile, Frankie never showed his hand. When he acted, it was always with a blindside. Pierre decided to watch his step from now on. He couldn't tell if Frankie was still playing the role they'd concocted, or if he really meant it. It was always possible Frankie actually suspected him. "When I was working with them, I never heard about anything they were investigating. I was as shocked as anyone. The only guess I have is this detective that disappeared before the takedown of the cops we had on our payroll. I'd have to look at my books to get his name, but we only used him once, and that was over three years ago. I don't know … it could be a coincidence."

Frankie paused for several seconds. "We know who the detective is and we're working with him as we speak. Shiv's been in contact with him for what really happened on our sting. So far, he seems to be in the program. I've got another test for him, and if it works out, then we'll put him to work when we do the heist – to make sure the cops are busy on the diversions."

"Say, since my phone is bugged, you got another one for our real conversations?"

"Yeah, here. Make sure you keep in mind which one you're using."

Pierre glared at him as he put it into his pocket. Then he decided to let it go. "So, what's the real job?"

"Now, about the job, I'll give you a quick rundown. It's over ten million worth of uncut diamonds. I want you to give the guys their assignments. Talk to Shiv. He can tell you what each of the guys do best so you can decide where to place them. He might be a good one to put in charge of Team Shepard."

Frankie's telltale idiosyncrasy flicked across his mouth. "We'll need almost everyone for this job. We we've got a couple of new guys, but since they're so new, we can't let them in on anything major until they're put through the ringer first. They'll be stationed with me at the warehouse waiting for the package to arrive."

Frankie folded his hands, leaned forward, and rested his elbows on the desk. "The time of the job is the same as the diversion. That way, the cops will be busy covering it instead of the jeweler. Most of the plans are fleshed out already. But we have some time to finalize the details since the diamonds won't be arriving for a while. We'll have three teams. Team Python will break in and load the truck. Team Shepherd will watch the streets for a clear getaway and transport. And I'm putting you in charge of Team Rhino, blowing the safe."

"Diamond stores usually have really good security systems, and it takes too much time to open their safes. How will we get around that?"

"We got the specs on the building and security. We'll disarm the alarm, enter the building, and then simultaneously blow a wall behind the building and the structure holding the safe. We've got a forklift to move the safe to the truck and then into the warehouse. That's where we actually blow the safe."

Pierre frowned. "Won't the explosions alert everyone?"

The crooked smile again. "Nobody will know the difference. One of my construction companies got the contract to demo a building in the next block. They're scheduling it to coincide with the time I gave them."

"How do we open the safe?"

"We'll drill into the top of the safe, fill it with water, light a stick of dynamite, put it inside, and blow the door off it from inside." Frankie chuckled. "I saw that in a movie once. There's no better way to get good ideas for major heists than watching movies!"

"Well, if there's anything that will survive a blast like that, it's diamonds."

"Right now, we're building the framework to contain the blast. That way no diamonds will get lost or picked up by greedy hands."

Pierre liked the plan, but he couldn't stop thinking about their other problem. "This is off the subject, but what's the update on the gold digger and her sister?"

Frankie glared at him. "How'd you hear about that?"

"The Feds were pretty accommodating. I was able to keep up on the news with newspapers and a TV."

Frankie's eyes narrowed slightly.

"So, what really happened?"

"The little druggie went off half-cocked. We had to fix it."

Pierre eyed him. "What aren't you telling me?"

Frankie's jaw tightened to match the rage in his eyes. "I know where the money went."

Pierre excitedly leaned forward in his chair with his hands on the edge of Frankie's desk. "Well? Where is it?!"

"Vera has it."

"What?! How?"

"Don't know yet."

"How do you know *she* has it?"

Frankie's neck veins pulsed. "Just before Jody pulled the trigger, Vera yelled at her, 'Don't do it, or I'll never tell you where I hid the money.'" Frankie's nose flared. "It had to be when Brent and Vera took that little vacation to Switzerland last year."

"What are you going to do about it?"

"Don't concern yourself about it. Since it's a family matter, I'll handle it."

Pierre leaned back and crossed his arms. "With all the news coverage, I'd say it's more than just a family matter. I'm guessing the cops have been here more than once, asking a lot of questions."

"She has amnesia and still doesn't remember what happened. But when her memory comes back, we'll make her tell."

"Don't you think we need to make sure of that so-called *memory loss*?" Shaking his head, he continued, "And what about that sister of hers?"

"Still in Salem. With her attitude, they still think she's crazy."

"I say we take care of it *before* it gets out of hand."

"You mean like you took care of Alice? You got caught! Remember?"

After a quick flinch, Pierre glared at him and said nothing.

"*I'm* in charge!" Frankie's nose flared as he pointed at Pierre as if holding a gun and commanded, "*You* don't need to get involved."

"She's a big risk. Both of them are. Just letting you know."

Frankie glared at him. "I will handle this. You focus on your part."

Pierre put up his hands in surrender. "Okay," he said and sighed. "So, what's the diversion?"

"I'll tell it to you on your bugged phone, so I won't have to say it twice. Go down the hill and call from there."

Pierre got up to leave. When he got to the door, he looked back over his shoulder and said, "Don't say I didn't warn you about her." Knowing Frankie would give him the evil eye, he turned to leave so he wouldn't have to see it and shut the door behind him.

Frankie's mouth pressed into a hard line as he headed for the den. "Cousin or not, he's getting just a bit too cocky. I'll have to keep an eye on him," he angrily mumbled to himself as he walked down the hallway. Refocusing on his mission, he controlled his breathing.

Like every night for the last two months, he closed the den door and prepared two cocktails, a dirty martini and a White Russian. He carefully took them upstairs and pushed the bedroom door open with his elbow.

Phaedra was still up. Always intense and full of energy, she recently had a downturn in her health. She had stopped micromanaging the staff, hadn't gone to the gym downstairs, and her appetite was gone. Frankie had taken note of every setback. Yet with all that, she still maintained that penetrating look in her dark eyes. Wrapped in a silk down comforter, she sat in her upholstered rocking chair in front of a roaring fire in the stone fireplace. He thought it was too warm for a fire, especially in summer, but he acceded to her comfort.

"I see Tanisha built a fire for you."

As she looked up at him, her once lustrous, brown hair draped softly over her left shoulder. A flicker of appreciation crossed her tired face. He noticed her skin recently displayed a definite pink, almost red tinge.

She nodded to the Duncan Phyfe end table to her right. His chair, a William and Mary wingback, was on the other side of the table. He always hated that chair, but Phaedra had insisted they buy it, and that he use it. He pushed the thought away and put on a smile. "Got your nightcap here."

"Obviously," she said dryly. She turned back to watching the fire, motioned for him to sit, and resumed rocking slowly. She pulled the comforter closer around her slim body and propped her slippered feet onto the footstool before the fire.

He looked at her flushed cheeks as he placed her drink on the table and he sat down. "You feeling any better?"

"It comes and goes a little. If I don't feel better soon, you should call the doctor again." She picked up the dirty martini and took a sip. "So, how did the meeting go with Pierre?"

He filled her in on what they said. "Since he's been away for so long, I told him about the plans for the heist." He set his drink on the table and turned to face her. "He's concerned about our little gold diggers. I told him we have the situation under control, but he won't let it go."

Definitely irritated, fire returned to her eyes as she slowly turned to him. "Why do you put up with that? If he talked to me like that …." She huffed. "… he wouldn't have to worry about talking anymore."

Surprised that she still had spunk, he paused before speaking. He didn't want to get her riled up, but the issue needed a solution. "What do you suggest we do with our problem? We really don't know when, or even if, she'll get her memory back." He saw her nod slowly, like she always did when deep in thought. She took another sip of her cocktail, rocking as she concentrated.

He waited as he watched her nodding; interrupting her train of thought would not go well.

After a few moments, she continued, "Get one of the guys to install a bug in her room to keep an ear on her. If there's even a glimmer of a memory, you know what to do."

"What about her sister?"

"Considering the security there, I'll have to think about it."

He paused for a moment before bringing up their biggest bone of contention. "Brent's up to his old tricks."

She looked towards him with a jerk of her head and winced. She put her hand across the back of her neck and moaned. A few seconds later, she mumbled, "Already? You're going to bail him out again?"

"Not necessary yet. Just keeping an eye on him for now."

She nodded slowly for a moment. "I'm beginning to think you were right about how to handle his scandals." Her breathing increased. "Who is it this time?"

"Some waitress."

She rubbed her temple as she frowned.

"You okay?"

"Just another headache." Her head lowered slightly. "I'm so tired right now. I don't want to think. Let's talk about Brent and his problem later."

"You need an aspirin?"

"Okay."

He retrieved the pill from the bathroom and returned. "Here you go."

She took a sip of her martini to swallow it.

As always, he sat with her until she finished her drink. He wondered what she was thinking because she shared only what she wanted you to know. For her, being sick was merely an inconvenience – until now. Being a type A personality, she had always been a talker, usually initiated conversations, and micro-managed everything. She had always been involved in the family business. But now there was little energy for conversation, much less for business. Although she didn't say so, he knew how depressed she must feel. Especially now, he needed to keep an eye on her condition.

When she was done with her drink, he helped her get ready for bed. After tucking her in, he kissed her on the forehead. "Good night, try to get some sleep."

She closed her eyes and mumbled, "Night."

He picked up the empty glasses and turned out the light as he slipped out of the room. He walked down the stairs, pondering the situation. He genuinely hoped Vera wouldn't remember what happened, at least for a while. He didn't want her dead, not yet anyway. Not until he got the money back and tied up some loose ends.

Phaedra hadn't heard what Vera said about the money, and he wanted to keep it that way. But if Phaedra decided to ice Vera to keep her quiet about the details of the shooting, then he'd have to tell her. Phaedra would be furious at his refusal, but her anger would be worth it if they could retrieve that money. Two million is a lot to lose. And nobody steals from Frankie without consequences.

Rudy sat with the Feds intently listening to the transmission. Cloning Pierre's phone to keep tabs on him was a snap with the Fed's equipment. This was even better than the app he had; no need to hide a bug on something the perp might leave behind.

Standing behind the agents at the screen, he watched the blip on the electronic map to see where Pierre went after being released. The GPS showed him stop at one location for a while and travel to another before making the call. When Pierre started talking to Frankie, he knew they'd hit the jackpot.

When Pierre's phone started transmitting, the road and traffic noise told them that he was driving. "Hey, Frankie, almost there, probably fifteen minutes."

"No problems then?"

"Nope. Went off without a hitch, just as we planned. So, what's our next job?"

"Electronics. There's a big delivery of TV's, phones, tablets, and laptops arriving in a few months at the Best Buy warehouse. We're going to ambush the delivery trucks before they arrive. We'll have several vans to split up the merchandise and take them to our warehouse in Tualatin." He gave details for the next ten minutes.

Shiv made an impromptu call on Frankie to tell him about new information. "I just got a call from our mole. Just as you suspected, Pierre's phone is bugged. The Feds know about the electronics heist. As you authorized, I promised him five grand for the info." He stood up proud when Frankie told him, "Job well done."

Chapter 10

Indigestion had never been an issue before and it was distracting. Roy decided it came with the territory, so he kept antacids in his pocket. No one at the station knew, and he had to keep it that way. The new captain might insist he see the doctor. Roy had already figured out that it came on with the increased tension, so the doctor wouldn't tell him anything new anyway. Besides, if he went to the doctor, he'd insist on an investigation into why. That could blow his cover.

Although four dirty cops were arrested, no one really knew if there could be others at the station, like himself, who were on the hook but hadn't come to the surface yet. The only people who knew about him were Rudy, the Feds, and the guy on the phone, and he called the shots for now. He called himself Shiv. What a name – Shiv! Roy assumed he had chosen it for the intimidation factor. Why else?

He couldn't talk to anyone about the plan, even if he wanted to. He wouldn't know his next step until after work when he checked in with the Feds. At least he wouldn't have to stress over it for long; he had to finish typing out a report before he clocked out in fifteen minutes.

Captain Carlos Hernandez came in. His small ears and face emphasized the long, hooked nose that seemed to reach down to his upper lip. He reached up to scratch at his curly, salt and pepper hair. It was a short, thick thatch that looked like a knit cap on his round skull. "Hey … Jackson, is it?"

"Yeah."

"Where do you store the bathroom supplies? Someone neglected to replace the paper towels."

"Storeroom. Fourth door on the left as you go towards the locker room."

"Thanks. Someone ought to create a 'where is it' sheet for newcomers."

"Yeah, that's what I thought when I first started. Oh, by the way, welcome aboard."

"Thanks. I guess I won't see you until tomorrow at the morning update."

"Right. Excuse me, but I've got to finish this."

Hernandez waved his approval and left for the storeroom. Roy's breath escaped in an involuntary rush as deep remorse returned. It was happening more often now, regretting that terrible decision he made three years ago. But he had to face the music, and it had the feel of a dirge, the dirge at his own funeral. Even though the deal he made with the Feds was to work undercover with them, anything could go wrong. Several scenes from the past flashed before him – that first meeting with his contact three years ago, meeting him in the poorly lit parking garage, the robbery that went wrong, Rudy confronting him …

A noise down the hall brought him back to the present, and he realized he only had five minutes left and he still had to change. The report would have to wait. He saved the report and signed off the computer.

That night, Roy couldn't concentrate. He needed to balance his checkbook, go shopping, and do laundry, but he had no energy to do any of it. He flopped into his recliner, clicked the remote, and let the TV drown out the silence. He leaned back, staring at the ceiling as the documentary droned on. *If only I'd known. I never would've done it.* He closed his eyes to shut out the world and grimaced. *But then Grandpa probably would've died.*

He thought back to that day – the day that changed everything. The doctors had told him and his brother that their grandpa needed by-pass surgery, but there was no insurance, and they didn't have the money to cover the astronomical bill. Even if the three of them had sold everything, it wouldn't be enough, even with charity. He and his brother talked for hours trying to solve this dilemma, but they couldn't see a way around it.

The next day, when he got that phone call with the offer, it seemed too good to be true. At first, Roy said no and hung up. But the seed was planted. So, when the man called again within an hour, Roy was ready to agree, but only if nobody got hurt. He always wondered about the timing of those calls. At the time, he thought the deal was perfect. This stranger would pay all his medical bills in exchange for Roy delaying his response to a planned robbery. Roy was counting on that promise that nobody would get hurt.

Roy was expecting the call on the police radio, but it still jolted him, "12-62, Veyonne Jewelers, Southwest 6th and Yamhill."

"Jackson here. ETA 5 minutes." *Okay, now just play it cool, slow down, and this'll be over in just a bit.*

"This isn't right," Roy mumbled to himself as he pulled up to the curb. Jumping out, he commanded, "Police, stand back." He pushed past several onlookers at the doorway. One of them shouted, "It's about time!"

No. No, it can't be! He promised! All the display cases were broken and empty, and the cash register drawer was open. A quick search found the owner on the floor behind the counter. A pool of blood. No pulse.

A loud crack startled him. Roy's eyes flew open to the flickering ceiling and walls of his living room. The TV was in the middle of the documentary on thunderstorms as the thunder cracked again. He sat up, rubbed his forehead, and swallowed hard. The flashbacks were becoming more frequent.

Hindsight is so clear. He should've known, but his judgment was clouded by Grandpa's needs. How could he have known that the stranger's promise was a flat out lie? And even worse, that the man who contacted him was connected to the syndicate. Although he knew his involvement wouldn't be a secret forever, he still tried to hide the fact that he was an accessory to robbery and murder. He had agonized over that.

At first, he was actually relieved when Rudy confronted him. Then, the first of his consequences hit – losing Callie because of it. The end was in sight, not a pretty end. He didn't deserve that. He wondered if he had the perseverance to go through with the plan. And what kind of a life would there be afterwards?

The sound of his phone ringing made him jump. He saw it was Rudy and hastily answered. "I'm so glad you called, I've been driving myself crazy!"

"Uh, ok. So, I was just wondering what you'd told the Feds about who the kingpin is."

"Uh, you mean what his name is?"

"Typically, that's what that question means."

"I told them it was Frankie."

"Did you talk to them after Pierre said it was Andre?"

"Of course, I wanted to make sure they knew it was him lying, not me."

Rudy moaned. "Ok, I guess I should do the same." He paused. "Do you want to talk about whatever you're driving yourself crazy with?"

Roy sighed. "I guess it's just being in this situation. I knew it'd be bad. I just didn't realize how bad it would get."

"Yeah, I hear ya. Hate to tell you, it's probably going to get worse."

Roy let out a pathetic laugh. "And here I thought I'd get something encouraging out of you."

"Sorry to cut this short, but I've got that call to make. Try not to be too hard on yourself."

Roy rubbed his forehead. *Thanks for making me feel worse.* "Yeah, right. Later."

Chapter 11

Sharon pulled out the box she had hidden in the cupboard.

Callie looked up from the clam dip she was making. "How did you get Dad to leave?" She smiled when she saw that devilish look in her mother's eye.

"I told him I needed some ice cream." She opened the box and looked at the cake she had ordered from Jack's favorite bakery. "You think he'll like it?"

"You put in a special order for it, didn't you?"

"How'd you guess?"

Callie put her hands on her hips. "Seriously? Nobody would have *that* as a stock design." Then, she laughed.

Together, they chirped, "He's gonna love it!"

Sharon just smiled. At least they still had this strange mind meld. It was one of the quirky connections they hadn't grown out of. Then she wondered if it would ever end. She hoped not; it made them feel even closer.

"I sure hope so." Sharon placed four sparklers on it, evenly spacing them between the fondant decorations: wheelchair, walker, false teeth, hearing aid, and prescription bottle. "Do you think the black icing was too much?"

"No. But the sparklers don't seem to fit."

"Well, this is the Fourth of July, and 'independence day' from work for the rest of his life?"

Callie rolled her eyes.

Georgia came in from the patio. "Rudy says he thinks the meat's almost done." She looked at the cake and grinned. "You really did it, didn't you? I thought you were kidding."

"Well, I only had one shot at this, so I figured that I'd do it up right." She patted Callie on the shoulder and held her other hand out to the cake. "You want to carry out your masterpiece?"

"Of course!"

When Callie got to the patio door, Mark called out, "Hey! You need to make a grand entrance. Wait until he's out here so we can get a good picture of his face when he sees it."

Sharon's face dropped. "He's right. Put it back and get the camera, would you?"

"Sure thing." Callie put the cake down and ran back to her purse. She was just returning when Jack drove up. Mark ran down the driveway to make sure he didn't go in through the front door.

Sharon waved Callie to the back yard. "Take lots of pictures now."

Callie beamed. "You can bet on that." She ran out just in time to snap the first one.

Sharon followed her outside just as everyone started singing "For He's a Jolly Good Fellow."

Jack laughed as he looked around at his beloved family. His parents, brothers and their families, Georgia and Rudy, as Sharon, Mark, Callie, and Gary all sang enthusiastically.

When everyone finished, he applauded. "Thanks, everyone."

Sharon went over to the barbecue to help Rudy put the ribs, chicken, sausage, and hamburgers onto serving platters. When she turned around, she was puzzled to see that Georgia was sitting down instead of organizing. Not that she expected her to help; it just seemed out of character. She helped Rudy put everything on the tables.

Rudy called out, "Come and eat! Everything's ready." He stepped back to get out of the way.

Jack whistled loudly. "Okay, let's make way for us elderly first."

Mark laughed.

"Don't worry. Mom and Dad get to go first, then me!" Jack laughed.

Chatter increased as everyone loaded their plates and sat in groups around the yard.

Sharon sat down next to Callie. "I'm really glad Ralph and Cora came. How's it going for them?"

"It's getting a little more difficult for Grandpa to move around. His energy seems off." Callie continued hesitantly, "Do you think it's just old age?"

"Could be. He really should see his doctor for a check-up." She took a sip of lemonade. "Speaking of parents, how is Gary's dad?"

"Okay I guess. He still doesn't talk much."

"That's no surprise. Is Marci still there?" She took a bite of her hot dog.

Callie's face lit up. "Oh yeah. And would you believe that she's crushing on Gary?"

"Ooh, tell me about it." Sharon's eyes gleamed as she leaned in to hear more.

"When I introduced them, she flirted and hung onto his every word. She would've talked all day, except she got paged. I tried to convince him he should ask her out for coffee, but he said no. I think he's just overwhelmed by his dad."

"What do you mean?"

"Gary's suspicious of everything his dad says. I wonder if he's worried he'll start drinking again. I think Billy's trying, but no matter what he says, Gary takes it the wrong way. He's so defensive."

Sharon frowned. "I guess it might be a while to see the change and realize it could be permanent. I can see Gary's viewpoint though, I think I'd be suspicious for a while, too."

"But won't Billy get discouraged?"

"Yes, that's possible. I wish Gary could see that his support could be the swing factor."

"The last time we were there, Billy gave him the keys to his car. And Gary took it as a slap in the face. He called it a rusty pile of junk."

Sharon grimaced. "Oh! I hope he didn't say that to his face."

"No, it was after we left."

"It looks like we're not done raising him yet. I'll have Jack talk to him."

"But if dad talks to him, Gary will know I said something."

"I'll make sure to ask Jack to bring it up in another way."

"There's more than one way to skin a cat," they said in unison and then chuckled.

Callie ate a bite of chicken and suddenly held up her hand. "Oh, Mom. I've got to tell you about this woman at the nursing home. She is such a busybody. She knows everything about everyone, but I wonder if she's got it right. Get this – she thinks one of the residents is an alien."

Sharon snorted. "You've got to be kidding!"

"Really! And she said another one accuses everyone of stealing her underwear!"

Sharon leaned back and laughed. "Oh, that's a good one! How do you keep a straight face?"

"It isn't easy." Callie grinned for a moment, but then her face dropped. "But there are some sad cases, too. One little woman always asks if she's had lunch. I feel so sorry for her. If lunch is the only thing she has to look forward to and can't even remember from an hour ago, that's awful."

"Aw, the poor dear. That reminds me of when we researched Alzheimer's. You know, when Alice had dementia. It'll probably just get worse."

Callie frowned. "But this next one really haunts me. Bertie – she's the busybody – she told me about a new resident that was shot by her sister. With a shotgun!"

Sharon gasped. "Her sister did it?!"

"But the woman can't remember what happened. I just can't stop thinking about that."

"Have you tried to visit her?"

"No, I've been so focused on making sure Gary sees his dad that I haven't tried yet." She grimaced. "I guess I should, huh?"

"I'll go with you next time. While you're in visiting Billy, I'll drop in on her. But how will I know who to see?"

Callie rolled her eyes, "Don't worry about that, Bertie will come up to you and introduce herself. And she'll update you on everyone. I'll bet she'll even escort you to her room."

"Okay. So, when's the next time you're going?"

"Tomorrow."

"I can hardly wait!" they chimed together.

As if from a script, Callie tipped her head down as she said with her mocking tone, "Get out of my head!"

Sharon chuckled. "Never." She smiled contentedly, reveling in their bond. Then, seeing Jack walk up to the food table, she stood up. "It looks like a good time to go talk to Jack about Gary."

She left to join Jack at the table, and Callie got up to take more photos.

Jack gave Sharon a shoulder hug and a peck on the cheek when she came up to him. He listened carefully when she described the situation with Gary and his dad. Looking to the ground, he said discretely, "I'll talk to him. Thanks for the head's up." He gave Sharon another kiss on the cheek and took his plate over to Gary.

Gary looked up. "Hey, Dad. How does it feel to be retired?"

"Good. And I'm glad to hear you haven't stopped calling me Dad."

"Here, sit down."

"You get your grades yet?"

"Yeah. I looked this morning and I've got a four-year average of 3.6."

Jack gave him a high-five. "Congratulations! I knew you'd do good."

"I have you to thank for it. If you hadn't made sure I got good grades in high school, I wouldn't have qualified for that scholarship."

"Just looking out for you, son. I saw the potential and I didn't want it to go to waste." Jack took a big bite off a beef rib. "Mmm, Rudy sure can cook."

"That's for sure. And these burgers are the best."

"So, what's next for you?"

Gary looked at him suspiciously. "Has Callie been talking to you?"

"Huh? No. What's that supposed to mean?"

"I just figured she pushed you to get me to take that job at the nursing home."

"There's an opening there?"

Gary sighed. "Yes, but I'm not taking it."

"Why not?"

"Are you sure she didn't put you up to this?"

"Callie didn't say anything to me. I'm just curious. So?"

He sighed again and looked aside. "Because I don't want to have to be around him any more than I have to. There, I said it."

"You mean your dad? You wouldn't have to spend all your time with him, just during his therapy. You can even get your visit in during the session. Look at it this way; you'd get paid for seeing him. Plus, when he's released, you'd still have a job. What's wrong with that?"

Gary hung his head. "Why do you have to be so logical? When Callie said it, it was like she was ordering me."

"Callie talked to you about it?"

Gary rolled his eyes. "Yes, but like I said, she said it differently, like she was twisting my arm."

"Looks like I'll have to give her a little lesson in tact."

"She needs a *lot* of lessons!"

Jack laughed.

"Something else is bothering me," Gary said. "You know his car?"

"Yeah."

"He gave me the key so I could fix it. I don't have any money. How am I supposed to do that? Besides, it needs so much work, it isn't worth fixing. What kind of gift is that?"

"So, are you saying he gave you his car?"

Gary nodded.

"Well, first off, you know I'm going to be restoring vehicles. That's why I retired. I've even got a shop all decked out for it. I can help you."

"But, like I said, it will cost more to fix it than it's worth."

"You're kidding, right? When that thing's restored, it'll be a classic worth thousands. Do you know how many looks you're going to get when you drive around in it?"

"Seriously?"

"Oh yeah! You go online tonight and look up the values of a restored 1958 Oldsmobile JetStar with a triple carburetor J2 engine."

"But, I can't ask you to pay for the costs of restoring it."

"Good, because I'm not paying for it. You're going to get a job, but you can still live here; that will cut your living expenses. Hey, I'll even help you do some repairs on your dad's house after your checks start to come in."

"Why do I get the feeling this was a setup?"

"Why? You mean because it wasn't what you already decided? I'm just using logic."

Gary sighed. "I'll think about it. Thanks for the offer to help, though."

Jack patted him on the back. "You know I'm always willing to help, especially one of my kids."

Gary leaned back and smiled. Then when he saw Callie, he squinted, got up, and went up behind her. "You talked to your dad, didn't you?"

She jumped and turned around. "Huh. What are you talking about?"

"You told him about the car, didn't you?"

"No. Why? What did he say?"

His eyebrows pressed down in disbelief. "Never mind." *She must be using some of that detective training to get what she wants. I'd better find out what she's learning.* "So, everyone says that you're learning how to be a P.I. What exactly do you do?"

She snapped pictures as she talked. "So far, it's only research. But I did talk to a lead once. And Georgia is giving me self-defense lessons, but you knew that." She turned around to look him in the eye. "She and Rudy are teaching me about body language so I can tell if someone is lying, acting nervous or guilty, or hiding something."

She peered at him as she leaned closer, and Gary's eyes got big.

"So, what are you hiding?" she accused.

"What are you talking about?"

"Your eyes. Something's up."

"Are you just making this up? Or can you actually read minds?"

"You had an autonomic reflex."

"A what?"

"It's the body's way of communicating. Kind of like when your heartbeat increases involuntarily, only it's visible. Your eyes told me something was up. What is it?"

"Well, it might've been from you lunging at me with accusations. Rudy said you did the research on the Governor. I was just curious how you did that."

"You really want to know?"

"I wouldn't ask if I didn't want to know."

"Okay. After the party, I'll show you how I found out about him." She turned around as she chirped, "Gotta go. More pictures."

"Good, that'll be interesting." Focusing on her swaying hips, he watched her as she walked off into the crowd. *Maybe I can tell her then.*

Sharon got up and sat down next to Georgia, but she had to be careful not to step on Lucky, Georgia's dog. He was curled around her feet and his tail was in the way. "Hey, are you okay?"

"Just a little tired. There's been so much to do, lately."

"Do you know what's with Lucky? He seems overly attached to you."

"I don't know. Sometimes, it's almost annoying. I've almost tripped over him several times."

Looking up into Georgia's eyes, Lucky sat up and rested his chin on her knee.

She put her hand on his head to scratch his ear. "And he's always doing stuff like this. He's got a vet appointment tomorrow, so hopefully he isn't sick. And then after that, I'm getting my annual mash job."

"Huh?"

Georgia leaned over to be discreet, "Mammogram."

"Oh, right." Sharon grimaced. "I heard it's like lying on a concrete slab and having someone drive over you."

Georgia laughed. "Well, maybe not quite that bad. Although it depends on the technician as to how uncomfortable it is." Georgia looked at her carefully. "Have you had one yet?"

"Not yet."

"You'd better. You're way past the age for getting the first one."

"I guess you're right. I'll call the doctor for an appointment."

That night, Gary sat down as he listened to Callie's explanation of how she started her research.

Talking the whole time, she became more animated as she pulled out her laptop and plugged in the flash drive. She set it on the table and Gary scooted up beside her.

He leaned over her shoulder and closed his eyes as he took in the scent from her shampoo. He was jarred from his reverie when she elbowed him.

"When Rudy asked me to see what I could find on the governor, he also gave me a list of other names to check out. He wanted me to get anything and everything that had been written about them."

"That must've taken a while."

"Sure did. At first, nothing seemed out of the ordinary, and I thought, 'What a waste of time.' But when I looked into one of the names on the list, there was an article in the 90's about a wedding, and it had a photo. One of the ushers looked just like the governor and was about the same age. But it wasn't the governor.

"There was also a story about the governor getting a dog bite. The picture in the paper showed a terrible wound, and I was certain that it would leave a scar. But, get this – the governor doesn't have a scar, not even a little one. That didn't make sense until I started comparing all the pictures of him with the guy in the wedding photo. I researched both of them and found a few articles during that time. After putting it all together, I found out that the guy in the wedding photo murdered the real governor before he ran for governor. Then he staged his own death, took the other guy's place, and ran for governor. He's a murderer and an impostor!" She leaned back glowing with pride. "And *I* figured it out!"

"Wow! I'm impressed."

"To top it off, he used his position to help the bad guys. I gave Rudy all the information I found, and he released it to the cops. It wasn't long before more evidence came out about him getting paid for favors." She turned to face him and almost bumped noses. She jerked back. "So, I helped in discovering all of that, and it's been in all the news reports since then."

"Show me."

She showed him all the articles and photos, and her eyes beamed with pride as she explained each detail.

He leaned back and let out a long whistle. "Wow, you're good."

"Rudy says I have a knack for putting the puzzle together." She beamed again.

"The next time you do research, can I watch? Maybe help?"

"I don't know why not. Next time Rudy gives me an assignment, I'll let you know."

"Awesome."

She looked at Gary strangely.

"What?"

"I just realized."

"What's that?"

"Rudy said he didn't have time to do the research, but I think he used it as a distraction."

"Distraction? For what?"

Her face fell. "Well, Roy and I had just broken up, and I was feeling pretty down." She paused and shook her head. "Yeah, that must be why he did it. I'll have to thank him. I think it did help me to not think about him so much."

Gary couldn't hold it any longer. "So, why'd you break up, anyway?" He regretted asking when he saw the sadness in her eyes.

She looked away before continuing, "He lied about taking a bribe."

"What? A bribe?! What happened?"

"His grandpa needed surgery, and there was no money or insurance for it. Someone offered to pay for everything to make him delay responding to a robbery."

"Whoa. That's pretty serious."

"It's even worse. The store owner died because of it."

Gary's jaw dropped. "What!" He could see her tears welling up.

She huffed. "You remember that job I had stocking shelves at Best Buy?"

"Yeah, what of it?"

"One of the warehouse workers approached me with an offer to join in a theft ring. They were skimming products and selling them. They wanted my help."

"You never told me about that!"

"You and Mark were still in college. Anyway, the point is that I went to management because I couldn't bring myself to do something like that. Just so dishonest! It goes against everything I believe in. So, when Roy told me about what he did, that just showed me he has a different set of standards, especially when someone died from it. And that he was willing to keep big secrets from me. I can't start a life with someone like that." She started to cry. "That was so hard."

He put his arms around her to comfort her. "So, what happened? Is he in jail?"

She gasped and jerked away. "I don't know." She immediately searched the Internet to find out. After looking for several minutes, she threw up her hands. "I can't find anything about him." She turned around to Gary again. "I can't believe it! He didn't tell them. He lied to me … again! He said he was going to turn himself in. I'm so angry right now."

"So, he's still pretending?"

"Obviously. I'm going to go ask Rudy about it right now." She jumped up and ran to get her purse. "You coming?"

"You bet!" *Now is not the time. I'll have to wait.*

Rudy was startled by the pounding on the front door.

Georgia rushed in from the kitchen. "What's going on?"

"I don't know. I'll get it." When he opened the door, Callie rushed in, followed by Gary. He stood back. "What's wrong?"

Callie put her fists on her hips and demanded, "What happened to Roy?"

He knew it was inevitable that she'd have to know. Although he didn't want to tell her until it was over, apparently he had to now, but not in front of Georgia. He turned to Georgia, "I'm sorry, but I'm going to have to ask you to let us talk about this privately." He could see she was hurt as they headed for his office.

Knowing Callie's lack of control when she was this incensed, Rudy held up his hand to stop her until after he shut the door.

As soon as it clicked shut, Callie exploded, "I just did a search, and he was never charged with that bribe. I want to know why." She pointed her finger at Rudy and demanded, "I *know* you know, so you tell me what's going on!"

Rudy was silent for a few moments, working his jaw. Then he started pacing.

Gary whispered into Callie's ear, "What's going on?"

She held up a hand to silence him. "Well? Are you going to tell me?"

Rudy pointed to the chairs in front of his desk. "Sit." Although she sat in the old chair that reminded everyone of an electric chair, Rudy knew she was so focused that the resemblance to an instrument of death wouldn't register. Too bad, he'd be glad to take advantage of any intimidation it usually generated. Shaking his head, he continued to pace. Only when he saw Callie's worried face did he realize that he'd neglected to put on his poker face. He saw her swallow hard. *I must be losing it. I'm doing this too often, showing my hand.*

"Why wouldn't you make him confess? You promised me!"

Rudy took a deep breath. "And I kept that promise. But, nothing said here can leave the room. You can't tell *anyone!* Understood?"

He could see the pulse beating at her neck as her eyes widened, she nodded quickly. "And what about him?" he demanded, eyeing Gary. "Callie, how much does he know?"

"I've told him everything I know."

"Okay, so you're going to keep your mouth shut. Right, Gary?"

"Yeah. I won't tell a soul."

Rudy sat down in his old wooden office chair with casters under the legs, picked up a pencil, and rolled it between his index finger and thumb. "He's working with the Feds ... *we're* working with the Feds. We're going to catch the guys who paid the bribe."

Callie's breath seemed to escape in a rush, and she fell against the back of the chair with a thump.

Gary's mouth dropped open, and mumbled something inaudible.

"He's actually the bait for them to offer another bribe so we can nail them. It's pretty certain they'll bite since the police station has been cleaned up. As far as they're concerned, he's the last dirty cop." Rudy let out a long breath. "Obviously, this is strictly confidential. Roy's life could be on the line."

Callie's hands flew up to cover her mouth.

Rudy noticed Gary look at Callie with an unreadable expression. Turning back to Callie, he repeated, "You absolutely will not say anything to anyone, not even a word on the subject."

Callie sank down and apologized. "I didn't know."

"A lot of people are doing their best to keep him safe."

She closed her eyes. "If he lives ..." She shuddered. "If he lives, what will happen to him?"

"We've talked about a deal in exchange for his help, but nothing is set in stone. So, I don't know how it will turn out. Obviously, I can't tell you any more than that." He turned on her, letting his anger show. "Next time, call me. I don't want you upsetting Georgia again."

Looking contrite, Callie looked down. "You're right. I'm sorry."

When they got home, Gary went straight to the basement while hopelessly shaking his head. *I can tell. She still loves him. I don't have a chance.*

He sighed as he took off his shoes. *Telling her now would only cause her more hurt. I can't do that to her.* He flopped down onto the cot, put his hands behind his head, and stared at the ceiling. *I wish I could do something to take away her pain.*

Chapter 12

Sharon drove Callie and Gary in the van to the nursing home. She pulled into the only available spot in the parking lot and shuddered. It was the same spot she used on that awful day when Alice died. Old feelings came rushing back: the anxiety when she had to put Alice in here, the dread that preceded each visit, the shock when she received the call that Alice had died, the horror when she realized Alice had actually been murdered, and the guilt she felt afterwards.

"Mom, are you okay?" Callie asked when she put her hand on Sharon's arm.

Sharon looked up quickly.

"You're thinking about Alice, aren't you?"

"I think you know me too well."

"We can wait for a minute if you need to."

"I'll be okay. Let's go."

As they got out and walked to the front door, Callie took her arm. "You're probably going to laugh when you're talking with Bertie, so be prepared to have a good time. Although, I'm not sure what you'll see when you visit the woman that was shot by her sister. You be sure to tell me about it, okay?"

"You're getting pretty good at that."

"Huh? What do you mean?"

"The art of distraction."

"Really? I wasn't even thinking about that."

Sharon nodded knowingly. "Sure, you weren't. But, yes, I'll let you know whatever I find out. And I'll drop in on Billy, too." They walked in, and Sharon made sure to pretend not to notice the job opening posted in the lobby.

As they approached the hallway, Bertie rolled up on her scooter. "Good morning, Callie and Gary. You brought someone new?"

"This is my mother, Sharon. Mom, this is Bertie."

Sharon shook hands with Bertie. "Hi, I'm very glad to meet you. Have you been here long?"

"I've been here long enough to know what's going on. If you need to know anything, you just ask me."

Callie walked off with Gary towards Billy's room, leaving Sharon to talk with Bertie.

Sharon caught the beginning of their conversation when Gary whispered, "What was that all about in the car?"

"Mom had a really hard time dealing with the last time she was here, when Alice died."

Sharon's mind drifted as Callie and Gary continued down the hallway. But when Bertie tugged on her hand, she came back to the present.

Bertie whispered, "I need to tell you; one of our aides is not doing her job. Tina always finds a way to get someone else to do the dirty work. You know, changing adult diapers, cleaning up messes – the icky stuff – like vomit and messy bathrooms, but I can't convince anyone. She's too sneaky."

"Really? You know, you can report that kind of behavior to the authorities."

"I can?" Bertie asked excitedly, and then she frowned. "But I don't know how to do that."

"I can show you the number later. It's usually posted on a wall somewhere."

Bertie glowed. "Oh, thank you. You are such a dear." She pointed a knobby finger at Sharon approvingly. "I can tell; you're one of the good ones. I'll bet you could cheer up some of the lonely ones here, too."

"Are there a lot of them?"

"Oh, dearie, there are so many. But the saddest one is Vera. I feel so sorry for her. She doesn't get any visitors. And what's worse, her own sister did her in, shot her in the stomach with a shotgun. Tore holes in her abdomen. I heard the doctor say she was fortunate to live through it. If it was me, and I knew my sister did that, I think I'd want to die. Just terrible.

"The police have even been here to talk to her. I heard her say she doesn't remember it, some kind of amnesia. You know, the kind that blocks out what happened. She remembers everything else, just not that day. Apparently, the rest of her family was all there when she did it. Everyone here is shocked by the whole thing."

"How awful."

Bertie leaned towards Sharon and whispered with her hand guarding her mouth, "I heard the police say her sister was high on drugs. That stuff is poison, you know. Makes you do things you normally wouldn't do."

Sharon nodded. Then, she pretended to have an idea. "I can go talk to her, maybe cheer her up."

Bertie's eyes beamed. "Oh, I knew you'd be a good one. I'll show you her room." She started down another hallway in high gear and calling out, "Right this way. She arrived last week, but since we don't have a physical therapist, she's not progressing very well. Her family wants her at home, but the police said no for now." She stopped and pointed towards the room at the end of the hallway. "Right in there."

"Thanks, Bertie." She shook hands with her again and then knocked on the open door. "Hello?"

An attractive young woman with long raven hair turned her head towards her. Her high cheekbones and rosy, full lips gave a pleasant, almost happy appearance. But her wide-set, dark eyes were turned down at the corners, looking incongruously sad. "Hello," she said with a confused look. "Do I know you?"

"No, but a friend told me you might like some company."

Her face softened. "Thank you, but you don't have to."

"But I want to." She walked up to the bed to shake hands. "My name is Sharon."

"I'm Vera, but you probably already know that."

"Yes, Bertie told me."

Vera's face turned red.

"Oh, don't be embarrassed. She's just concerned for you. I thought I'd introduce myself and maybe chat a while. Is that okay?" She pulled up a chair and sat down next to the bed.

"Why? You don't even know me."

"I used to work in a nursing home. It was a long time ago, but I'll never forget how some of the residents needed more attention than others. Some didn't even get visitors."

Vera closed her eyes and turned away.

"I'm sorry. I didn't mean to make you feel bad. I was hoping to cheer you up a little."

Vera swallowed hard.

"If you want to tell me anything, I can keep it to myself."

Vera's brow furrowed. "I feel so alone."

Sharon picked up her hand. "I'll be your friend."

Vera struggled to hold back tears. "Why? You don't really know me."

"Oh, Honey, it's because you need someone."

Vera looked down, "Like a stray dog?"

"No, no. Not at all. If only you knew about all the lonely kids I've taken under my wing. And I've loved them like my own children. My heart goes out to you. Please, let me be your friend."

Vera pinched back tears and winced.

"Is something wrong?"

"It hurts when I cry. I'm trying not to."

Sharon took her hand and squeezed it lightly. Vera squeezed back.

"Just breathe slowly, in, then out. Slowly. That's right."

After a few moments, Vera regained her composure. "I'd like that, to have a friend."

"And anytime you want to talk, don't hesitate. I'll give you my phone number, too."

"That's very kind of you, but if I could see my sister, that would cheer me up." She put her hand to her forehead. "I'm sorry I'm so out of it. I was told I was in a coma for a while, and I really haven't caught up yet. Then with the pain meds, I'm pretty loopy."

Sharon took her hand again. "You have nothing to apologize for. I completely understand. So, tell me about your sister." She was prepared for the worst.

Vera's face softened as she turned to look at Sharon. "Jody's so pretty and smart. I worry about her, though. She's been having a hard time getting a job. That's why we let her move in ….." She looked away to think. "… last year sometime? Just to help her get on her feet."

"What about your mom and dad?"

She turned away. "Mom's dead, and Dad's in jail."

Sharon grimaced. "I'm sorry. How long ago?"

Vera pulled her hand back and fidgeted. "I was eight and Jody was seven. When dad went to jail, mom got sick and died. Then, we were shuffled around to different relatives until we turned eighteen. At least, we didn't have to go into a foster home." She frowned. "Although, I sometimes wonder if that might have been better. It was hard, especially with changing schools so often. But I made sure Jody did her schoolwork." She smiled. "I'm really proud of her. She graduated last year, even with all the moves."

Sharon mulled that over. "If she just graduated, why couldn't she stay with your relatives until she found that job?"

Vera glowered. "Because when she turned eighteen and graduated, the state stopped paying support."

Stunned, Sharon was speechless for a moment. She couldn't comprehend selfish behavior like that and wanted to lash out. But she had to keep Vera calm, so she whispered, "I'm sorry."

"Well, that's how it was."

Sharon patted Vera's hand. "It sounds like you took good care of her."

"We were all we had. That's why I wonder why she hasn't come to visit."

"Maybe she doesn't know."

"She must know. Brent surely would have told her … but then, maybe not. At least, one of the servants should have said something to her."

"Having servants must have been quite a change for you."

"Yeah, but I didn't care about that. I just wanted a family." She gasped. "I wonder if she got kicked out. Brent's parents really didn't want her in the house to begin with." She closed her eyes. "That must have been what happened."

Sharon grimaced. "Isn't she the one who …."

"I don't believe it for a second!" Vera's quick turn to Sharon made her wince in pain, apparently from trying to hold back instant tears.

"Are you going to be okay?"

"I guess," she squeaked.

"So, why don't you believe she did it?"

Vera took some soothing breaths and continued, "After Mom and Dad were gone, we realized that we were all we had, just each other. We helped each other, depended on each other, we loved each other. That's how I know. She couldn't have done what they say. And she would never desert me like this."

"I can go visit her if you'll give me your address."

"You'd do that?"

"Of course. I know I'd want someone to help me if I were in your situation."

Tears started to well up in Vera's eyes. "I don't know what to say."

"Say yes." Sharon dug in her purse. When she looked up, she was glad to see the hopeful look in Vera's eyes.

"That would be great."

"Here's a pen and paper. Just write down the address, and I'll check it out."

With her lip quivering, Vera took the pen and paper and wrote down her sister's name, their address, and the house phone number. "I should probably tell you that we were living with my husband and his parents. They have a man at the gate, so you probably won't get in if you go unannounced." She turned away again after she finished.

Sharon took the paper and pen. She glanced at it. *Skyline? That's a pretty swanky neighborhood.* "Is there anything else I should know?"

"I've tried to call, but no one will talk to me. I don't know why."

Sharon's eyes and mouth popped open. "Are you saying your husband won't talk to you?"

She nodded.

Sharon resisted the urge to race out of there to Vera's house and demand to see her husband. *I've got to find out what happened, so I can help her. I'll ask Rudy for help. He is a detective, after all. Maybe Callie can help too. A domestic squabble is probably an easy job for her to train on. I'll get as much information as I can from Vera first.* "Maybe you should write down your husband's name and his parents' too, so I'll sound more legitimate. I don't want to try to contact them and not know who to ask for." She handed the paper back to her.

"Oh, right. I didn't think of that. I'm still foggy, I guess." She wrote down everything she could remember, including the names of all the servants and their positions.

As Sharon took the paper, she said, "So, tell me about your family."

"My mom died right after my dad was put in prison …"

That's odd. I mention family and she talks about her parents instead of her husband and his parents. I'd better listen carefully. Maybe there's a clue there.

"… that was almost fifteen years ago. Our grandparents are dead, so we were shuffled around to different relatives. Did I already say that?" Her lips pressed to a quivering line. "Nobody wanted us for very long. And most of them were pretty mean to us." She shrugged. "Jody and I had to stick together. That's why we're so close. We really have only each other."

"But what about your husband and in-laws?"

"We were married early last year, but right from the start, his parents didn't approve of me. His mother actually called me white trash." Her face pinched with emotion. "I tried so hard to prove myself. I made sure to keep myself pretty for him, I tried to learn how to meet their standards, but nothing was good enough. His mother actually treats the maids better than me." A tear trickled down her cheek.

Sharon fumed inside. *How can anyone treat anybody with such horrid behavior?* She reached out to hold Vera's hand.

Vera turned to look at her and another tear rolled down her cheek. "Please don't pretend like you care."

Huh? Pretend? "Vera, I'm not pretending! My dad taught me to respect everyone, regardless of age, class, race, gender, or anything else. It works out better for everyone, and everyone feels better."

"Well, I'm glad you have a nice dad."

Sharon heard a note of sarcasm in her voice. "Had. He died about twenty years ago."

"I'm sorry. I didn't mean to be so snappish." She started to cry and then flinched. She held her stomach and moaned in pain. "Jody would never do this to me," she whispered through her tears.

Sharon looked at the paper again. "So, your sister still lives with your husband and his family?"

"Yeah … maybe. She moved in with us about a year ago. She was out of work, and, well, Brent's parents have rooms to spare, a lot of rooms. But they actually think less of her than they do of me. I don't know if they'd let her stay since I'm not there."

"I'll see what I can find out, and I'll make sure to let her know where you are."

Vera looked at her quickly. "That must be it! I'll bet they wouldn't tell her where I am."

Sharon struggled to control the urge to cry for her. *I've got to distract her.* "Would you like me to brush your hair?"

"You'd do that?"

"Of course. You'll feel better."

"My things are in the top drawer here." She pointed to the stand next to her bed.

Sharon made small talk as she brushed, commenting on the nice texture of her thick hair. After a few minutes, she could see that Vera had relaxed some, so she put the brush away. "I have to go now. My daughter and her friend are visiting someone here, and they're probably waiting for me by now. It was very nice meeting you. I'll be sure to come back, and I'll let you know what I find out about your sister."

Vera reached out to take Sharon's hand. "Thank you. You don't know how much that means to me."

"I'm glad to do it." Sharon patted Vera's hand. "If you'd like, when I come back, we can talk some more. I'll still see what I can find out, but I'd really just like to get to know you."

Vera's eyes glistened. "You mean that?"

"Of course!"

"No one's ever cared before. I don't know what to say."

Sharon smiled. "Just say, 'yes.'"

Vera nodded quickly as a tear trickled down into her ear.

Sharon waved as she walked towards the door. *It doesn't make sense. Her family wants her at home, but they won't visit her? Something is wrong.* As she left the room, she almost ran into Marci. She stopped to talk for a moment.

Marci smiled. "Visiting Vera?"

"Yes. She's such a sweet young woman."

Marci leaned forward to whisper, "I'm glad you're visiting her."

"It's my pleasure."

"She really needs it."

"And I'll see her again."

Marci grinned. "That would be awesome, thanks."

When Sharon approached the lobby, Callie was waiting. "Where's Gary?"

Callie's eyebrows shot up and she grabbed both of her mom's hands. "You will never guess!"

Sharon cocked her head. "Did he go in to apply for that job?"

"He didn't say that's what he was doing, but I'm pretty sure." Callie let go and put her fists on her hips. "Wait, how did you know?!"

Sharon shook her head. "I didn't, but I know how convincing your dad can be."

Callie giggled. "I've got to thank him."

"While he's in there, I'll go say hi to Billy."

Sharon had gone and returned by the time Gary emerged from the office. She and Callie both feigned disinterest.

"What? You aren't going to grill me?" he asked defensively.

"Grill you? About what?" Sharon asked coyly.

He looked at her for several seconds and then said, "I start Monday."

Callie jumped up and down. "That is so cool! I'm so happy for you!"

"And I'm so proud of you," said Sharon. "You even got a job before Mark."

"Then you did know!"

Sharon shrugged. "Callie told me."

Just then, Marci walked up behind him. "Did I hear you say you're going to start work here?"

Gary jumped and turned around. "Uh, yeah."

"Don't tell me you're going to be the physical therapist?"

"That's okay, isn't it?"

"Of course." She shook his hand and let hers linger in the grip. "I look forward to seeing you again."

Looking uncomfortable, he let go. "Monday, then. Thanks."

Sharon sensed that Marci was watching them as they left the building.

As they approached the van, Gary did a double take when Sharon chuckled. "Okay, what's so funny?"

"You. You're so oblivious."

"What do you mean?"

Sharon turned around to face him in the back seat. "Gary, that young lady likes you. The least you could do would be to ask her out for coffee."

"So, you want me to lead her on?"

"I'm just saying, it would be nice."

He rolled his eyes. *Great. How do I get her off my back?* "I can't."

"Why not?"

Well, I can't exactly tell her I like Callie. That wouldn't go well if I don't tell Callie first. "I don't have a car."

"You can borrow the van."

"You'd do that?"

"Of course. Besides, I'm not going anywhere. And if I did, we have other vehicles."

Great. That didn't go as planned.

"So, go ask her."

He reluctantly sighed, turned around, and went back inside.

I can't believe I'm doing this.

Marci was removing the help-wanted sign when he walked in.

"Marci?" he asked.

She looked up and smiled. "Yes?"

He took a deep breath and let it out. "Would you like to go for coffee sometime?"

Her dark brown eyes seemed to glow. "Okay," she said, obviously using self-control to keep from cheering. "When?"

"What's your schedule?"

"I get off at seven. Maybe then?"

"Okay. See you then."

When he turned to leave, he could've sworn he heard her giggle. He climbed into the van and buckled his seat belt.

Sharon turned around in her seat. "Well …?"

"I'm supposed to take her to coffee tonight and …."

Callie laughed and clapped. "All right! I *knew* she'd say yes." She turned and stared at him suspiciously. "You don't look very excited."

"He's probably just nervous, Callie. Let him be," Sharon counseled.

He looked out the window. *What have I done?*

As Sharon drove, her thoughts returned to Vera. "Callie, you were right."

"About what?"

"That woman Bertie told you about – Vera."

"How bad is it?"

"Bertie was right on the money. Vera hasn't had a visitor since she's been there, and she's really lonely. But something else isn't right."

"What do you mean?"

"Bertie said Vera's family wants her at home. If they're that close, why won't they visit? But if they aren't close, and no visits shows to me that they don't care, so why would they want her at home?"

Callie frowned. "That's odd. I wonder what the story is."

"And another thing – she's convinced that her sister, Jody, would never have done anything to hurt her. She's really upset that she hasn't been in to see her. She thinks that either Jody doesn't know where she is, or she must be hurt too. Otherwise, she'd be here. Whether or not that's the case, I'm concerned for her. People don't heal very well when they're stressed like that. I think we should try to help her."

"I could try to find her sister. At least find out what happened."

"I was hoping you'd offer."

"Thing is, on all the other research I did, Rudy always told me where to look. I'm not sure where to start."

"Honey, he'd be honored to give you some hints. He'd probably join you if you want. You know he loves to dig. And right now, he's not busy with any cases."

Sharon noticed a strange look on Callie's face when she explained, "But he's retired."

Sharon waved her off. "You know Rudy; he won't ever really be retired. Besides, I've got some information for you to start. Look in my purse, Vera wrote down everything we need for now."

Callie found the paper and looked at it. *Carelli? That name sounds familiar.*

Gary offered, "Callie, I just happened to think. I'll be starting on Monday, and I'm going to have her chart when I work with her. I can get all her personal information …."

"I don't think that's legal, is it?" Sharon quickly added.

"Oh. Right. I forgot about that."

Callie's face lit up. "But if I come around when you're working with her, I might accidentally see something when the chart is open."

"And if I'm looking the other way, I wouldn't know, and I wouldn't be able to report you."

"Remember, I'm not saying that I'm going to do that because then you'd know and have to say something. I'm just saying … if."

"Yeah. Don't tell me what you're going to do," Gary said with a telling catch to his voice.

Sharon rolled her eyes. "You really shouldn't be saying anything when I'm within earshot. I might get the wrong impression."

"You're right, Mom. Forget we said anything." Callie turned to wink at Gary, and he nodded with a grin.

Pierre shut the door and sat down across from Frankie's desk. He noticed the light indicated that an audio feed was on as usual, but it was silent. "Hear anything interesting?"

"Not yet. Just the same old things. Apparently, she still doesn't remember."

"That's good."

"So, what brings you here?"

"Got the latest."

"And?"

"Good news. It looks like our plan's working. The Feds have swallowed every fake lead we've given them. Every time we talk about a job, they're on it, and arrest the man we sent. So, we're killing two birds with one stone – make the Feds think they've got us, and we're culling the unimportant men from the organization. Just like we planned, only better."

"Good. When it comes time for the big job, they'll all be across town on our diversion."

Just then, voices came from the speaker.

Frankie held up his big hand, "Hold on. I want to hear this."

"But you said it was just the same old stuff."

When Frankie glared at him, he knew to be silent. He shrugged, waiting for whatever it was to be over with. But as the audio went on, Pierre felt nervous.

After listening for a few minutes, Frankie gritted his teeth. "What does that broad want?"

"I'll have Fingers get the security footage at the home to find out who she is." It had been a long time since he'd seen Frankie this angry. They couldn't have somebody snooping around. And they certainly didn't want an outsider getting close to Vera. Vera was always a wild card. Monitoring her was especially urgent since her memory could come back at any moment.

When the conversation ended, Pierre stood up and asserted, "I'll get right on it."

Chapter 13

For the last half hour, Gary had been pacing in the basement. He jumped when Sharon called down from the hallway, "Did you want a bite to eat before you go?"

"No thanks. I'll be fine." *I wish. I should've told Callie right away. Mark was right. Now look at me.* He put his hands on the sides of his head as he continued to pace. He looked at his watch and stopped in his tracks. *Just great. It's time to go.* He climbed the stairs and was surprised to see Sharon standing there with the keys in her outstretched hand.

"Oh. Uh, thanks."

"Have fun now." She gave him a hug.

Mark walked with him on the way out to the van. "So, this is how you tell Callie?"

"Geez man, loud enough? I don't think the neighbors down the street heard you."

"Just sayin.' I thought you'd man up by now."

"Don't worry. Nothing's going to come of it."

"You do know that going on this date is not going to make you very convincing to Callie when you do tell her."

"You think I haven't thought of that?"

"Then why'd you ask Marci out?"

"You don't know? It's like I was blindsided."

"Marci did that?" Mark asked.

Gary stopped and glared at him. "No! Mom and Callie!"

"Well, that explains a little. But you've got to stand up for yourself. Don't let people push you around." Mark put his hand on Gary's shoulder and said, "Tell me what happened."

"Sure," Gary murmured gloomily.

As he drove off, his breathing increased to match his anxiety level. He considered calling off the date. Realizing that would be cold-hearted, he vowed to let her down easy. Just tell her, "It isn't you, it's me." *Yeah, like that's going to work.* He was there before he decided what to do.

He pulled into the parking lot five minutes early, so he went inside to wait in the lobby. He sat in one of the chairs and picked up a magazine; he didn't want to look anxious or eager. He was mortified when he realized his foot was jiggling, making his leg look like it was in a spasm. He forced it to stop just as Marci came out from the hallway on the left. He took a breath and stood up.

"Hi, Gary. I'm ready."

He moaned inside. *She looks so happy. How can I disappoint her?* "Hi. I hope it isn't too late for you. I know how hard you have to work."

"Oh, no. It's fine."

He opened the door for her so they could leave. *At least be polite – don't be a jerk.* "You're probably hungry after a long day. Is pizza okay?"

She grinned. "That would be perfect. I am really hungry."

As the hostess led them to a table by the window, Gary's stomach tied in a knot.

"I've always liked this place, nice atmosphere," Marci said after they sat down.

A waiter came by to take their order. She ordered a root beer, and he ordered a cola. They decided on a half pepperoni, half Hawaiian medium pizza.

"So, you don't drink beer?"

His stomach flipped. "No." He froze for a moment. "I'm driving, so – you know." *I hope that went over. I don't want to talk about my dad.*

"Oh, of course."

"But if you want one, that's okay."

"No, I'd probably get sleepy. I'll pass."

Gary fidgeted as the small talk continued laboriously. Finally, their pizza was delivered. Since she carried the conversation as they ate, he allowed himself to zone out. He thought about Callie, her still unresolved feelings for Roy, and he wondered how or if he'd find a way to bring up his feelings for her.

"Are you ready?"

He looked up with a start. "Ready?"

Looking frustrated, she put down the slice of pizza she was eating. "Are you okay?"

Feeling trapped, he stammered, "Uh, yeah. Why?"

"You haven't heard a word I've said, have you?"

He frowned and swallowed hard.

"Something's bothering you. What is it? Are you nervous about starting work?"

"That could be part of it."

"Do you want to talk about it?"

He looked down. "It's my dad."

"Aw. You're worried about him."

He looked up sharply. "No. That isn't it." He spent the next twenty minutes telling her about his family history, about his mom passing, but mostly about his dad's lack of involvement. He ended up telling her how Jack convinced him to take the job.

She grimaced. "So, you really don't *want* to work there?"

"I need the job. I just feel odd about working with him."

"So why didn't you look for a job somewhere else?"

He looked at her blankly. "I don't know."

"Well, you better decide pretty quickly. You have to do orientation tomorrow so you can start Monday."

"Oh, I'm going to keep the job. I'm just not sure how much I'll enjoy it."

"Once you get started, you'll get to know the patients and it'll pick up from there."

"I guess."

She watched him as she took another bite. "You really don't want to be here, do you? Here with me."

His breath caught and his pulse raced. A guilty smile grew on his face.

"Can we be honest with each other?"

"Uh," he half-whispered. His breath escaped as he hung his head. "Okay. You got me." He looked up again, pleading, "I'm really sorry. I didn't mean to hurt your feelings. I just got in this... uh ... weird situation."

She frowned. "You think us being together is a weird situation?"

"I'm sorry, I said that wrong. It's not you. It's me." He picked up a napkin to wipe perspiration from his brow. "I don't know how to explain it."

"So, what's the weird part?"

He took a deep breath and huffed. "I feel bad. I didn't mean to lead you on. I'm sorry."

She leaned back in her chair. "You like Callie, don't you?"

He flushed. "Uh ... how'd you know?"

"Seriously? I could tell from the first time I saw you. I guess I was just hopeful. And then when you asked me out, I really thought we could make a go of it." She leaned forward. "So, why did you ask me out?"

His ears turned red and he swallowed hard. *Oh, great. How am I going to tell her I was tricked into asking her out?*

"Just spit it out."

He looked up. "Promise you won't hate me?"

"Of course not."

He took a cleansing breath. "Well, Mom saw how you acted and thought it would be a good idea for me to ask you out. There, I said it."

She gasped. "Callie's your *sister*? I knew she had a brother, but *this* is just *weird*."

"What? Wait! No. I just call Sharon my mom because *my* mom is dead. She and Jack are the ones who helped raise me. They were always more like my parents than my dad ever was."

She forced a breath out between tight lips. "Okay. You scared me for a minute. But, if you like Callie ... wait, she doesn't know, does she?"

He shook his head as his defeated eyes focused on his plate.

Marci took a bite of pizza and eyed him. She took a drink of her soda as she squinted at him.

He wondered what she was thinking. Perhaps, how she was going to throttle him and dispose of the body, his body?

"Do you want me to help you get her?"

Incredulous, he stammered, "After I humiliated you, you'd be willing to help me?"

"Sure. It might be fun."

"You're pretty amazing. Most girls would probably toss their drink in my face."

She shrugged. "You don't gain much when you burn your bridges. So, what's the plan?" She took another bite.

"I don't know. I've never done anything like this before."

"First off, you have to spend more time with her. Even though you know each other, you'll create a stronger bond. Friendship and trust are the first steps."

"How do you know so much about relationships?"

"I've taken some psychology classes in my studies. It helps with the patients. I'm not an expert, but I know a few things."

"I have been trying to make up reasons to be with her. I even asked her to show me some research that she …" He stopped mid-sentence, realizing he might say something that shouldn't be shared.

"And?"

He shrugged. "Um, she showed me. Now, I'm kind of wondering what else to come up with."

"Play it by ear. If you push too much, you could look like a stalker." She shook her head. "You really don't want that."

After getting some suggestions, Gary paused. "Mom told us about one of your patients."

"Oh, which one?"

"I don't remember the name, but she was shot by her sister."

"Oh yeah, Vera. She's going to be one of your patients when you start work. What about her?"

"She said Vera hadn't had any visitors except for her. Is that true?"

Marci frowned. "Unfortunately, yes. I think the family's pretty well off. I heard they pay everything in cash. I don't know anyone that can do that."

"Cash? *That* sounds strange."

"I'll say."

"This might sound weird, but would you tell me if anything strange goes on?"

"Are you kidding? I've wanted to have someone to talk to about all the crazy stuff that happens. Nobody wants to get involved."

"What kind of crazy stuff?"

"I suspect there are some caregivers stealing from the center and from the residents. Then there's elder abuse, you name it. By myself, I can't do anything. Makes me wonder if the administrators are involved, maybe even in Medicare fraud. And I'm always suspicious of families that hire their own caregivers."

Although he thought she was going to reveal crazy stuff about Vera, he thought it would be wise to let the conversation flow naturally. No point in creating suspicion. "Why is that?"

"A lot of the same reasons – Medicare fraud, theft, spying on the facility. Maybe other reasons."

"So, about the family that pays in cash. If they're so well off, why doesn't someone visit her?"

"Seriously? The really rich ones hire nannies for their kids and pay others to do their jobs. If they're willing to pay someone to look after their kids, do you think they'll care about the elders? It galls me to think they don't have any real feelings for others. It takes too much time away from making all that money," she scoffed.

He shook his head. *I've got to tell Callie. Wait, I can't let Marci think I'm interested only in Vera. I'd better ask about others.* "What can you tell me about the other residents I'll be working with?"

"You've probably seen the 'lunch' lady. She has plantar fasciitis. The only way we know it's bothering her is when she limps. She doesn't say anything because she just can't think to tell us what's wrong."

"I'll be able to help with the plantar fasciitis with therapy."

Marci's face perked up. "We'll schedule it then." Too soon, she looked somber again. "Her family doesn't visit either. They prepaid for two years. I think they're hoping she passes away before the bill comes up again. But I'm pretty sure she's going to have to go into the dementia wing. We have to hunt her down several times a week." Marci laughed. "You've probably already figured this out, but she always forgets that she's eaten and then sneaks snacks, so she's gained a little weight. Once when I was helping her get dressed, she whispered to me, 'Don't tell anyone, I'm pregnant.'"

Gary laughed out loud. "Seriously?"

Grinning, Marci nodded. "She pointed to her belly and said 'see.'" Then, she looked somber again. "But I worry about her. The family is not involved. I can see how people can get discouraged when the patient loses their ability to recognize and communicate, but that doesn't make it right."

"I agree."

They passed the rest of the evening discussing more of the residents.

Chapter 14

While Gary was out with Marci, Callie called Rudy for advice. "When I did research for you last year, you told me where to look and who to look for. What suggestions do you have for me?"

"What do you need to know?"

When she explained about Vera's situation and asked what she should look for, Rudy was silent for several seconds. Finally, she broke the silence, "Where do I start?"

"Surveillance. Observation. I know you're already good at putting pieces together. First, you have to get names, and sometimes that can be tricky – making sure it's not an alias. Find out where they live, follow people. Are they renting, or do they own the place? What's their schedule? Where do they go? Who do they talk to? You talk with the people they meet, but don't be obvious. Always have an alibi for that. Then research *them*. Sometimes the littlest bit of information will lead to the evidence that cracks the case. And document everything. Never rely on your memory."

"That takes a lot of time."

"That's what a P.I. does. A lot of leg work."

"So, when you gave me all those names to research, you'd already done a lot to get them, right?"

"You're getting the picture. There's a lot of digging involved."

"What I'm hearing is that being a detective is a full-time job."

"Not necessarily. Start out with small jobs. Get the feel for what you are doing. In the meantime, you work at a paid position because you can't support yourself when starting out, especially when you're investigating something on your own. Even with paying clients, it's tough getting started."

"So, what do I look for?"

"Patterns. Inconsistencies. That's why it's important to learn all you can. That's how you found the connection with the governor and his impostor."

"Okay."

"So, tell me about this Vera person."

Callie explained all the information she had on Vera. She assumed he was absorbing what she was saying, for he was silent the whole time and even after she finished. So, she went on, "And Gary's going to start work there Monday as the physical therapist."

When he said okay, she wondered about the change in his voice.

"If you or Gary can get your hands on her application records and chart, get every bit of info you can from them. Copies are ideal, but making them is not always possible. Use a phone to take pictures, but don't use the facility's copier. Copiers can store images of what is copied, and you'd get caught."

"I wouldn't have known that. Thanks. Can I come to you in case I get stumped?"

"I'd expect you to."

"Thanks, Rudy. I really appreciate your help."

"Just be careful. There's always a possibility of digging up more than you bargain for, no matter how small the job is."

"Okay. Thanks again."

They said their goodbyes, and as she ended the call, her eyes brightened. She opened her laptop and created a file for everything she would find on the Internet.

Let's see what we can find. Since she was shot by her sister, there should be tons of coverage on that. Scandals involving rich people always make the news.

She searched for Vera Carelli, and dozens of articles came up. *Whoa!* Realizing she didn't have time to read all of them, she saved them for later. There were a few articles on the engagement from almost three years ago and then the wedding over two years ago. She noted from the wedding announcement that Vera's maiden name was Perkins.

In addition to the engagement and wedding, Callie found several older articles about Vera's husband, Brent, mostly about him being a party boy and slipping through a few scrapes with the law. One article, in particular, from four years ago made her jaw drop. It was a shocking, stand-alone article in an obscure paper. After looking for several minutes, she found no other articles about the incident. She wondered why it didn't produce more coverage or interest. With a family that influential, the reporters should have been all over it. She read it carefully a second time:

PLAYBOY ARRESTED

Well-known trust-fund playboy, Brent Carelli, was arrested Thursday on charges of rape. Carelli's parents, Anthony and Phaedra Carelli, were attending a charity dinner, and the rest of the household staff had been dismissed for the evening, leaving him and Angela Pelayo, the family maid, alone in the mansion.

Miss Pelayo claims that Brent Carelli told her to stay after hours in order to "discuss benefits". He then forced her into his bedroom where the incident allegedly happened.

Carelli insists that any intercourse between them was consensual, and she had planned from the start to extort money from him. He claims that when he refused to be blackmailed, she pressed charges. Questions by the reporters to the parents and other household staff remain unanswered.

All charges were dropped yesterday when Miss Pelayo insisted she had made a mistake. Attempts to contact her for an explanation have been in vain. The Carelli family states that Miss Pelayo decided to return to her home in Mexico instead of facing the media.

With charges dropped, Carelli was released.

What a jerk! Why would anyone marry a man like that? Vera must not have known. But why is there only one article? I wonder if the whole media circus was squashed, and this story was missed? And why would she file charges and then drop them? Did she lie? Was she scared of revenge? Maybe they paid her off? I should track her down. Callie copied the articles into a special file for follow-up.

Looking up Vera's sister, Jody Perkins, brought up several articles too. Most of them revolved around the shooting, but a few in particular caught her attention. They dealt with a bout of depression resulting in her being hospitalized, and another reported on arrests for drugs when she was a teen. All of the stories were written by the same reporter. She scratched her head. *I thought juvenile issues weren't accessible after reaching adulthood. I wonder how the reporter discovered all that.* Then she realized the articles had been written about the time of the engagement. *I wonder why they were written then.* She slapped her forehead. *Well, duh ... prominent family with a connection to a depressed druggie? Of course, they'd capitalize on that juicy piece of news. Anything that might sully the Carellis' name? Apparently, Brent did a pretty good job of that all by himself. But he wasn't publicized for everything he did. Something doesn't add up here. I think I'll look up that reporter, maybe talk to him.*

She created a document listing things she wanted to follow up on.

She went back to a couple of the articles on the sister's drug charges; resisting arrest, the diagnosis of her mental issues, and ultimately her placement in the Oregon State Hospital for the criminally insane after the shooting. *Wow! Poor Vera. Not only did her sister really shoot her, but she's nuts, too. I guess you'd have to be crazy to shoot your own sister. Or really mad. No wonder Jody doesn't visit her ... she's locked up and can't.* She groaned. *How do we tell her about this situation? I'll have to talk to Mom first and maybe Rudy.*

Callie searched for anything regarding the sisters' history. Finally, she found an obituary about their mother from over ten years ago that named Vera, Jody, and their father as survivors. Getting the husband's name from the obituary, she eagerly looked him up and found some older articles showing several arrests through the years, with the last one stating that he was sentenced to prison for drug dealing. She frowned. *I wonder if that's how Jody got into drugs.* She saved all the articles.

Then Callie looked up Vera's in-laws. Having verified their names, Anthony Carelli and Phaedra Carelli, from the wedding articles, she found numerous news items. Anthony Carelli came up more times than she could count. He'd received an award for several donations to Oregon Health Sciences University, hosted numerous charity dinners, was named benefactor of the year, plus dozens of other awards and social events.

She spent the next few minutes sorting the articles by 'Vera,' 'Jody,' 'Brent,' and 'Carelli' and putting them in separate folders, in addition to the separate folder needing additional research.

Callie heard the front door shut at eleven. She closed her laptop and ran to the living room. Energized with anticipation, she blurted out, "Well, how did it go?"

Gary shrugged. "Okay."

"That's all you're going to say?"

He sighed loudly. He explained how his date with Marci had gone leaving out the discussion about Callie.

"Is that all?"

"It looks like we've got a partner in figuring out what's going on with Vera."

Callie's eyes widened incredulously. "Really? *That's* what you talked about?"

He frowned. "Yeah," he countered defensively.

She shrugged. "Okay." Then, she brightened. "Oh, guess what?! Speaking of Vera – you won't believe what I found. Come here, I have to show you!" She grabbed his hand, dragged him to the den, and opened the files she created.

He spent the next half hour scanning everything. "Wow, you've been busy." He pointed to the article on Brent's arrest, "That's creepy and suspicious looking."

"Just what I was thinking. And I've only started."

"Do you think that maid really just *left*?"

"We won't know until we dig some more. Rudy says, 'Never make assumptions.'"

"So, how do you find someone that disappeared? How do you know where they went? Yeah, the article said she went back to Mexico, but that's a big country. I doubt they have very good records."

"We've got to try."

"I'd better get ready for bed. I have orientation tomorrow at nine."

She waved as he walked out. "Night." These articles had piqued her curiosity, and that trumped being tired. She worked until her battery died at 3 a.m.

When Callie hung up, Rudy inhaled deeply. *Carelli? Where do I remember that name?* After thinking about it for a while, he stopped cold. *Oh, I hope not.* He opened his safe to look for the name Carelli in the research he'd previously done on Pierre's family tree.

Chapter 15

Jack had taught Gary well; he was early for orientation. Being late is career suicide, especially on the first day. He really did need this job, so he came in with a cheery demeanor.

He shook hands with the administrator, Patrick Hughes, and he led Gary to the break room. He sat Gary in front of a pile of papers and left him to his paperwork. As Gary filled out each form, he occasionally glanced up. Just through the door, he saw Mr. Hughes working at his computer, his deep-set, dark eyes focused on the monitor.

When Gary first applied for the job, he noted Hughes' deep tan, classic features, and charismatic personality. That image, along with the tailored suit, manicure, and perfectly styled black hair, added to the professional look that seemed more suited for a lawyer than an administrator. Gary wondered why this man worked here. He wondered if Mr. Hughes might do better as a model, maybe a politician, or perhaps as a motivational speaker. He returned to his paperwork, which took over an hour.

After giving Gary the facility polo shirts with the nursing home's logo that he would wear while on duty, Mr. Hughes escorted him on a tour of the facility and introduced him to all the staff. Gary wondered how long it would take to remember everyone's name.

Besides the residents' rooms, Mr. Hughes showed him the therapy room, supply room, rest rooms, dining hall, nurses' station, med room, offices, as well as the location of all safety equipment. The physical therapy room was located between the break room and the nurses' station. He noted that the equipment and supplies were mostly up-to-date. Hughes told him that he would have access to coffee as desired, and he would be allowed to eat lunch for free as long as he was scheduled during those hours. Because this was a part-time position, there would be no other benefits.

When they were done with the tour, Mr. Hughes asked him to stay for lunch to observe the process. Gary stood against the wall as everyone worked. As he watched everyone busily performing their duties, he noted that the dining hall had large windows looking out to a spacious garden-like commons area that had concrete paths to make it easy for a wheelchair or walker to navigate. Trees, shrubs, and blooming flowers decorated the lawn's edge, two birdbaths, tiki lights for evenings, and signs pointing to different areas of the grounds. He wondered if residents could actually get lost out there. The scene gave him a sense of peace, reminding him of Georgia's back yard. He smiled thinking how relaxing it must be for the residents.

When Bertie wheeled in, she waved to him with a big smile on her face. She came up to say hi. "Are you having lunch with us today?"

He nodded and extended his hand. "Yes. I hope you don't mind."

She giggled. "Of course not." She motioned for him to bend towards her and she whispered, "Don't order the meatloaf. It tastes like sawdust."

He chuckled. "Deal."

She wheeled over to her designated table and waved again.

Mr. Hughes explained, "As you can see, some of our aides take meals to the residents that are bedridden and they feed them in their rooms. When they finish, they return to the dining hall to help with cleanup. You'll sit at my table today so we can talk." He led him to a table in the corner. After they sat down, he added, "Remember, the residents always come first. Make sure your personal needs are taken care of before you work with a resident. It isn't safe to leave them unattended even for a few minutes."

Gary nodded. As Mr. Hughes continued, Gary watched as aides asked each resident which choice they wanted to eat, chicken strips or meatloaf. Remembering Bertie's warning, he chose the chicken, but even after adding salt, it was still tasteless. *Not much better than sawdust*, he thought. Canned peas were the vegetable of the day along with instant mashed potatoes, and he hated both.

Gary asked for milk, but he could have sworn it was watered down. A soft white roll was served with a butter substitute, but the roll had little flavor, and when he took a bite, it squashed into a glob of dough. Dessert was either pudding or a serving of ice cream. He chose the ice cream, which was more like ice milk. It was the half-cup-size, cardboard-enclosed pull-top with a wooden spoon, like he had in grammar school. He vowed to bring his lunch from now on. Even a peanut butter sandwich would be better than what he was served today.

As the residents finished, aides helped them back to their rooms while other aides cleaned up the lunchroom. Gary volunteered to help. Even though the serving sizes were meager, he noticed that several residents left food on their plates. *I don't blame them. I didn't want it either.*

Mr. Hughes shook hands with him in the lobby. "See you Monday," he said, and handed Gary his schedule.

It was not an easy schedule. Monday was the start of the next bi-monthly pay period. The split-shift meant that most of his day would be shot. At least, he would be there only three days a week, Monday, Wednesday, and Friday. One good thing – the only good thing – was that he wouldn't have to worry about being here during lunch.

Thinking about that stroke of luck, he shook his head. He'd get only 18 hours per week. It would be a long time before he'd earn enough money to fix that car. He almost wondered if the job was worth it. He sighed. *At least, it's a start. I can always go somewhere else after getting experience.*

Chapter 16

Rudy was barbecuing ribs and chicken on the grill. Jack had prepared them with his special rub and marinade, brought them over three hours ago, and left right after that. Rudy had been experimenting with the recipe for the sauce but still hadn't gotten it right. So, it was Jack's responsibility to do the preparation until Rudy was able to master the sauce.

Although the temperature was still in the mid-eighties, it was comfortable with all the shade trees in the yard. He reached over to tap on the frame of the screen door, "They're here," he called out. He looked in to the kitchen and saw Georgia wave an acknowledgment, and then she almost tripped over Lucky at her feet. Normally, she would have been ecstatic to have company, but the joy didn't bubble over like usual. *She's been so tired lately. Maybe she's overdoing it. She doesn't look it, but she is nudging seventy.* He had started thinking how to get her to slow down and asked if it would be wise to continue hosting dinners here. Sharon and Jack were more than happy to take over, but she had insisted. Worried about her health, he sighed.

Even Lucky was acting differently. He seemed so clingy with Georgia lately. Although the vet had given him a clean bill of health, Rudy found it curious.

He turned his attention back to the grill and flipped the chicken just as Sharon, Jack, Mark, and Gary entered the back yard carrying their contributions to dinner. Although they called it a pot luck, everyone always brought their favorite dishes. The boys, however, were still novice cooks, so they were allowed to bring store-bought.

He looked up as Sharon carried a large bowl of potato salad to the picnic table. Mark put drinks in the cooler, and Gary set the chips and dips on the table. Of course, Georgia always made dessert. Rudy was always amazed that she had such a large selection in her recipe box that they seldom saw the same dessert twice.

Sharon went into the house to help Georgia prepare for the barbeque. The boys set up the folding table next to the picnic table, brought out the folding chairs, and set them around the tables.

Jack stood next to Rudy to monitor how the ribs were going. "I think you're really getting the hang of this."

"Well, look at my teacher." He chuckled. "So, is Callie bringing your parents?"

"Yup. And Cora insisted on bringing something too. She wouldn't tell me what it is, but it'll be good." Jack glanced up from the grill. "If she brings a dessert, do you think Georgia will mind?"

"Pssh. Nah." He turned the ribs. "Say, I've got a question. Since you guys have been married so long ...."

"Trouble in paradise?"

Rudy elbowed him. "No! I'm just concerned about Georgia. She doesn't seem like herself lately. Is there anything I should be aware of?"

"You two talk over everything, don't you?"

"Yeah. I'm pretty sure she isn't keeping a secret ...." He stopped, certain he didn't want to discuss *that*. "Nothing current that I know of, that is." He realized that Jack picked up on his change in voice, but didn't say anything. He leaned over to whisper, "Look. You've probably noticed that Georgia is hiding something from her childhood, but that's not what I'm talking about. She seems so tired, and I'm getting worried."

"Has she been checked by the doctor?"

"She's going in for her mammogram tomorrow. I know, that isn't a checkup, so I'll make sure she makes an appointment for one."

"Make sure you rule out the physical possibilities first."

"You're not implying she has a psychological problem, are you?"

Jack held up a defensive hand. "Hey, I'm not going there. Just making sure." He turned around at the sound of car doors closing. "Sounds like Callie's here. Hey, Mark, Gary? Would you help your grandparents?"

They trotted down the driveway to help.

Rudy looked at Jack quizzically. "So, how come you say they're Gary's grandparents?"

"Hey, we're like his parents. So – why not? He's family."

"What you've done for that kid is awesome." He gave Jack an approving pat on the shoulder.

"Well, if we hadn't, I'd hate to think what kind of person he would've turned out to be. It was hard on everyone, but we've gotten as much out of it as he has. What a reward!"

Callie brought her fruit salad and Gary followed with Cora's dish, macaroni and cheese. Mark brought up the end of the parade with Cora on his arm, followed by Ralph who shuffled down the driveway with his walker.

Cora hadn't changed much from last year, keeping the pixie haircut; but she had stopped dying it blonde. Since she had been cooking more healthfully, she'd dropped a few pounds and could walk easier. She had made it her job to take care of Ralph even though Callie had moved in with them.

Ralph, on the other hand, had chronic health issues resulting from all those years of drinking and poor eating habits. Although he stopped drinking over a year ago, his skin was still grey from the liver damage, and the wrinkles had deepened. He was developing cataracts in his yellow-tinged eyes that hadn't progressed enough for surgery, but had gotten bad enough to keep him from reading. His mood was somewhat better, but he had developed a little dementia with confusion, yet he was clever enough to sneak treats, and that played havoc with his diabetes. His gray eyes seemed to have lost some color in the last year and he had lost more of his hair, so that only a narrow fringe wrapped behind his head from ear to ear. Because it was still a battle to cut his notoriously wild eyebrows, they stuck out like disorganized antennas over the top of his horn-rimmed glasses.

By the time the kids helped their grandparents sit at the picnic table, Georgia and Sharon came out with big pan of peach cobbler. Lucky circled Georgia's feet, almost causing her to trip.

"Great timing – meat's done," Rudy announced. Jack helped him plate everything and added it to the bounty. Everyone else sat down and passed around the dishes.

Georgia started the conversation. "Cora, that smells wonderful. I can hardly wait to try it."

Cora grinned. "I used four different cheeses. It's Ralph's favorite."

Ralph was already spooning a big helping of mac and cheese. "Yeah, ah could eat this ever' day." Then he poked a rib, put it on his plate, and started to eat.

Gary smiled at the spread as he reached for a chicken leg. "You guys spoil me. This is awesome."

"Gary, I heard you got a job," Rudy said as he dropped some potato salad onto his plate.

"Yeah. I start Monday. I've already done the orientation, and I've got my uniform shirts. But I'll have to get some black or khaki pants to go with them."

"Any first impressions?"

The look on Gary's face seemed odd, almost like he'd been caught red-handed in something. "It's clean and organized ...." He hesitated, and his pupils shrank.

"But?"

He shook his head. "The administrator asked me to stay for lunch to observe the routine. Well, the food is awful. I actually wanted to spit it out. They tell me I'm allowed to eat there if I'm scheduled at mealtimes. Thank goodness, I'm not. And speaking of hours, they're terrible." He shrugged. "But it's a job."

Jack smiled. "Hey, at least you've got a foot in the door. After you get some experience, you'll be able to pick where to go from there."

"Yeah. That's what I thought, too."

Sharon looked up with a glint in her eye. "So, tell us about your date."

Cora's eyes brightened. "Date? You had a date already?"

"Yes." Gary rolled his eyes. "Mom made me ask her."

Sharon grimaced. "Was it *that* bad?"

"No. No, I meant ... well, it turns out we're just going to be friends."

Callie's eyes gleamed. "Tell them what you told me. You know, about how you're going to collaborate?"

"Oh, yeah."

Rudy was confused. "Huh? Collaborate? About what?"

Gary sighed. "Marci – she's the girl I asked out – she works at the nursing home. After we talked a bit, we both think something odd is going on with one of the residents."

Rudy's breath caught. *Please don't let it be Vera Carelli.*

Cora shook her finger at him. "Well, if that's what you talked about, no wonder you didn't hit it off!"

Callie snickered.

Rudy frowned. "Wait. How would you know about any of the residents before you actually start working there? Are you talking about your dad?" He really hoped it was.

Gary shook his head. "No. When Callie and I first went to see my dad, we met this resident, her name is Bertie. Well she's a big gossip; she tells you about everyone in the place. She told us about a new resident – Vera Carelli's her name …"

Rudy inhaled quickly, and a piece of chicken stuck in his throat. He managed to cough it up and then took a big gulp of lemonade. *Just great! Now he's involved too!* His research had showed there *was* a Carelli in Pierre's family, not a common name, so Vera's probably related.

"… and she gets no visitors. So, Mom went with us the next time to visit her."

Rudy wilted inside.

Callie interrupted, "Gary told me about the date when he got home. When he said that he and Marci were going to collaborate, I couldn't wait to tell him that I'd already been researching her – Vera, not Marci. I took your advice, Rudy. I looked up everything I could think of, and you won't believe what I found!"

Rudy struggled to keep the poker face, but he managed. He dared not alarm anyone.

Everyone's attention focused on Callie as she continued, "I know where Vera's sister is." She leaned forward for emphasis. "Turns out that she's in the loony bin in Salem. She was high on coke when she shot her sister, *and* she has a record of arrests for using drugs from when she was a teen. Their mom is dead, and their dad is in prison for dealing drugs. I think that's how she got hooked. The psychiatrist that examined her pronounced her criminally insane. So, that's why she hasn't gone to visit Vera. She couldn't!"

Mixed reactions followed.

Cora set her fork down. "They ought to ban those drugs. People do the darndest things because of them."

Ralph nodded and pointed his fork at the group. "Worse'n liquor, ah tell ya. Somebody's gotta *do* somethin'." He nodded with a frown as he went back to eating his mac and cheese.

Georgia's face dropped. "How awful."

Worry lines etched Sharon's face. "How am I going to tell all that to Vera?"

"Well, I'm pretty sure she knows about the arrests ...." Callie paused and then added quietly, "... maybe." Then she frowned. "But telling her about Jody being in Salem, that will be hard."

A few moments of uncomfortable silence followed.

"There's more," Callie continued. "I looked up her in-laws. The Carellis are a pretty prominent family, heavily involved in charities, community service, and local politics." She leaned forward.

Rudy held his breath, worrying about what could be next.

"But the most interesting detail is Vera's husband, Brent Carelli." She paused for emphasis. "He gets a *lot* of news coverage – a real party boy. The most shocking piece of news only had *one article* in a remote newspaper. I wondered, well, *more* than wondered about that. I'm pretty sure someone tried to erase the incident, but missed this one article."

Rudy asked cautiously, "And why do you say that?"

"Because it was such a shocking story that I would've expected the reporters to be all over it in *all* the papers. That's why I think there had to be a cover up."

Rudy's instinct told him she was on the right track, and his concern ramped up to anxiety. But since everyone was focused on Callie, he was thankful nobody noticed the change in his expression.

"So, what was the story?" Jack asked with anticipation.

Callie leaned forward again, her voice firm, "Four years ago, their maid accused him of raping her. But she withdrew the charges and returned to Mexico. I think they paid her off." Callie frowned. "Or she got scared. Maybe they threatened her?"

Rudy made sure not to reveal anything yet. Trying to look natural, he stirred his lemonade with his straw. "So, what's your next step?"

Callie's eyes lit up. "I was kind of hoping you'd give me some pointers on research."

"I think you're doing just fine."

Callie put on a pleading look as she tilted her head towards her left shoulder. "Maybe you could make some suggestions on what to look for next?"

He needed to know her plan of action before giving any warnings. "What do *you* think would be a good search?"

She huffed and knitted her eyebrows. "I guess I could look up more information on her sister. Maybe visit her and find out what she has to say?"

Sharon gasped. "Seriously? She's in Salem! For being criminally insane! Won't that be dangerous?"

Rudy held up a hand. "That place has excellent supervision and security, almost *too* good. However, if you do go, there are several things that have to happen first. First, you have to be added to the visitor's list and that has to be approved by the patient as well as the staff. You'll have to think of something pretty good to get in there since she doesn't know you. Only relatives and friends are allowed, and you're neither." How they'd get in wasn't what made him nervous.

Callie sighed. "Oh, great! Getting in to see her isn't going to be easy, is it?"

Rudy shook his head. *Hopefully, you won't be able to get in.*

"Maybe I can find something in the news reports that I can capitalize on?"

"There's a thought."

"I really thought you'd help more."

"If I tell you what to do, you aren't using your imagination." He hoped that explanation would discourage her. He really didn't want her to find out everything, but that probably wouldn't happen. However, if she truly found out the truth, she might retreat. He prayed for that conclusion. "Rely on your own curiosity; it will serve you well. Get to know your subjects, their personalities, their ways of thinking, and their habits. Always think about why things happen, why people make their decisions. When you know the person, that's when you see what doesn't fit, and that's where you focus. Just keep in mind that even the most insignificant bit of information could lead to a goldmine. Keep me informed." *Maybe she'll be kept busy until the storm blows over.*

Callie shrugged. "Thanks a *lot*, Rudy," she grumbled.

Mark turned to Callie. "So, with all this P.I. stuff you're doing, does that mean your college courses are going to be useless?"

"Not really. If I really do decide to be an investigator, it'll be a business, and I'll still need the business courses, and the photography will come in handy too."

"Are you going to have enough time for classes while working *and* taking care of Grandma and Grandpa?"

"It's only another year of classes, and they don't start until September. Besides, Grandma and Grandpa are still pretty self-sufficient." She turned to her grandparents, "You are, aren't you? You're not hiding any problems, are you?"

"Pssh." Cora waved as if swatting a fly. "We're fine. Just having you living with us is more than enough."

Turning back to Mark, Callie defiantly straightened her back and lifted her chin. "I'm doing just fine, thank you." She took a sip of lemonade and returned to her plate.

"Hey Dad, I almost forgot to tell you. Those parts for the truck you ordered are supposed to be delivered tomorrow. They didn't give a specific time, so we should be there before eight."

"Oh, thanks, Mark. I appreciate you keeping tabs on the emails. If they're delivered early enough, we should be able to get them installed the same day."

Glad for the change of subject, Rudy added, "Since you're going to be at the shop tomorrow, can I come by? I want to check out your security system. You've got a lot of nice equipment there. I'd hate to see someone take off with any of it."

"Sure. Glad to have your input."

"Georgia, what time are we leaving for your mam ..." Sharon stuttered, "... uh, office visit tomorrow?"

Georgia snickered. "Being discreet?"

Sharon shrugged. "Well, you know, the kids?"

Mark laughed. "Are you talking about a mammogram? Come on, surely you know we're aware of what a mammogram is?"

Sharon turned red. "Sorry. I guess I just put more attention on it than if I'd said it to begin with."

Georgia laughed. "If you're driving, pick me up at ten."

"Got it." Sharon quietly resumed eating.

Chapter 17

When Rudy opened the door at 7:30 the next morning, he called out, "Hey, anybody here?"

Jack stood up from working under the hood of the old truck, wiped his hands on a shop rag, and waved. "Come on back." He shook hands with Rudy and led him into the bay.

Mark stopped sanding the chassis to wave, and Rudy waved back.

Jack spread his arms as he proudly announced, "This is my baby."

Rudy nodded his approval as he looked around. "Nice. Is everything set up now?"

"Not quite. I still have to set up a paint booth, but I'll have to hire someone to do the actual paint work until I get the hang of it. It'll go over there." Jack pointed to the back corner of the large warehouse. "After doing some research, I decided that would be the best spot for it, considering ventilation and power access."

Rudy looked into the pit. "Make sure the lift works properly. I'd hate to see it fail with you in there."

"I've already got some leads for maintenance. I'll just pay to have them instruct me on the upkeep. Maintaining it shouldn't be too much different than what I've been doing for twenty years."

"With all this equipment, have you made sure of security? You know, alarms, cameras, maybe a dog?"

"A dog? That's an idea. But I've got the alarms and cameras. Wanna see them?"

"You bet."

"They're inside and outside, motion activated, so we're being recorded right now." He took him to the locked security room to show him how the system worked. There was a large monitor showing the feeds from each of the cameras. Jack demonstrated how he could select one feed and enlarge the picture or choose a frame to print.

"High definition?"

"You bet. I'll show them to you," Jack said as he led him out the back door. As they walked around the building, he pointed out all the cameras and the angles they captured. "I got the ones that'll last, the fisheye lenses to get the wide angles and steel cages to survive impact, in case someone tried to slam it with a bat or something."

Rudy nodded again. "Impressive. Got a backup system?"

Jack grinned. "Yup. I've got an online system that backs it up to the cloud as it records."

"Glad to see you've done your research."

"Well, Callie's the one that researched it. She helped me find the right fit."

"Looks like she's really improving her skills."

"Aw, come on. I know you've been training her."

"Hey, the research skills are her own. I only pointed out a few things. That girl has got researching down to an art. You should be proud of her."

Jack grinned. "I sure am. And I tell her all the time."

They had just started to go back inside when a box van drove by. Rudy's attention turned to it when the passenger gestured as he talked on his phone. Rudy did a double take and watched it drive by until it turned into the open bay of the third building on the next block across the street.

"Do you think that truck'll be on the camera feed?" Rudy asked quickly.

"I don't know. Let's go check." When they got inside, Jack punched a few buttons and ran the recording.

"Can you run it slow motion?"

"Sure." He pushed some more buttons. "That okay?"

"Uh-huh. Is it possible to zoom in on the passenger?"

"If you want. What are you looking for?"

"I'll tell you if I'm right." Jack ran the playback slowly and when it got to the van, Rudy leaned in close. "That's him!"

"You mean the guy with the blonde ponytail? Who is that?"

Rudy put on his poker face.

Jack's breath caught, but he managed to ask, "This is serious, isn't it?" When Rudy didn't answer, he urged, "Well, are you going to tell me?"

"I guess I have to; you're too close not to. But you can't tell *any*one! I mean *no* one! Not even Sharon or Mark."

"Is this as bad as what we found out about Sharon's dad?"

"Worse."

Jack's face dropped, and he groaned.

"Give me your word first."

"You're scaring me."

"Your *word*?!"

Jack nodded quickly. "Yeah, sure. I won't tell anyone."

"That guy is bad news." He saw Jack's worry lines deepen. "Seriously, a *really* bad guy. He was connected to Pierre. We didn't know it back then, but I found out later that they're part of a crime syndicate."

Jack seemed to go limp. After a moment of silence, his eyes and mouth popped wide open and he stammered, "Does that mean Alice was part of it?"

"I don't know if she knew about the connection or not, but she was involved in a lot of illegal stuff."

"Are *we* in danger?!"

"Not if you keep a low profile."

"What are you going to do?"

"I can't tell you, but I can say that I have connections. And I'll need a copy of that video."

"You got it."

Rudy pulled out a flash drive that he always carried with him. "Put it on this."

As Jack copied the video, he looked up at Rudy. "I don't know if this is important, but there've been a lot of materials being delivered there, and that noisy construction's been going on for over a week. I didn't think anything of it, but if it means something, I thought you should know."

Rudy nodded his acknowledgment. When he received the flash drive, he admonished, "Remember, mum's the word."

When Rudy got home, Georgia was on the phone. She looked puzzled then, and after talking a little bit, she became serious, took some notes, and hung up.

"What was that all about?"

"I have to go in for a biopsy."

"What?! Why?"

"There's a spot on the film they did today."

"When do you go?"

"Tomorrow."

His heart sank. *So soon?! This has to be bad.* He knew he couldn't show any anxiety, for it would surely make her more nervous if he did. He had to buoy her up. "Hey, I was thinking, how about we go out for dinner?"

She eyed him, then walked up to him, and put her arms around him. "It's okay. You don't have to put on this brave front. Remember, I'm a tough old gal."

As he held her, he squeezed his eyes shut. No words could come out through his compressed lips. He couldn't even manage a sufficient breath.

She patted him on the back, "It's probably just a cyst. I'll be okay. You wait and see." She looked up, and before she could say anything else, Rudy managed, "I'm going with you. No argument."

Chapter 18

Being the first week in August, Monday night was still hot. Callie arrived at her parents' house with a salad. She had left Ralph and Cora at home because they were too tired from their weekly trip to the grocery store. Plus, the heat always wore them out.

When she first heard they were having an impromptu family dinner, she was excited about sharing the news she had just gotten. When she approached the back yard, she had expected Mark to make some crack about her being late. At first, she was relieved when he didn't, but then, she realized everyone was uncharacteristically quiet. Something was in the air, and she groaned inside. With this atmosphere, she'd have to be careful how to introduce her news, if at all.

Jack looked up, "Hey, thanks for the salad." Just then, the doorbell rang. "Must be the pizza," he said as he got up.

Callie sat down across the picnic table from Georgia. "Dad ordered pizza?!"

Sharon patted her hand and gave her the look that conveyed a 'shush!'

"All right," Georgia announced. "This is just ridiculous. I know you all want the diagnosis."

"Diagnosis?!" Callie exclaimed, her eyes wide.

Georgia explained about the mammogram and biopsy. "I don't have a diagnosis yet. The biopsy results won't be in for a while."

Callie whined, "Why do they have to make you wait? Then you have to worry so much!"

Georgia patted her hand. "They have to grow the cultures. Hey, we're all here, so let's have a party!"

Callie was suspicious when she saw Rudy acting strangely reserved. *What're they keeping from us?* Now was the time to change the subject, so she sat up straight, took a cleansing breath, and put on the pleasant face she had been practicing. "Hey, *I* have some news!"

Georgia smiled. "Well, let us have it!" It was obvious she was relieved to have the attention on something else.

Jack walked out with four pizzas and placed them onto the picnic table. "Dig in, everyone."

Georgia piped up, "You serve while Callie tells us her news."

"I contacted the State Hospital to set me up as one of Jody's visitors. Apparently, it's okay for a friend of a relative to visit patients, so I just told them Vera and I were friends. Now the visit's in the process. If they get Jody's okay, then I'm in."

Rudy groaned inside. *And I was really hoping she wouldn't get approved.*

Gary held up his hand as if he were in first grade. "My turn. You know today was my first day at work."

Sharon chimed in, "Oh, that's right. Tell us how it went."

"I did three therapies today. Vera was one of them. She about talked my ear off. I guess she's pretty lonely."

Alerted, Callie looked up quickly. "What did she say? Anything we can use?"

"Mostly about missing her sister. Oh, Marci told me something. Vera's husband tried to have her served with divorce papers yesterday, but the administrator stopped him in the lobby." He cringed. "I told Vera about what he wanted. She didn't take it very well."

Sharon moaned. "Was she angry, sad – what?"

He sighed. "Mostly hurt. At first, she was surprised; but afterwards, she said she sort of expected it." He scratched his head. "Say, you haven't met any of the night shift crew, have you?"

Puzzled, Sharon frowned. "No. I usually visit mid-morning. Why?"

"Vera said the strangest thing. She told me that the night aide mentioned you by name, that you'd been grilling her. You know, getting names and phone numbers? Neither of us could think of a time when she would have seen or heard you. So, that was pretty strange."

"Grilling her?" Sharon looked genuinely puzzled. "We were just talking. And she couldn't have heard it from someone else because there was nobody else around that could've heard us."

Georgia squinted. "There must have been someone nearby. Otherwise, how would she know?"

Rudy felt like the rug had just been pulled out from under him. The only explanation was too serious to discuss now.

Callie frowned. "There's something else. From what Mom said, Vera's description of her sister doesn't match what I've been reading in the newspaper reports. If I can get in to visit Jody, I think I can find out."

Rudy pointed at her. "You be careful. If the Carellis are as important and influential as you say, they might not *want* you to learn anything." He had to make her cautious without frightening her, but even saying *that* in front of everyone may not have been wise.

Sharon's face dropped. "Is this going to be dangerous?!"

"One never knows what's under the surface of any investigation until you uncover it. So …" He shrugged. "I don't know." He hoped that explanation would allay any fears.

"If anyone's interested, I've got something to add," Gary added cautiously.

Callie's face lit up. "Well, what is it?"

Gary's shoulders slumped. "I talked with Marci after my shift. Don't worry; she was on break, so we didn't get in trouble. Marci talks with Vera, too. We figured that she'd be more likely to confide in Marci. I think if we need to find out anything, Marci's the one that can do it, and she's willing to help."

Callie thought for a moment. "Let's wait until after I talk to Jody. Maybe there will be some clue in there for the next set of questions."

Rudy squinted suspiciously, "I was about to say the same thing. And find out all you can about the Carelli name." Hopefully, she'd find out enough to keep her on her toes, maybe scare her off. All the same, he would do his own research as well. *Looks like I've got more to tell the Feds.*

Callie nodded. "I was thinking that, too."

Sharon interrupted, "Since we're talking about weird stuff, I think someone might be following me."

Jack chuckled. "Nerves getting to you?"

She elbowed him and huffed.

Rudy was certain he'd put on his poker face, but Callie seemed to be watching him. That made him wonder if his control was slipping. She'll want to know, so he said, "Callie, I think we'd better change the conversation for now. I'll talk to you tonight." He encouraged everyone to continue eating.

Callie was itching to know what Rudy had to say, and she could see that everyone else was curious. It was a challenge to hold her tongue, but she had learned that the expression on his face meant this had to be confidential. So, she took a bite of pizza and chewed it slowly. *Is this his way of teaching me patience?* Her breath caught. *Maybe it's so dangerous that no one else can know?* She shook off a shudder and forced herself to breathe normally. *If it's that bad, should I be involved? But I've got to know.* She wanted to jump up and shake him for torturing her like this. *Just be patient,* she repeated to herself. Deciding to try to relax, she focused on the meal. She had to at least *look* calm for Georgia's sake.

Time drug on slowly, stretching into dusk, and then evening. She couldn't concentrate on the card games or the light-hearted conversations. It finally became too difficult for Callie to maintain the act any longer. "Say, I'd better get home and make sure Grandpa and Grandma are okay." She got up to leave and said her good-byes. As she left, the rest of the family decided to go home, too.

She was glad to see that her grandparents were in bed when she got home. While she waited for Rudy's call, she cleaned the kitchen and bathroom. She practically jumped out of her skin when her phone rang. She grabbed it before it finished the first ring.

"Hey, Rudy. What took so long?"

"Well, I had to help Georgia wash our dishes and help her get ready for bed. She wasn't going to leave them for tomorrow, and I didn't want her to do them alone."

"Oh, of course. I'm sorry. Look, I've been dying to know what you wouldn't say in front of everyone else."

He chuckled. "I noticed. You still need to work on your body language."

Her shoulders dropped in disappointment. *Rats. And I thought I was pretty convincing.*

He paused. "I'm going to give you some information, but I'm putting it on a flash drive," he stated seriously. "I don't want it going out in an email. Just cautious, I guess. Did I ever tell you that I did a family tree on Pierre?"

"Uh, maybe?" She gasped. "Wait! Are you saying those people are related to Pierre?"

"Good guess. I took another look at my research the other day, and the Carelli name is in there. So, when you get the flash drive, you can figure out the missing pieces. What's more important is that we figure out what's really going on in that family."

Her eyes popped. "Wow. I had no idea." Then she gasped. "Wait! Are you saying that you waited to tell me this because the rest of our family could be in danger if they knew? Or is it that they'd worry too much?"

"Possibly and probably." He paused. "But, there's more."

Callie held her breath.

"I wasn't going to tell you this, but you're getting very close to an explosive situation."

She gulped.

"Pierre is part of a crime syndicate and several of his family members, too. It's very likely that place is a den of thieves. I'm pretty sure Vera's in-laws are the same family that the Feds are investigating."

"Oh-h-h …." Her voice was punctuated with a sudden escape of air.

"If that's the case, they'll be keeping a close eye on Vera. In fact, since that aide mentioned your mother by name and cited other information during their conversation, they probably placed a bug in the room. So, if you talk to her, you have to be *very* careful and *never* discuss anything in there. And, warn your mother not to talk about any details when she's in Vera's room.

As for you, talking to Jody could be tricky, too."

Callie grimaced. "Okay. But about Vera. Would it be better to ask Gary to talk to her? I could – uh, we could let him know what to ask."

"Why? Are you afraid?"

She paused, looking down at her feet. "Actually, I just thought that since he has to be with her anyway as her therapist, it wouldn't look suspicious. He *has* to talk with her." She grimaced. "But that would put him in danger, wouldn't it?"

"I don't know. He hasn't had any training. It's too much to ask of him."

"But if they're watching her, I wouldn't have a reason to talk to her."

"I think you should talk with the sister first before we think about you talking with Vera."

Callie gasped. "Rudy!"

"What?"

"They already know Mom's been visiting her! Won't they be focusing on her?!" She heard Rudy sigh and then silence. After several seconds passed, she panicked. "Rudy, is mom really being followed?! How bad *is* this situation?"

"We don't know for sure. I'll take care of it. Okay?"

"Okay," she said reluctantly.

"Be aware that when you are actually in the Salem hospital, you will never be allowed to be alone with Jody. And there's the potential that someone is watching her, just like Vera."

"Oh. Uh, okay." She grimaced. "Rudy?"

"Yes?"

"Do you think I'm really ready for this?"

"I can go with you. Although I don't know of a relationship that would get *me* in the door."

Callie thought for a moment. "Do you think my fiancé would be allowed?"

She heard him groan. "Callie, Callie. Nobody is going to believe we're engaged."

"No, I'm thinking Gary can go with me as my fiancé."

"But he hasn't been trained," he emphasized. "Remember?"

"You could give him a crash course. Right?"

"I guess that could work." He sighed. "Okay. Since tomorrow's Tuesday, have him come over about eight. No, I'll call him."

"Thanks." She paused. "Rudy?"

"Yeah?"

"How's Georgia?"

"She's still tired. But waiting on the diagnosis, we're a little edgy."

"Tell her I love her, okay?"

"Sure."

They said their good-byes, and she put her face in her hands. "What have I gotten into?"

Chapter 19

Thursday afternoon, Gary fretted while Callie drove. *I don't know about this. Seeing a nut case doesn't sound very appealing to me. The last few days with Rudy have been disturbing. To think Callie knows all those things — self-defense, reading body language, seeing what isn't there — I can't believe she likes it. I realize I have to know all this if I'm going to escort her, but this cloak and dagger stuff is alarming. I sure hope there's no real danger.*

To top it off, we're pretending we're going to get married. I know she doesn't realize it, but she couldn't have picked a more painful scenario, but I guess it was the only way to get me in the door too. He sighed. *I wish I knew why Rudy suggested we play house. I get that only relatives and friends of relatives can visit here, but why me? Yeah, I enjoy being with Callie, but this is a lie.* He shook his head. *Oh, how I wish we really were engaged.* He sighed again. *Get a grip. It's never going to happen.*

"Something wrong?"

He flinched and glanced over at her.

Callie looked concerned. "Are you worried that we could get hurt?"

His eyes darted over to her again. *If you only knew.* As an afterthought, he nodded. "I'll be okay, as long as you do the talking."

"It's a good thing Rudy gave you that crash course in being a P.I., at least, so you'll know what to expect. Don't worry. I'll protect you." She grinned.

He rolled his eyes. "Thanks," he scoffed. *Just what I need, to use her as a bodyguard.* He closed his eyes. *Real macho, Gary.*

She glanced over to him, "You still have that awesome memory, right?"

"Yeah," *I guess that's why I'm here. Not because you* want *me here.*

"Well, when we get back to the car, I want you to put everything onto this recorder. I know you'll remember; I just want it there for me. I don't want to forget anything. Okay?"

He frowned. "We already went over that."

"Sorry, just nerves. But I still want it on the recorder. That way, I can refer to it at any time."

She frowned. "You're okay with coming with me, aren't you?"

"I guess. Why do you ask?"

She grimaced. "Well, you know. Crazy people and all." She cringed. "After all, this is where they put the criminally insane."

He looked at her with an arched eyebrow. "I already said it makes me nervous. We *should* be safe, right?"

She glanced at him. "I'm sorry. I didn't mean to sound so macho – you know, when I said I'd protect you. Rudy said they supervise everything and there's always a guard around. So, I'm pretty sure we'll be okay."

"Is that the place?" he asked.

"It must be. Sure is huge."

"The grounds look so nice. Must be to make the residents feel at home. Peaceful maybe?"

"If they get to go outside. Wait! There's no fence, so probably not."

"They must have a secured area for them. Even prisoners get to go out in the yard, don't they?"

"I guess." She drove around the lot and finally found a space. "Looks like we're in for a walk." Callie sighed and popped the trunk. We can't bring in any electronics, or anything that could be a weapon. Besides, they make us check in everything. We can put our belongings in here till we get back."

He smiled as they put everything but their wallets and keys into the trunk. "You're going to feel lost, aren't you?"

"What do you mean?"

"*Hello!* No purse, no phone."

She gave him a punch on the shoulder and glared at him. "Shut up! I'll be *fine*," she declared.

He rubbed his shoulder and chuckled. "If you insist."

She grumbled as she shut the trunk lid. "You sure know how to put a damper on everything."

"You take everything so literally."

"Well, sometimes life does that to you."

He stopped dead in his tracks. "What?!"

She turned to face him. "Sorry, I was thinking about that trip Rudy and I took yesterday."

"You mean to talk to Vera and Jody's relatives?"

She nodded. "You wouldn't believe it. They're all welfare junkies, jailbirds, scam artists, rednecks. We didn't find a single one that did an honest day's work. The only reason any of them took the girls in was to get the paycheck from the state." She bowed her head and sighed.

"I figured it wasn't so good for Vera and Jody, but I didn't realize it was that bad."

"I'm just surprised they came out of that mess as well as they did."

He put his hand on her shoulder and they headed for the front door again. *Diversion.* Gary looked back to where they parked. "I can't even see the car. What is this, about two blocks?"

She turned to look. "That looks about right. With this much parking, I guess there must be a *lot* of visitors."

"I was thinking plenty of parking for staff."

"Oh, right." She pointed to the right of the building. "Hey, looks like there are some employees over there on break. How about we try to see what we can find out from them?"

He smiled to himself that it worked. "You really think they'll talk to us? You know, privacy laws?"

"You'll never know if you don't try."

He shrugged as they changed course.

They walked up to a stout, middle-aged woman with short black hair. Smoke blew out her turned-up nose, and her dark eyes looked them over. Her underbite made her look angry.

Callie introduced herself, "Good morning. This is our first visit here. I'm Callie and this is Gary. My friend's sister is here. Do you have a few minutes?"

"For what?"

"Can I ask you a few questions about her?"

The woman eyed her. "Now, what could I tell *you*?"

"I don't want to take time from your break, but just a few questions, please?" Callie smiled sweetly.

The woman put her fist on her hip. "Okay, shoot." Then, she took another drag from her cigarette.

"Can I ask you your name?"

"Harriet. I'm one of the aides."

"Hi, Harriet. I don't suppose you know my friend's sister?"

"The name?" she barked. As if Callie were a moron.

"Jody Perkins?"

Harriet's eyes got big, and her mouth opened slightly. "I don't have anything to do with *that* one. Not unless they've got her doped up or tied down. And that's most of the time."

"What do you mean?"

Harriet looked over her bifocals like Callie was the dumbest clod on the planet. "That girl's a wild one, that's why. Otherwise, she could hurt one of *us* when trying to take care of *her*."

"So, what do you mean by 'wild one?'"

"I was just starting my shift when they brought her in. I'm just glad *I* didn't have to deal with her."

"What happened?"

"It's what I *heard!* She was screaming something about her sister, and they'd better help her or she'd ... well, she said she was going to ... let's just say it took several guards to transport her to a room and get her secured. Finally, one of the doctors gave her a shot to put her out." Then Harriet's eyebrows arched and she quickly added, "It was for everyone's *safety!* We can't have the loonies hurting themselves or *us*, you know."

"Have you seen her since then?"

"A couple times. She won't take care of herself. I've never seen the likes of her. Me? I've had to bathe her, but I'll only do it when she's unconscious. The ward doctor warned us about her. So, we're not takin' any chances." Harriet glowered. "She shot her own sister, you know."

"She did?!"

Harriet's hand dropped as she glared at Callie. "So how come you don't know *that*? *If* you're a friend of her sister?"

Callie face was concerned as she interrupted, "Vera's got amnesia. *She* doesn't even know what happened. She's going to be devastated."

"Oh, honey, I'm sorry to be the one to tell you. You be careful in there. Okay? I've heard stories." Harriet peered at her as she said, "I'm just glad she's been sedated. I wouldn't want to be her next victim. No sir-ree."

"So, you're saying they keep her drugged?"

"Well, I understand she ain't screamin' no more, if that's what you mean."

"So, she's pretty much comatose?"

"Well, I wouldn't say comatose, but pretty close. I heard she's been in the medical ward the last couple of days. Something about being contagious." Harriet looked at her watch and frowned. "Oh, *great!* My break is almost over, and I have to get back to work." She crushed her cigarette on the ground, spun on her heels, and marched off.

"Thanks for your time, Harriet."

Gary shuddered. "That does *not* sound good."

Callie let out a big sigh. "I know, but we've got to find out Jody's side of the story," she whispered to keep the retreating staff from hearing.

"If we can believe it," he retorted.

The other employees had already returned to the building, so Callie and Gary headed for the Communication Center. After they signed in, the clerk checked their IDs against the visitors' list, and they were cleared through security. The clerk said, "Everything in the tray. When you bring back your visitor's badges, everything will be returned."

They sat in the waiting area along with all the other visitors. Within a few minutes, everyone was split into groups, depending on which building housed the resident they were visiting. Callie and Gary were led to another building, which seemed like another couple blocks away, then through several security doors, and finally to a cafeteria. They sat at a round table that could accommodate four people.

Within a few minutes, Jody was led to their table, and she sat down with a thud. Her dark brown eyes looked empty as she stared at them. Her t-shirt and jeans were baggy and worn. The cut of her brown hair looked like it had grown out from a pixie and the ends were showing signs of fading from being dyed neon green. Flecks of neon green polish remained on her short fingernails. She was short, no taller than 5'2". She seemed unsteady.

The guard walked away to join another guard at the door to observe. Each of the three doors had two guards standing alert.

Gary frowned, wondering how heavily they were keeping her drugged. She didn't seem incredibly out of it, but she wasn't all there either.

Jody was quiet as she seemed to study Callie and Gary. "Who are you?"

Callie put on a smile, but Gary could see it was from nerves.

"I'm Callie, and this is Gary, my fiancé."

Even though they had discussed this scenario, Gary's heart skipped a beat when he heard her say it. *If only that was true.*

"We know your sister Vera."

Jody's lip quivered. She swallowed hard and looked down. "You mean you knew her," she mourned.

Callie was silent for a moment. "You mean you don't know?"

Jody looked up slowly. "Know what?"

"She isn't dead; she's recovering in a nursing home."

"You're lying!" Her eyes became even darker as she squinted at them, almost as if she was trying to focus.

"No. If I'd been allowed to bring my phone, I would've shown you a picture I took of us," Callie reassured her.

Jody started to shake as her eyes teared up. "If you're lying to me, I swear ...." She looked at the guard and clamped her mouth shut.

"I can have her write to you."

Jody seemed to hyperventilate. "I ... I can't believe it. Really?! She's alive?"

"Of course. But she doesn't remember anything about the shooting. Can you tell us what happened?"

Her lower lip pressed up, nearly covering her upper lip as the corners of her mouth pulled down. Her hand whipped up to cover them. Tears welled in her eyes as she said shakily, "It's true. I shot her." She closed her eyes, hunched over, and sobbed.

Callie leaned forward to touch her arm, but a guard rushed to their table and announced, "No touching. When you leave, you can give a hug, but nothing else." After he saw Callie retreat, he went back to his place by the door.

Gary cringed when he saw Callie suppress her urge to help. He knew she was hurting too, not being able to comfort her. Her compassion was one of the many qualities that drew him to her.

Callie seemed to switch gears when she asked, "So when did you move into the Carellis' home?"

Gary knew Callie was using one of the tricks that Jack had taught them: create a diversion to help reduce tension.

Jody sat back, and the change of subject seemed to pull her out of her sorrow as she tried to think. "Around the end of February, about a year and a half ago, I guess."

"How did everyone feel about that?"

"I was relieved, and Vera was happy."

"What about the in-laws?"

Jody's thin eyebrows knitted. "Uh …."

Gary couldn't figure out if she was trying to think, or if talking about Vera's in-laws was a difficult subject.

"Not too good." Her words were drawn out and seemed to be an effort. "The servants were nice. Brent, but mostly his parents, I could see they didn't like me. Right away, I didn't think they liked Vera either."

"What was it like living there?"

She spoke haltingly as if she was struggling with the words, "It was a big change from what we knew before. We were so poor, so, living in a mansion was uncomfortable. We didn't fit in." Jody squirmed. "But the worst was trying to get along with the family. Vera and Brent argued a lot. She tried so hard to please everyone, but I guess she just didn't know how to act like … like a spoiled rich kid. *I* sure didn't.

"After a while, that Brent's parents *really* didn't like either one of us, and they wouldn't let us forget it. Vera told me it was like that before I got there, but it got worse when I moved in. On good days, they just put up with us."

"What was it like growing up?"

"Our parents died when we were just seven and eight. Then, we were passed around to different relatives. When one family got tired of us, we were sent to the next." Her eyes took on a beaten look. "Living like that made going to school really hard. We even had to move in the middle of a school year a few times. But Vera insisted I graduate. I don't think I would've done it without her." Jody smiled weakly, "She was my guardian angel – *is* my guardian angel." Then she looked at Callie with a great sadness, "We're all either of us have." Jody closed her eyes and went limp, "That's why I could just die after what I did."

"What do you mean?"

Jody's lip quivered. "I shouldn't have done it, but I couldn't help it. I was so *angry*."

"Couldn't help what? Why were you angry?"

Gary frowned with confusion when he saw Jody pinch her lips shut and jump up from her chair, knocking it down and almost throwing herself down with it. She clung onto the table as she turned to shout, "Guard, I'm ready to go back to my room now."

Callie stood up as the guard approached. "But, we're not finished."

Jody swept her arms out as if pushing through a crowd and growled, "*I'm* finished." She turned around, and the guard escorted her out.

Callie turned on the recorder when they got into the car. "That woman we talked with before we went in, do you remember what she said?"

"Which part?"

"Didn't she say Jody was always drugged?"

"Yeah. 'Cause she's a maniac."

"She didn't look drugged when we talked to her. I'm wondering why."

"Actually, it looked like she *was* under the influence of something. But I don't know of any drugs that doctors would prescribe that would cause the symptoms I saw, at least for mental reasons."

"What symptoms?"

"Didn't you notice a little bit of slurring, eyelids at half-mast, taking time to think, unsteadiness?"

"Well, I don't know her, so I didn't want to assume anything."

"Maybe one or two symptoms, but all of them? I think they've got her on something."

"Well, the employee said they had to keep her drugged." Callie raised an eyebrow as she turned to Gary, "So, if she's so dangerous that they need to keep her drugged, why take her off the drugs and endanger *our* lives? But then, if she isn't dangerous – and she didn't look dangerous to me – why keep her drugged?"

"I don't know. Maybe she *is* dangerous. The guards were right there." Gary arched his eyebrows. "Did you see how angry she got?"

"There was something else about her body language; I wonder if she's hiding something." Callie pointed at him for emphasis as she added, "Drugging her would be an easy way to mask everything and keep her from talking."

"Then why take her off the drugs when they knew we were coming?"

"Because we'd be able to see she was drugged and get suspicious."

Gary's eyes popped open. "Are you saying there's some kind of conspiracy?"

"We can't eliminate anything yet."

He thought it strange to see her rub her chin like Rudy always did when he was thinking. He wondered if she had told him everything.

"If they were hiding something, wouldn't it be risky to take her off the drugs? 'Cause if they *were* hiding something, it could slip out, whatever 'it' is." Callie shook her head. "I don't know. Something isn't right here."

"So, how come you asked her questions that you already knew the answers to? You know, about her past?

"I wanted to see what she'd say, if her answers matched up."

He nodded. "You know, just before she stopped the conversation, you asked her what made her angry."

"That's right! I knew your memory would come in handy. So, she's *still* angry. But why? We've got to find out what happened."

Gary grimaced. "What could make you so angry that you'd shoot your sister?"

Callie started the engine. "The answer to that question is the key." She handed him the recorder. "Here, record everything you heard with Harriet *and* with Jody."

Callie drove silently while Gary repeated everything that was said, including what they saw. She was amazed at his memory retention, it was like hitting the replay button. When he finished, she said, "Thanks for being there. You really are a big help."

He shrugged. "I guess when you have a talent, you get used."

She cringed. Glancing at him, she fretted, "Do you think I'm using you?"

"Can I plead the fifth?"

"Ouch."

"No, it's okay. I know you need help. I'm glad to do it."

"Thanks for your help."

"Uh-huh." He looked out the window.

Oh great! I don't want him to think I'm just using him. How do I fix this? If I ask for help, it'll just be more of the same. For the next few miles, she drove in silence, thinking.

"Gary?"

"Yeah?"

"I tried to find that reporter, you know, the one that wrote about Brent Carelli and the rape?"

"What about him?"

"He seems to have vanished ..."

Gary jerked to stare at her.

"I know, it sounds suspicious. I'm not sure what to think about it. There were lots of articles of his before that, and after that one, nothing. Not even other papers, in or out of state."

He squinted. "I know what *I* think."

"I have a pretty good idea what that is."

"Oh? And you still want to keep investigating? Seriously?"

"And what do you suggest?"

"Oh, you're actually asking *my* opinion?"

"Come on. Don't get all huffy. I really *do* want your opinion."

He huffed. "Well, I'll tell you. But I doubt you'll do what *I* think. I think we need to stop doing this. Apparently, people disappear when butting heads with this family! Just saying, I'm not much interested in disappearing. I'd like to live a long life with no complications. Have a family with no worries. And I'd be happy with an ordinary, uneventful existence ..." he stopped short.

"So, you'd just desert Vera and Jody? They'd like to live an ordinary life too. And what makes you think an ordinary life is without complications? We have to fight for what we want and help when we can. Besides, could you live with yourself if you opted out?"

He held up his hands in surrender. "Okay. I get it." He shook his bowed head. "I guess I'm just really scared. You do know, that we could …." He closed his eyes. "… we could die," he whispered.

She bit her lip for a moment. "I'm sorry."

"For what?"

"For pulling you into this. I'm scared too. But I can't just let go, knowing I can do something."

"I know. But can we please be careful?"

Chapter 20

Sharon stopped by to see Billy for a few minutes on her way to see Vera. As she talked with him, she realized he seemed different lately. She knew he would be different after he quit drinking because she recognized the signs of change from when Ralph sobered up. All people are different and react differently, but there was more than the initial crankiness and becoming more lucid and reasonable. Billy seemed sad, a deep sadness that made her wonder if he was depressed. She became worried, wondering if Gary's rejection was the reason. She thought about that as she left for Vera's room. Marci was changing her bed when she walked in.

"Where's Vera?" Sharon asked in a lower pitch.

Marci looked up and smiled. "She just left for therapy. I thought I'd take advantage of her absence to take care of her bed. I'm sure she won't mind a visitor, so go ahead. The therapy room is in the C wing, second door on the left."

"Thanks. You're a peach." Sharon waved as she turned to leave. She was grateful that Rudy had talked to her and Gary about the possibility of a bug in the room. Obviously, Marci had been warned too since she didn't flinch at Sharon's disguised voice and didn't address her by name. As Sharon approached the therapy room, she heard Gary's voice. "We're going to continue with light exercise since you're so weak. The doctor said that if you worked on it, but not overextend yourself, you should improve pretty quickly."

Sharon walked into the room, waved at Vera, and sat down in a chair.

As Gary helped Vera onto a table, she looked at Sharon.

Gary turned to see who came in and he waved. "Oh hi, Mom. We should be done in about ten minutes."

Vera looked at him strangely. "I thought your mom was dead."

He explained their relationship as he helped Vera through her routines.

Sharon noticed the odd look on Vera's face as Gary told her about their background. She'd heard that Rudy and Callie learned about her past, and she wondered if Vera was feeling shortchanged, wishing she could feel that close to someone. She vowed to herself to do what she could to support the young woman. She admired Vera's determination to do everything that was asked of her, even when it meant a lot of pain. It reminded her of last year when she had to help Ralph with his therapy. Only he was not cooperative.

When they were done, Gary picked Vera up and put her into the wheelchair. He looked up at Sharon, "She's not ready for walking yet."

Sharon said, "Would you like to go for a ride outside? I can wheel you back to your room when we're done."

He placed a support pillow on her lap. "Only if you call for an aide when you get to her room," Gary insisted.

"Of course. I wouldn't want to take a chance on her getting hurt."

Gary patted Vera's hand. "You stay out of trouble, now."

Vera looked up at him with an appreciative smile.

Sharon stood up, walked to the back of the wheelchair, and said, "Where to, m'lady? Or is it Swiss Miss?"

Vera laughed. "Oh, don't do that. It hurts too much." After a few calming breaths, she asked, "Where did you hear that?"

"One of the aides told me they gave you that nickname. You know, because you were pumped full of holes, like swiss cheese."

Vera smiled sadly as they headed for the garden.

Sharon used the handicap power assist to open the door to the garden. "I hope you don't mind, but I was watching you while you were doing your therapy. I think you've made some real progress, even since I saw you last time. Even right now, you're sitting up without help. Remember last time you needed pillows to hold you up. Even though you don't need them, I see they still insist you have one for support, just in case."

"I'm still not that steady."

"And I'll bet you don't have as much pain either," Sharon said as they wheeled past the birdbath.

Vera thought about that for a moment. "Yeah. I think you're right again." She paused. "Thank you."

"For what?"

"For being so encouraging. Except for Jody, I've never gotten a kind word from anyone." Vera's shoulders dropped. "I'm getting really worried about her. Something must have happened to keep her away."

Sharon's heartbeat increased, pounding in her ears. She stopped Vera in front of a bench, locked the wheels, and sat down in front of her. She dreaded this moment, but it had to be.

Vera looked worried. "You know something, don't you?"

Sharon's breath caught.

"Okay, give it to me."

"I don't know how to tell you."

Vera's brow furrowed. "How bad is it?" Suddenly horrified, she blurted out, "Is she dead?!"

"No! No, nothing like that!"

Vera closed her eyes and sighed with relief. "Okay then, what is it?" She looked up, "Please, tell me."

"Vera ... Jody's in the state hospital."

Vera's eyes became intense. "What? You mean the nut house in Salem?"

Sharon nodded and averted her look from Vera's stare. She took a deep breath and continued, "Since you don't remember what happened, I'll just have to tell you everything. Everything I've been told, anyway. My uncle is a private investigator; he looked up the news releases and the police reports. According to the witnesses, Jody was high on drugs, she started yelling at you, and ... well, she shot you with a shotgun. Then you hit your head when you fell. Apparently, Mr. Carelli had to wrestle Jody to the floor. She's been in Salem ever since. They're keeping her there until the trial. But with all the witnesses, it's pretty certain she'll be pronounced criminally insane."

Vera's horrified expression made Sharon's eyes well up with tears.

"That's not ... it can't be ... she would never ... how could anyone believe...? No-o-o!" Vera bent over as she wrapped her arms around the pillow. Anguished moans turned into heart-wrenching sobs.

Feeling her pain, Sharon stood up, bent over, and held her as she grieved.

Chapter 21

That evening, Callie drove Gary to Rudy and Georgia's house. Rudy greeted them, and they visited with Georgia for a while. Callie sensed a general uneasiness, almost tension, in the house. She decided it was probably nerves because they were still waiting for the diagnosis, so she didn't say anything. No sense in pointing out the obvious. She was thankful she had her mom's guidance in how to handle uncomfortable situations.

Soon enough, Rudy led them to his office to discuss what each of them found. Callie volunteered to sit in the "electric" chair; she knew it would be too much for Gary right now. He was practically ready to call it quits as it was. She had finally accepted that he was stressed over all this cloak and dagger stuff. After all, he hadn't willingly chosen the lifestyle of a detective.

Rudy began, "We know that Vera married into a family that, uh, isn't exactly in legitimate business."

Callie huffed. "Why don't you just say it? That family is just a bunch of criminals."

Rudy continued, "I got the copies of all the police reports around the shooting. Actually, three copies, one for each of us." He gave them their copies. "Study them tonight, look for any irregularities, and we can talk about them next time."

Callie flipped through the pages, let the pages close, and then looked up. "When we visited Jody, we both thought something was off with her." She sat up straight when she remembered, "Oh! We actually got to talk to one of the aides. She was outside on her break when we got there. She said something that didn't seem to add up." She knew she had Rudy's attention when his eyes darted in her direction. She needed that boost of confidence; it reassured her that she was learning well and that she had discovered something he didn't.

"She told us that Jody has to be sedated for her safety and for the safety of the staff. However, when we met with Jody, she did seem drugged, but not the way that aide said." She turned to Gary. "Why don't you describe how she acted?"

"Yeah. She seemed unbalanced in a physical way, like she was dizzy. She talked slow, as if she couldn't think – fuzzy and almost incoherent. I don't recall studying any meds for use with psychological problems causing that kind of response ..."

Gary leaned forward. "... and I've been thinking about it. That aide said Jody was in the medical ward for two days because she was contagious. I'm wondering if maybe they had her there to take her off those meds, knowing we were going to meet with her. We'd had that appointment set a few days in advance, so I think they didn't want us to know about the sedatives, and her symptoms were consistent with sedatives that hadn't completely worn off." He paused. "I don't know her, but something seemed odd – other than her appearance. I'd like to see what kind of sedatives they've got her on."

Rudy's eyes lit up. "So, if we find out *what* they're using, you'd know *why* they're using it?"

"Being a physical therapist, I have to know drugs and how they affect the body. If I'm not familiar with what they're using, I can find out. So, yes."

"I'll see if I can find out and get it to you as soon as I can. What else do you have, Callie?" He looked down to write himself a note.

"This is something we've got to figure out. Jody said she was angry just before the shooting. When I asked her what she was angry about, she jumped up out of her seat. She looked so agitated. She said the visit was over and asked the guard to take her out. Maybe something in these police reports can give us a clue."

Rudy rubbed his chin. "I wonder. If there *was* something suspicious going on, do you *really* think that family would let any witnesses make a statement?"

Gary leaned forward. "So, we're looking for something that doesn't click?"

Rudy pointed at him. "Exactly."

Callie raised an index finger. "One other thing. Remember, that night aide that knew about Mom? We discussed it with Mom, and she's making sure she only talks to Vera somewhere other than her room. Right now, it's in the garden or the cafeteria." She swallowed hard. "Today, she told Vera about Jody being in the state hospital. She was pretty broken up."

"It's a good thing they aren't talking in her room," Gary piped in. "I spoke with Marci right after we discussed talked about the possibility. She said that she checked the room when she changed Vera's bed. There's something behind the headboard that doesn't belong there."

Rudy sat up straight. "She didn't mess with it, did she?"

"Oh no, she knew better than that. But someone is definitely listening in."

Rudy nodded slowly. "Obviously, they're looking for something, or trying to hide it."

Chapter 22

Being the one in charge of technology and security, Fingers was a key player in the syndicate. He did research, managed security, and made sure the equipment was up to date and working properly. He was good at his job. The only part that made him doubt himself was actually meeting with Frankie face to face. He always dreaded that. Those meetings made him feel inferior and threatened. One could never tell how Frankie would react. Although he was bringing benign news, there was always a chance Frankie wouldn't like it, especially since it had already been six weeks since Frankie asked him for this report. Although Frankie would look at it as a delay, Fingers had to make sure it was complete and accurate.

He stood outside Frankie's office for a few minutes trying to shake off the anxiety. With his file under his arm, he shook his hands at his sides, took a deep breath, and then knocked.

"Come in."

He entered, stopped short of the chair in front of Frankie's desk, and waited. One never just sat in the chair unless invited or commanded to do so. As usual, Frankie feigned being busy just to make him sweat. Frankie had a full bag of tricks on how to intimidate his men; making them wait was one of them.

When he was new, Fingers forgot to wait before sitting – *that* would never happen again. Occasionally, someone was used as an example for the rest of the men, and he thought he'd be the one. Thankfully, Frankie was in a good mood that day, and Fingers escaped his wrath.

After a long wait, Frankie finally pointed to the chair, and Fingers sat down.

Fingers kept his anxiety in check: no fidgeting, no slouching, no crossing the legs or arms, and no swallowing excessively, and he looked

Frankie straight in the eye. It was a lot to remember when trembling and not showing it. "I did a full background check on this Sharon person."

Frankie looked down his nose and bellowed, "And ...?"

"And I followed her everywhere. Sharon Cooper is just a housewife doing ordinary things. She's been visiting her neighbor who's in the same nursing home. Apparently, there's a resident there by the name of Bertie Hill. She's a real busybody and accosts all the new visitors. She told Mrs. Cooper about Vera, said she was lonesome. So, Mrs. Cooper visited her. Since she hasn't shown up or called here, it looks like she only asked questions to make Vera feel better. I don't see anything to worry about."

"I'll decide that!"

"I have a full report here." He held up the file, waiting for Frankie to either take it or direct him where to place it.

Frankie pointed to an empty spot on his desk. "That'll be all."

Fingers set the file down and stood up. Even though all looked well, there was always the chance Frankie could change his mind, so Fingers left as if nothing was wrong. He dared not show any nervousness; that would certainly arouse suspicion. He knew where all the security cameras were located, so when he got to a blind spot in the hallway, he took a moment to shake off the tension before he went back to his office.

Chapter 23

Rudy washed the breakfast dishes, but his mind was in the next room. The phone had rung. He knew it was the doctor's office because he could hear Georgia talking softly. He braced himself against the edge of the sink. When she didn't cheer, he knew the verdict. He heard her hang up, walk into the kitchen, and pause. He turned around and her fallen face said it all. He tried to look brave for her. "That was the doctor's office, wasn't it?"

She nodded blankly. "We're supposed to go in to get the diagnosis in person. In half an hour."

Bad news. If the diagnosis was benign, they would have said so. He dried his hands and pulled his keys from his pocket as he led her to the door and then to the car.

Neither of them said anything on the drive. What could either of them say? Besides, he couldn't think. Everything seemed hazy; he didn't even remember how he got to the clinic.

As Rudy held Georgia's hand, Dr. Mercer's voice became a muffled drone. When the doctor's face showed the telltale sympathy lines, Rudy knew it was bad. Georgia seemed to wilt. The thirty-minute appointment seemed to take hours. He certainly wouldn't have been able to recall much of what the doctor said. At the end, he was just thankful that they had paperwork to take with them so they could absorb everything at their own pace, the diagnosis, the plan of action, and the list of upcoming appointments.

No coherent thought crossed his mind until they got home. Then, his one thought was to try to comfort Georgia. Nothing from his past – no case, no trials, no dangers – nothing up to this point in his life could compare to this horror. How could he survive, cope, and still give her the support she needed? He refused to consider the worst. As he sat on the couch holding her and rocking in place, he slowly gave in to sorrow. Stroking her hair, he wept with her.

Later, she stood up and announced, "I've been thinking about this for several days now." She looked down at her wringing hands as she spoke. "Whether my DNA shows a disposition towards cancer or not, I have cancer. So, I've decided to have both breasts removed. I don't want to worry about it starting up in the other one."

He stood up next to her and gave her a mighty hug. His red eyes wept anew. He was in awe of her courage. "You are my hero. Nothing I've ever done in my life can compare to your fearlessness."

She looked up at him. "Not fearlessness. I just want to do everything I can because I *am* afraid, *very* afraid."

He held her tightly. His next words were merely a squeak, "I'll be here for you."

She nodded quickly, "I know. That's why I love you."

The next day while trying to help, Rudy ran the vacuum over the rug. The busyness seemed to help abate his distress, but disturbing thoughts kept nagging at him. Lately, he'd been dying to tell her. Even though she was sick, he couldn't keep the secret any longer. He had to tell her, just in case he waited too long.

He turned off the vacuum and sat down beside her. "Sweet Cheeks, I've got to tell you something."

She looked up at him with a trusting smile. "What's that?"

"Remember when we went to Switzerland last year?"

"Mmm-hmm."

"Well, it wasn't just for the vacation."

"I know. You had to do some business."

He flushed. "Well, it's the business I have to tell you about."

"Did it have anything to do with that extra suitcase?"

He looked down at her. "I should've known you'd notice."

"I saw it before we went to the beach house, but I didn't see it when we packed up and came home."

"You're pretty observant; I guess I underestimated you." He sighed.

"So, it's still at the beach house?"

He nodded.

"Well, are you going to tell me what's in it?"

"That suitcase, it, uh …" He took a deep breath. "… I did something illegal."

Her mouth dropped open, and she leaned back. "Seriously?!"

He nodded. "Remember when Sharon and Callie inventoried Alice's house, and they found that file on her and Pierre?"

"Yes," she said hesitantly.

"Well, at the time, nobody knew that Pierre had connections with a local mob."

She gasped. "Are we okay?"

"Oh, yeah!"

"So, your secret was that Pierre's with the mob?"

"Yes, partly. But there's more, a lot more."

"And?!" she asked with alarm.

He shifted his weight. "One thing led to another, and I found something that belonged to him. He'd hidden a ledger in Alice's garage. It had information about him skimming from the mob and then putting the money in an offshore account. I took the money."

"What?!"

He looked aside. "Then later, I happened to get hold of some information about the mob's account. So …" He closed his eyes. "… so, that trip to Switzerland was to take two million out of *that* account."

Her eyes popped. "From the mob?! You've got to be kidding! If they find out …." She put her face in her hands and shuddered.

He held her tight. "Nobody knows. Actually, the kingpin thinks someone else did it."

She shook her head. "Rudy! How *could* you?!"

"I knew Pierre would never let on that *his* swindled money was taken. He couldn't tell anyone, not the police, the mob, nobody. So, I figured that was safe."

"But, the *mob*?"

"I know, it was stupid."

"And what do you plan to do with it?"

"Well, since it came from people's pain and suffering, I thought I'd use it to help people."

"But, how? Won't you have to show where that money came from?"

"I've been thinking about it. I'll come up with something."

She closed her eyes and shook her head.

"I'm sorry. I know you're feeling sick, and right now isn't good timing, but I couldn't hold it in any longer."

She started to sob.

He held her again. "I'm sorry," he moaned.

"It's not that," she said between sobs.

He brought her face up to his by lifting her chin. "What, then?"

With tears in her eyes, she pulled back. "I have a confession too." She squirmed a little. "Since this cancer thing came up ...."

"Don't you worry about it. I'm here for you, you know that."

"I know, but it's not about that." She looked at her hands as she fussed with her afghan, as if she didn't know what to do with them. "Since this cancer thing came up, I've been thinking, and I have to get something off my chest."

He squinted at her. "Is that a joke?"

A pained grimace crossed her face. "I wish it was. I've been thinking about the past, us, and the future, and I need to tell you something that happened a long time ago." She swallowed hard. "I figured that if I'm going to die ...."

"No!" Rudy interrupted. "No, that's not going to happen."

She looked up at him. "Look, I'm getting older, and I know it's a hard subject, but anything could happen. And we could all die anytime; some are just sooner than others. So, I need to clear the air."

He didn't want her to see his anxiety, but the poker face seemed unattainable.

"It's not about you. It's about me. It's about when Alice and I were kids; I was eleven and she was twelve ...." She wrung her hands.

Rudy held his breath.

"... You know we had a stepfather. Mom had married him the year before." She fidgeted with her afghan again for several seconds. "She was working two jobs, and he was supposed to take care of us while she was at work. Rudy, he …" She closed her eyes and tried a shaky cleansing breath. Her voice trembled as she whispered, "he abused us."

Rudy's eyes darkened as he put his arms around her and held her tightly. "I suspected as much."

Her eyes shot up at him. "How?!"

He leaned back, feeling guilty for figuring it out. "Well, it was a lot of little things. You always shut down when his name came up, and you sound like a vigilante whenever you hear about someone that could be an abuser. Then, there were all those pictures that were torn in two. I just put two and two together." He hung his head. "I have another confession."

"What's that?"

"I looked up Mick's other stepdaughters. It seems he had married two other women with daughters before he married your mom."

Georgia closed her eyes and groaned.

"Most of them turned out pretty messed up, and I couldn't contact them, but the one I talked to … she didn't say so, but I'd be willing to guess he did the same with them."

She held her face in her hands and groaned again, "Oh, those poor girls."

"I'm sorry; I should've told you sooner."

"I should've known you'd figure it out …" Instead of going limp with the release of pent-up guilt, she seemed even more tense as she whispered, "… but, that's not the worst part."

That stopped him cold. He had been so confident that he'd figured out what happened that he never imagined there might be anything else, let alone something worse.

"Alice and I wanted it to stop so badly. We argued constantly over whether we should tell Mom. But she had struggled so hard financially, and she must have loved him to marry him. We decided we couldn't do that to her. So, we came up with another plan. We even went to the library to make sure it would work."

Dread made Rudy's heartbeat increase, but he forced himself to breathe normally.

"It was part of our chores to make dinner every night. He was diabetic, so we purposely cooked something with low sugar levels. After dinner, I brought him coffee that Alice had laced with four crushed up sleeping pills. We were really scared when he complained that the coffee tasted funny. We thought for sure he caught on."

Georgia started to breathe faster and tears welled up. "Then ... then he said we'd have to pay for giving him such nasty coffee. He looked at me with those horrible, lusting eyes. We knew what that meant." She started to tremble. "Alice saw that I was frozen with fear, so she grabbed me and rushed me to our room. There wasn't a lock, so she pushed the dresser in front of the door to keep him out. I just knew he'd be able to force the door because he'd done it before, so I started to cry. That's when Alice showed me the syringe and the insulin. She told me that it was ready, and we just had to wait for him to fall asleep. With her taking charge, I dared to hope ...."

Rudy recalled the nightmare Georgia had last year when she was delirious with fever. At the time, it didn't make any sense to him. Now he understood: *'I think he's asleep. Are you sure it'll work? ... It better. ... Yeah, he's snoring, so he's definitely asleep. ... Lissy, I'm scared. ... No. I know it's got to be. ... but still.'* He shuddered inside.

"... It seemed like we waited forever, listening. Finally, we heard him snoring and she said we had to act fast. He had trained her to give him his shots; I think he just liked having her hands near ...." Georgia grimaced and her hands whipped up to cover her face as she continued, "She knew how much insulin to use, but instead, she filled the syringe and put the whole thing into his thigh. Then, again and again to make sure." She looked up at Rudy, tears streaming down to her neck. "When Alice did the research, she told me what to expect, but I never imagined how awful it would be to see it and hear it. The convulsions were so bad that I freaked out. Alice pulled me back to our room and held me until it was over."

She became limp as she sobbed convulsively in Rudy's arms.

Although he tried, he couldn't think of one thing to say. Frozen in time, the mental picture played slowly in his head.

Finally, Georgia broke the silence and brought him back to the present. "We washed the coffee cup so there'd be no evidence." She grimaced as she looked up at him and shook her head slowly. "I couldn't think. Alice did everything. She made me get ready for bed, told me what to say to Mom, how to act. I guess ...."

Rudy swallowed hard.

She reached for a tissue to wipe away her tears and blow her nose. "... I guess it's true, one never really knows how killing someone will affect you. 'Cause after that, Alice was never the same. *I* sure wasn't." She shuddered.

A few moments passed before she continued, "When our real dad was alive, he was so loving. You know, like a real father should be. I was pretty young when he died, but Alice remembered and told me how much she loved him and missed him. At first, when Mom married Mick, he gave lots of hugs and Alice was happy to have a dad again. Then when ..." She shuddered. "... Then when he started ... you know, the abuse ..." Her voice cracked, "she changed. Later, I told everyone that she was always sullen and moody ... oh, she was a little bit ... but that's when she changed. She told me that she was never going to let anyone treat her like that again, like a victim.

"It all happened about the time she started to develop, and the boys got interested in her that she decided men were only interested in one thing. She actually said she was going to use it to her advantage to be in control. She vowed to get what *she* wanted, and nobody was going to stop her. Right away, she started manipulating people. I didn't like seeing her that way, all distorted with so much hate. I guess she figured that if she could kill someone, she could do anything to get what she wanted. I'm pretty sure that's how she got Don to marry her."

Rudy controlled the urge to react. He didn't want to let on how much he knew.

"She was careful not to write any of it in her diaries, in case somebody might read them. She said it was to protect me." Her lip trembled. "But it was more than just protecting herself or me. It was like a vendetta against men. I didn't recognize her anymore. She was so angry and hateful. She kind of made me feel that if our secret came out, I'd be the one to pay. I was almost afraid of her."

Rudy clamped his eyes closed, tightened his jaw, and his lips pinched into a thin line.

"Eventually, she wouldn't talk about it. I'm certain she didn't want to be reminded about that part of her life – our life – anymore, and I guess I didn't either. I think that's why she cut me and Mom out of her life. I also think that when she cut that cancer out of her life ..." She huffed. "... ironic, huh? That's when she put up walls, the emotional armor, she didn't ever want to trust anyone enough to truly fall in love. In a way, instead of getting rid of that cancer, she buried it inside, and it festered."

She blew her nose again. "I'm just so thankful it didn't spread to Sharon."

She was silent for a few moments, thinking, and then continued in a pensive tone, "I sometimes wonder if she had anything to do with Don's death. I wouldn't put it past her."

Since Georgia was cradled in his arms, he was certain she could feel his heart thumping in his chest. When she looked up at him, he knew she had. Her eyes became wide when she saw his red face.

"It's true. *Isn't* it?!"

"What makes you say that?" he bluffed.

She sat up to face him fully. "Tell me! I have to know."

"We don't know that! How could we?" he stammered.

"You *do* know! I can tell!"

He knew that look. He couldn't lie to her. Besides, he'd never be able to pull it off. So, he spilled the beans. "I didn't know at first, not even after all those years I followed her. Don was looking for something that he could use to make her let him go. That's when I found out about her affair and gave him the evidence. You knew about that part. Later, Jack told me about the timing of Don's accident. At the time, I just assumed it was a terrible tragedy! So close, he was almost free. But I didn't put it together until after Jack asked me to look into what happened." He tried to swallow the lump in his throat. "There's no concrete evidence, but I'm pretty sure she hired a thug to kill him." He swallowed again. "Pierre was the go-between. She asked him to hire someone to do the job."

He looked into the horror on his wife's face and he grimaced. "I'm sorry. I wanted to protect you and Sharon. That's why I didn't tell," he quietly pleaded.

She seemed to go limp and looked down. She covered her eyes and shook her head slowly. With her head still down, her voice quavered, "Does Sharon know?"

"No. Jack and I vowed not to tell anyone. We didn't want you to suffer any more than you already have."

"Thank you," she breathed.

He put his arms around her again and rocked with her.

She started sobbing again.

He held her tightly and a tear ran down his cheek as he stroked her hair.

She cried until she couldn't cry anymore, and then he helped her to bed.

Rudy spent the night churning the toxic mix of emotions, ranging from sorrow, to angst, to rage. He envisioned beating Georgia's stepfather into oblivion. He told himself that although he hated violence, this was the only way he knew to protect her. But that thought only made him feel worse. He ached to have been able go into the past to rescue them; but of course, that wasn't possible. He groaned inside, thinking about the torment she had to live with all those years.

He cried for her.

He would occasionally look over at her as she tossed and turned that night. He smiled sadly whenever she had a peaceful moment, but then the restlessness would start again. Sometimes, she would whimper, and he would cringe. Whenever he tried to hold her or just put his hand on hers, she flinched and recoiled. He assumed his touch was perceived as the lecherous groping of her abuser. Seeing her reliving those horrors wrenched at his gut.

In the morning, still groggy from lack of sleep, he got up and made coffee while Georgia continued to toss and turn in bed. Never in a million years could he have guessed Georgia's confession. He had spent the night thinking about all the little hints, looks, and comments that Georgia had made and how it all made sense now. He wished he could erase all of it from her memory.

He thought about what she'd said about Alice. When Don hired him to follow Alice, he got a quick education on that callous so-called-woman. She used men for whatever whim that crossed her mind, and she seemed to have no pangs of guilt for her actions. The more he learned about her, the more he despised her.

Now, having learned what she went through, her actions made sense in a warped way. When Alice cut her family out of her life, instead of protecting herself, she isolated herself. Too bad she didn't realize that she and Georgia would've been able to support each other.

When he heard Georgia stir in the bedroom, he poured her a cup of coffee and put it on the dinette table. Georgia came out, her robe loosely tied and her hair uncombed. She sat down at the table. "Thanks for making coffee." She took a sip.

He sat down next to her, and took her hand. "Are you okay?"

She smiled weakly. "As good as can be expected."

A thousand thoughts ran through his mind during those long seconds of silence that followed.

She looked at him with tired eyes. "I didn't sleep very well. I couldn't stop thinking." She took another sip of coffee and looked down. "I've been worried about something."

"I'm listening."

"How do you think this surgery is going to affect you?"

"Hey, I'm supporting you in however you want to proceed."

She wrapped her hands around her coffee cup and looked into it. "What I mean is, after my breasts are gone … I worry that you won't be interested anymore," she suggested in an uncustomarily quiet voice.

He reached out and squeezed her hand. "Sweet Cheeks, it doesn't matter. I'll love you the same even without both breasts, both arms, and both legs."

She let out a weak chuckle and put her free hand on his cheek. "You'd just love that, wouldn't you? Me being stuck in bed all day, just waiting for you."

He couldn't help but laugh. "Actually, you know I'm more of a leg man. So, maybe don't lose your legs."

She chuckled again. "I'll do my best."

He gave her a lingering hug. "You have to know I'm going to love you the same regardless of whatever part has to get removed. It was never about your body; I fell in love with *you*." He stroked her hair as she leaned against him and cried.

As she sobbed, she said, "You know, I'll probably lose that too."

"Huh?"

"My hair. Chemo."

"Oh, Sweet Cheeks, we can have so much fun with wigs." He smiled as he gave her a squeeze.

She smiled as she sank into his arms, her tears smearing onto his shirt.

Chapter 24

The Labor Day family picnic had bolstered Georgia's mood. She had needed some fun after getting that awful diagnosis. Everyone in the family had come, but it had been difficult to put the gloom out of mind, so the party ended sooner than expected. Besides, Georgia tired easily, and that was the excuse given by the majority of the extended family.

That's when Callie refocused. She spent two weeks in surveillance, taking pictures of all the people who entered and exited the Carelli mansion; she wanted to make sure she got everyone. It was no easy task. She had hidden in a tree down the street and used her telephoto lens. By the time she was done, she had leg cramps and stiffness that would take a while to get rid of. She decided that running again would solve the problem.

She gathered a lot of information. Surveillance cameras were at the front gate and around the grounds, mounted in obvious and not-so-obvious places. At the end of a long driveway was a three-story, stone mansion with ivy growing along the walls and around the windows. Several lights lit up the grounds at night. Everyone who came and went, even the regulars, had to use what looked like an electronic key in addition to getting by the attendant at the front gate. This was no ordinary residence.

She took pictures of everyone who arrived. Later, she sent the pictures with her mom to have Vera identify them. Besides the family members, the tall black woman with short hair was the maid, Tanisha Brown. She always arrived in her uniform around ten and left just after six. Selena Cortez was the cook. She had black eyes, a long, hooked nose, was of medium height and build, and wore her long black hair in a bun. Since Rudy's equipment was very helpful in hearing everything at a distance, Callie could tell she was Latina and spoke limited English.

There were several men who came and went sporadically. The gardener arrived most often. Vic Parsons had pale blue eyes, a blonde ponytail, was of average height, and was well-built. Once, one of the guards called him 'Shiv.' When she got a partial shot of a tattoo on his hand, she took notice, but she never got another clear shot of it. She was sure that tattoo was the same one that Rudy asked her to discuss with the tattoo artist last year. She made a mental note to ask Rudy about it.

She was excited when she met with Rudy with the photos and attached names. They sat in his office, and she handed him the information. Her foot bounced as she leaned forward with eager anticipation. When he turned to the photo with the tattoo, she anxiously asked, "Is that the same tattoo from last year?"

His intense eyes turned up to her so quickly that she flinched. "How did you get these?!" he demanded.

She had never seen him that angry before and she was suddenly worried. She shuddered inside. Meekly, she offered, "I did surveillance."

His jaw set.

She'd seen him give that intensity to those he wanted to intimidate, but it was different this time, more like dread. She was afraid. She tried to swallow, but her mouth was dry. "Why? What's wrong?" she managed.

"Did anyone see you?" His voice had a sense of urgency.

"No."

He exhaled quickly.

She assumed it was from relief. Actually, she *hoped* it was from relief.

Looking intent, he leaned forward. "I don't want you over there again – ever! Understand?"

She hesitated. "I guess. But why?"

He looked at the photo of the tattoo again and took in a deep breath. He let it out between pursed lips. "This is, let me just say, the man that lives here, he's *dangerous*."

Her eyes widened. "You know who he is?"

He slowly nodded. "Remember, I told you the Feds were involved?"

Her mouth dropped open. "Oh …." she managed.

"If needed, I'll take care of any additional contact with them."

"So, this is about the tattoo?"

"Yes," he confirmed sharply. "And a *whole* lot more."

"I just thought …."

"No, you *weren't* thinking," he barked.

"I did it because I knew you were busy with Georgia."

"I've already arranged with your mother to sit with her when I need to go out." His hands were firmly pressed on the desk." So, you agree that you will not go there again?"

She nodded. "Okay." She looked down at her hands; they were gripping her knees. "Are we still meeting tonight to discuss what we've found in the police reports?"

"Yes. Be sure to bring Gary."

Before leaving, she visited with Georgia and made a light meal for her. Having never seen Georgia so weak, she fretted as she prepared it. Yes, she understood that chemo makes a body weak, but it still worried her.

Callie had looked forward to this meeting. She and Gary had discovered two important things in the police reports, but since her impromptu meeting with Rudy earlier today, her enthusiasm was shattered, like a china cup thrown against a concrete floor. She had decided not to tell Gary about her poor judgment. She didn't want to dampen his enthusiasm. Besides, he'd probably chew her out, too.

So, here was Gary sitting next to her in the passenger seat. He couldn't stop talking about their grand discoveries. He was so animated, his eyes exuded the thrill of digging and achieving the 'eureka moment,' and he gestured wildly as he babbled on. She could relate to that feeling, just not right now. Rudy's scolding was still smarting, and she couldn't muster up the excitement.

When she parked at the curb, Gary stopped talking and looked at her. "What's wrong with you? I thought you'd be so happy with what we found. Instead, you're a real downer." Suddenly, he paused, and the blood seemed to drain from his face. "Do you think we're wrong?!"

She grabbed her purse and avoided his eyes. "Come on, we're going to be late." She climbed out of the car.

He jumped out and grabbed her arm as she stepped up on the curb. "Wait. One minute won't make a difference. You're going to tell me what's wrong. I don't want us going in there looking like fools!"

She sighed. "It isn't about what we found. I'm certain it's real."

"Then what is it? You're driving me crazy."

She threw her hands up and huffed. "Okay!" She explained what happened in Rudy's office earlier. Then, she stood there looking at her feet.

Several seconds passed before Gary said anything. Finally, he put his hand on her shoulder and said slowly and deliberately, "Yes, that was pretty stup- um, foolish. But it's over now. And you learned your lesson. Right?"

"Yeah. I guess so."

"So, we move on. Okay? But you aren't going to do *that, again? Right?!*"

She nodded her head and then looked up at him. "He was so disappointed in me. I felt like a real fool." She frowned. "And yes, I heard you. You were about to say I was stupid. Well, I guess I was. And now you don't want to work with a stupid, unthinking, impulsive, risk-taker. Right?"

He chuckled.

Her eyes flared with indignation. "Is that what you *really* think?! That I'm a stupid, unthinking, impulsive, risk-taker?"

This time, he laughed. "No. I was just surprised that *you* thought of yourself that way."

"Oh," she murmured contritely.

"Come on. We're going to be late."

She smacked him on the arm. "Not very original, are you? I believe *I* said that first."

"So, sue me."

Rudy let them in. Georgia was already in bed, sleeping.

Callie felt bad about coming and not being able to say hello to her, but Georgia needed her rest. She shuddered as Rudy led them to his office. Only a couple of hours had passed since she had been reamed out in that room. They all sat down, but this time she let Gary sit in the 'electric chair.' She was already stressed.

As soon as Gary sat down, he started. "We found something in those reports! And we think it's pretty important. Actually, two things."

Rudy nodded.

Callie was suspicious. *Rudy doesn't look right. This is not his poker face. Could he still be thinking about this afternoon? No, that look doesn't fit. I'll bet he already knows what we have to say! Is he letting his real feelings show lately? Either I'm getting better at reading his expressions, or he isn't trying as hard to hide it. Or maybe he's too distracted over Georgia being sick.* She wasn't sure.

Gary continued, "We read the statements from all the witnesses around the shooting. Except for a varying word here or there, they all said pretty much the same thing, almost word for word. Isn't that pretty unusual?"

"So, you found it."

Yup, he already knew.

Gary's face fell. "If you already knew, why ask us to look at it?"

"Training. And you're learning well. So, with those statements being so similar, what does that tell you?"

"It sounds like a script?"

"And?"

Gary paused, eyes brightened. "Collaboration?"

Rudy nodded. "Or someone just dictated to them what to say?"

"So, why haven't the police picked up on that?"

"They have. And the Feds are in on it, too. But they have to gather more information and evidence, solid proof."

"Oh." Gary glowered at him. "You could've told us."

"But then you wouldn't have used your minds to figure it out for yourselves. It's like exercising a muscle. After a while, you'll recognize the clues without having to think about it."

Gary looked at Callie. "And to think we thought we had found something he didn't know."

"Pigs will fly before that happens. You said there were two things. What was the other one?"

"The gardener said he was in the kitchen when it happened. He gave a lot of details about the maid, and I'm wondering why he would be noticing her and what she was doing, when there's a crazy woman waving a shotgun in the room. I know that's something I wouldn't be thinking about. I'd be making sure I wasn't in the line of fire."

"Good, you saw that one, too."

Gary let out a defeated sigh.

Rudy chuckled. "I've been at this for decades. Not much gets by me, so don't feel bad. You should be proud of yourselves."

Gary looked at his feet and mumbled, "I guess."

Callie noted Rudy's ambiguous smile when he said, "Have you been able to arrange another visit with Jody?"

"Actually, we're going there tomorrow."

"Good. Keep me informed. Her statement could be important."

"I just hope we get something this time," Callie lamented.

Gary looked at Callie as he reached for his seatbelt. "Feeling any better?"

She shrugged.

"I think you did pretty good, even though it *was* foolish. You didn't get caught, you put names with faces, and you made the connection with that tattoo. By the way, you have to tell me more about that."

She let a faint smile slip through. "Thanks. You're a good friend. No, you're *more* than a good friend."

He almost told her, but something nagged at him to keep his true feelings about her to himself for now.

Chapter 25

Callie's head was swimming with everything going on at once.

First, there was Georgia's illness and the possibility of … she didn't want to think about that. Her mom would be so devastated if anything happened to her; Georgia had become her mother figure. After growing up with Alice for a mother, Sharon relished the fact that Georgia was everything Alice wasn't. It had been only three years since they found each other. Losing her would be a cruel loss. Besides, Callie loved her, too.

Then there was Vera's awful childhood, her unfulfilling marriage, and being shot by her sister. Callie's heart ached for her. If she could find some way to alleviate any of her pain, she had to try.

Recently, she had been questioning her choice of work. There were so many pros and cons. She desperately wanted to help people like Vera, but thinking about the dangers made her waver between continuing and quitting. She would have to find some way to make a final decision on that. When Rudy chastised her for her foolish escapade, her poor judgment was brought home with a demoralizing blow.

Finally, Gary was acting so strange lately. She wondered if being around his dad was too much for him. She shouldn't have pressed him to take that job. Maybe the fact that Rudy pushed all that training on him was more than he could handle. Being a detective wasn't his choice, and he'd said so.

"Gary," she asked quietly.

She saw him squint at her as he answered, "Yeah. What's up?"

"Is all this too much for you?"

"All what?"

"All the things I've pushed you into – the job, being around your dad, going on these fact-finding missions, the danger Rudy trains you for? Did I miss anything?"

When he took a big breath and let it out slowly, she knew she must have pushed at least one button.

"I've seriously thought about all of those issues."

She noticed an awfully long pause and almost said something.

"The thing with my dad isn't as bad as I thought. I don't see him that much, and when I do, I'm learning to deal with it. I'm starting to let go of some of that anger I had. And I'm getting to know him better. He does *seem* to have changed.

"Even though I resisted at first, I'm glad I have the job. It's a good start." He looked out the window. "About this detective stuff, though. I was really nervous at first ... no, I'll admit it, I was scared. Then, when Rudy gave me that crash course, I was terrified. But, I guess I needed it." He gave her an enigmatic smile. "I think I might be stronger because of it, not just physically, but mentally."

From the corner of her eye, she saw him frown and look out the window again. "There's something else, isn't there?"

He huffed. "Nothing gets past you, does it?"

She shrugged. "You want to talk about it?"

"Not right now. Besides, we're here."

On the walk from the parking lot to the State Hospital entrance, Callie was still pensive. "You want to tell me about that other thing? We've got a few minutes till we reach the building."

"Maybe some other time."

Gary folded his hands in his lap when they sat down at the table in the big room. "How many tries did it take to get her to say yes to this meeting?"

"Just once."

"Well, I hope it's more productive this time."

He was surprised when he felt her shoe bump his until he realized it was to alert him that Jody had entered the room. Callie smiled at her.

Jody sat down. She looked more alert this time and had her arms crossed tightly. "So, what do you want?"

Callie put a picture on the table. "This is Vera and me in the therapy room. She wanted you to know how much she misses you."

Jody leaned forward to look at the picture and grimaced. "She looks so tired." She sighed. "How's she doing?"

"She's always asking about you."

At those words, Jody's eyes welled up. "You know I'd go see her if I could."

Callie nodded. "I know. Vera's made that very plain."

Jody turned around to the guard, and Callie tensed.

Gary groaned inside. He thought she wanted to leave again.

"Guard, can I keep this picture?"

The guard walked over and picked it up. "We have to have security check it. If it's okay, then yes."

Callie looked up at him. "It's already approved. The security at the front desk already said she could have it." She wondered what was going through his head when he frowned.

"Do you have the written okay?"

"Yes. Right here." She held up the paper, and he snatched it. After looking it over, he gave it and the photo to Jody. "Okay," he mumbled. He frowned as he walked back to the door.

Puzzling over that reaction, Gary wondered if he was always in a bad mood or if something else was the cause.

Jody beamed while trying to control her emotions. She mouthed, "Thank you."

Callie leaned forward. "There's something that's been bothering me."

"What?"

"It doesn't fit, and I can't believe it."

"Believe what?"

"That you would deliberately shoot her."

Jody stiffened. "Didn't you hear?" she stated sarcastically. "I was high on drugs. So, it wasn't deliberate."

Callie lowered her voice to ask, "Why don't you tell me what really happened?"

Jody's face dropped as she looked aside to the floor. "I deserve to be here."

"Why?"

"For shooting her, of course. It's a criminal act."

"I think there's something you aren't telling me."

"Now where would you get an idea like that?"

"From Vera. And you."

Jody eyeballed her. "I didn't say anything."

"No. But your body language does."

"What does that mean?"

"Let's just say I've got a gut feeling. So, what gives?"

Jody sighed and tightly crossed her arms.

That's right. What gives? Gary wondered. *She's a lot more lucid than last time.* He made a mental note to talk to Callie about it.

Callie changed the subject. "Did you know that Brent is filing for divorce?"

She jerked her head, her nose flaring, and fire seemed to shoot from her eyes. "Seriously?!" Then, she mouthed, "The creep!"

"And I found out some things about him. I did some research, and apparently he isn't a nice man."

"Well, duh." She rolled her eyes.

"You must have known about all the partying and minor scrapes with the law."

Jody nodded disdainfully. "It's no secret. Mr. Carelli wants to do something about him, but Mrs. Carelli won't let him."

From his lessons on body language, Gary could tell that Callie restrained the impulse to react.

Callie paused and then asked cautiously, "She won't *let* him?"

Jody scowled with the tilt of her head, and she raised an eyebrow as she spat, "Duh!"

"Does that happen often, him getting outvoted?"

Jody harrumphed. "Are you kidding? Everyone over there thinks *he's* the big cheese, but Vera and I have heard them going at it in private. She *definitely* wears the pants in *that* family."

"Any examples?"

"Mostly it's about Brent, on how to handle him and all the bad publicity he gets." She sighed. "Then they fought about *us*." She shrugged. "The way they talked, you'd think we're worse than him. We didn't do *anything* like him, but they hated *us* even *more*." She looked aside angrily.

"That must've been hard."

Jody looked at her with a raised eyebrow. "What do *you* think?"

Callie's breath escaped. "I discovered something else about him. It's pretty serious."

"What's that?"

"About four years ago, Brent was charged with rape."

Jody's eyes flared. "Who?"

"She was their maid. But she withdrew the charges and left town. I'm looking for her now to find out why she did that."

Jody was livid, "So, he raped someone *else*?!"

Gary saw Callie freeze. He really wasn't expecting her to lose her composure like that.

Callie recouped, but neglected to hide her shock. "What? Are you implying he raped someone *other* than that maid?"

Gary wondered, *did she just imply* she'd *been raped?* He watched eagerly as Callie handled the conversation. They would definitely discuss this when they got back to the car. But there was no mistake, Jody was angry, and he wondered if this was what her anger was about at the last visit.

Her voice seemed strained as if holding the reins on a wild horse, "Let's just say he did. *That's* why I was angry ...."

Damn! I really didn't want to be right, Gary thought.

"... *That's* why I got the shotgun. It had everything to do with Vera ...." Her breath seemed unsteady, and she was trembling.

Gary could see that Callie wanted to say something, but even *he* remembered Rudy's lesson, 'be quiet and don't push.' He admired Callie's restraint.

"... After it happened ..." Jody seemed to be struggling with the horror of the memory. "Everything was my fault. If I hadn't let Vera know I'd lost my apartment ... if she hadn't insisted that I stay there ... he wouldn't have .... So, I had to pretend." She bowed her head. "It's my fault, I need to be punished. That's why I have to play the wacko." She put her hands over her face and wept.

Callie reached out to comfort her as a reflex, but when she saw the guard step towards them, she pulled her hand back. "The rape is *not* your fault. You shouldn't blame yourself. The only one to blame is Brent."

"But I shot her."

"Were you trying to?"

"Of course not! I was aiming at him. I wanted to see him suffer … to beg!" She sobbed and then blurted out, "But I wasn't going to *shoot* him! I was only going to put a hole in the *wall*. I just wanted to scare him, to make him see how much pain he'd caused."

"Have you used a gun before?"

"I'm an excellent shot. I *never* miss. My Uncle Fergus made sure of that. I guess he was the closest to a mountain man you'd see around here. He taught us how to clean a gun, hunt, dress an animal, protect ourselves. I only missed because Mr. Carelli came running in. If he hadn't done that, I would've hit the wall behind Brent." She put her face in her hands.

"So, he tackled you?"

When Jody put her hands down, she looked deflated. "Yeah. I guess he was trying to stop me."

"Can you describe where everyone was?"

She ran her arm across her wet nose and explained, "Sure. I was at the doorway to the dining room. Brent and Vera were having breakfast."

"Where were they sitting?"

"He was on the left of the table, and Vera was on the right, opposite each other. When I came in …" Jody covered her face with her hands and trembled. "I guess I was a little crazy with anger and lack of sleep. I had the shotgun pointed at him while I was yelling at him. They both stood up, and Vera started to walk towards me. That's when Mr. Carelli ran into me."

"Where did he come from? What room is on the left? Did he have to run around a corner?"

"No, he came from my right …." She stopped. Her expression slowly changed from sorrow to rage. "*Wait!* He did it on *purpose!* The scum bag *pulled* on the barrel instead of *pushing! He's* the one that made me hit her!" Jody stood up with her fists thrust down at her sides, "It was him! Why didn't I see it before?!"

The guard rushed over and grabbed her and a second guard came running. "Okay, back to your room."

"Please, don't take me away! I'll calm down! I'll be good! Please, I have to talk with them," Jody pleaded frantically.

The guard turned to Callie and Gary, and said, "This visit is over!"

Callie stood up. "Could you give her a second chance? Please?" She gave them a mesmerizing look that mixed 'sad hound dog' with 'damsel in distress.' Gary had seen her use that look on her dad when she really needed him to change his mind, and it always worked.

Wavering, the first guard hesitated as he stared at her.

The second guard stopped and asked, "What do you think, Jeff?"

Several seconds later, trying to look firm, the first guard admonished Jody with an accusing finger, "Next time, it's over! So be careful."

Gary thought, *Good job, Callie!* He made a mental note to be aware of her wiles.

Trembling, Jody sat down. She spoke with hushed tones, "Thanks. I really mean it. But how do we prove it?"

"The police reports have three other witnesses besides the immediate family. Do you think any of them will come forward?"

"I don't think so. Everyone's afraid of the Carellis. Except for some of the muscle, they seem to be in on the control thing."

"I have to ask this …" Callie tipped her head down, leaned forward with a grimace, and asked in barely a whisper, "You hinted at it before, but did Brent rape you?"

Gary knew it was true when tears started to fill Jody's eyes, and he felt so sorry for her.

Jody's lip trembled, and she nodded slightly. Her voice was barely above a shaky whisper, "I just lost it." She shrugged. "When Vera got married, we both thought our troubles were over. She would have a nice family, and we wouldn't have to worry any more. Things looked pretty good."

She looked down and shook her head. "We had no idea it would be even worse than what we came from. That and the humiliation. The rape was just the last straw; I was *so* angry." Her shoulders slumped. "Afterwards, I started to think I deserved to be here 'cause I thought I'd killed her and lost everything." She sat up and inhaled deeply. Her eyes filled with deep hatred and she leaned forward. "But now I know I have to get out of here and *nail* that scum bag."

"I want to help you, but I need more information. Can you answer some more questions?"

Jody looked up at the ceiling without seeing, and huffed. "Okay."

"You said it was worse than before. How's that?"

"Before, when we were with our *real families* ..." she rolled her eyes and made air quotes, "we knew we were better than them and we'd be free when we turned eighteen. We had hope. But with the Carellis, we were made to feel inferior, never good enough. And there was no way out. We knew it wouldn't ever end." Sadly, she looked to the window, "Mrs. Carelli," she shook her head again. "She actually *told* Vera there'd be no escape. Vera told her she didn't care about the money, that's why she signed the prenup, but Mrs. Carelli said she'd just have to learn to live with how things were 'cause there'd be no divorce, no separation. She didn't want the scandal." She shrugged. "No end in sight." She shook her head. "I guess she changed her mind about the divorce."

Gary thought about that. *There was no way to avoid scandal, the shooting itself caused that. Apparently, the only way to appear blameless would be to divorce Vera.*

"So, there's no way any of the servants will talk?"

"Not a chance. You don't know how scared they are." Her face pinched in worry. "So am I, *now*."

"The way I see it, we have to find a way to get them to tell the truth." She looked hard at Jody. "Vera doesn't remember what happened that day. Tell me everything you know. Let's start with the reports. First of all, how did the drug screen show you with cocaine in your system?"

Jody's cheeks flushed, and her shoulders tensed. She looked around to see how close the guards were.

Gary looked without turning his head, making sure they didn't see him looking. One of the guards was talking to a man in a white coat, probably a doctor, and the guard nodded towards them. *Hmm, that doesn't look good.* He made a mental note of the appearance of the man in white, about 5'10", slim face, graying black hair, dark brown eyes, sunken cheeks, and pock marks, probably from a bad case of acne. Although he was wearing a name badge, Gary couldn't make it out. The man in white was definitely studying them.

Jody took a slow breath, apparently to stay calm before she whispered. "As soon as the shotgun went off, Mr. Carelli wrestled me to the floor, and Mrs. Carelli made a phone call. I guess to call 911."

Callie's eyebrow shot up.

So much for a poker face. Gary would have to remind her about that, later.

"The gardener came running in with a syringe and injected me with it. That's how. I don't remember much after that."

Gary was as alarmed as Callie appeared to be.

"How did all the scars get on your arms?"

He was impressed that Callie managed to maintain a steady voice.

Jody's eyes darted around desperately. "Okay," she said defensively. "I used in the past, but I had to stop after I came to live with them. And I *did*. That was hard, but I *did* it." She huffed. "Some trade-off." She slouched with resignation. "If you were able to check my juvenile records, you'd see I had a problem with drugs for a while. That's why everyone believed I was using." She looked Callie straight in the eyes. "That syringe *must* have had the coke in it because *I* didn't do it. *They forced* it on me."

Callie nodded. "I know about the priors. I found articles."

Jody frowned. "But that's when I was still a minor. How'd that come out?"

"I suspect the Carellis pulled some strings to make their story believable."

"I knew they were mean, but that's *way* beyond evil." Fear seemed to overtake Jody's eyes and she pleaded, "You have to *help* me. *Please!*"

"We'll do all we can."

Too soon, time was up for the visit and the guards escorted the patients out one by one.

Callie looked at Gary with her mouth open. "I can't believe it."

"We've got to help her. I think learning this detective stuff could be worth it," Gary whispered.

When they closed the doors to the car, Gary cleared his throat. "Something bothers me."

"What's that," Callie asked as she started the car and backed out.

"After the guards went back to their positions, I noticed one of them talking to a guy in a white coat. I don't know, maybe a doctor? I made sure they didn't see me watching, but they were looking straight at Jody while you two were talking. They were close enough that I think they were listening to what she was saying, even with her whispering."

She stopped the car and stared at him. "So, what are you saying?"

"I don't know, it just didn't feel right. The look on that man's face, it could've been worry, certainly concern, maybe even fear."

"Are you sure?"

"Well, after all the stuff Rudy and Georgia taught me about body language and autonomic responses, I'm pretty sure."

"Put that on the recording too." She started to leave the parking lot. "Better yet, call Rudy right now and fill him in. Just tell him everything that happened."

"Got it." Gary called Rudy and gave him the details of their visit with Jody. "Okay … Yeah, I understand … That's okay, I figured you'd want to know … We're leaving Salem right now. Bye."

"What did he say?"

"He's going to talk to some guys, wouldn't say who, but he said he'd get back to us. Oh, and he said thanks."

She cocked an eyebrow. "It's a good thing you called, then."

"Why's that?"

"Because your radar picked up on something important. Good work."

"That's what Rudy said." Satisfied, he smiled. He picked up the recorder and documented everything about their trip to the hospital.

When he finished, Callie frowned. "At least, we know why the police and hospital reports show she was so high on drugs and almost overdosed."

"Unless she was lying just then. Users can be pretty devious."

"I don't think so. You can't fake that kind of rage."

He paused. "Hey, I just thought of something."

"What's that?"

"If Jody overdosed so badly that she almost died, how did she manage to get the gun, load it, bring it to the dining room, and threaten

Brent before it knocked her out? She would've been comatose way before that."

Callie blanched. "That's right. We have to figure out how to get the servants to talk. But the gardener is out. I'm pretty sure that the phone call Mrs. Carelli made was to him to bring the syringe, not to 911 because the timing is wrong."

Gary nodded as he added their thoughts to the recording. "Oh, one more thing. You showed your hand in there. You're face said everything several times."

She frowned at him. "After what she said, can you blame me?"

"Just keeping you in the know." He allowed a smirk to form as he looked out the window.

Chapter 26

After talking to Gary, Rudy called Brooks and told him about Gary's phone call. Brooks assured him that they would take care of it. Then, he called Sharon to come sit with Georgia and get her ready for her next chemo session, which would be in two hours. Since he knew Georgia would be in good hands, he had to go to the warehouse in person to find out what the plan was. Jody's life was on the line, and although Georgia understood he had to make these sudden secretive trips, he still felt guilty for leaving, especially now that she was getting sicker from her treatments.

This latest trial, Georgia's cancer, had tipped his hand on the ultimate decision. *When this case is over, I'm going to retire – actually retire. I don't want to waste any more precious time away from her. I just have to get past this last case.*

He sat on the couch with Georgia until Sharon showed up ten minutes later. Georgia practically pushed him out the door, saying, "I know that whatever you need to do is important, so go." She blew him a kiss.

Sharon offered to make tea, but Georgia insisted she sit down. "Thanks for coming."

"You know I'm available whenever you need me. Like you told Rudy, it has to be something important for him to leave."

Georgia closed her eyes, and Sharon hugged her. "It's okay. Don't worry about him."

"It's not that."

"Feeling overwhelmed by everything?"

"That's probably part of it. Maybe I just need to talk." She leaned forward and put her head in her hands with her elbows on her knees.

Sharon became concerned. When she needed to talk, the first person she would consider was Jack. She groaned inside worrying that Georgia may not be confiding in Rudy. They had been married only a short time, so maybe they hadn't developed that closeness yet. Thinking back, with her own past, it was several years before she finally told Jack everything about her past. She rubbed Georgia's back. "Whenever you're ready."

"I'm not what you think."

Puzzled, Sharon flinched. "What do you mean?"

"I know you think of me as this self-sufficient, confident, modern woman. But I'm not." She leaned back to look at Sharon. "I doubt myself. I wonder if I've made right choices. I'm not the wonderful mother figure you seem to see when you look at me."

"I'll decide that for myself. You're just tired and sick. You're just not thinking clearly right now. It's okay. It'll pass."

Georgia shook her head. "No. I've had a lot of time to think in the last several weeks. You see only what I choose to let you see. But it's getting too hard to put on that face anymore, so I have to burst your bubble."

Sharon shuddered inside, dreading what could come next. Her breath caught with toxic anticipation.

"Alice was always the leader because I didn't have the courage to make decisions. So, I followed along. Some of it wasn't good or right, and I'm ashamed of that." She looked up quickly. "You know I'd never do the things you found out about her, but I didn't stop her either."

Sharon wondered about that since it was only after Alice married her dad that she cut off all ties to Georgia. *How could she have stopped Alice from anything? They weren't even on speaking terms.*

Georgia sighed. "I guess I just started putting on a face to hide behind. I suppose I didn't want to really admit to myself the part I played."

"But that was a long time ago. You're not that person anymore. And you were never like her."

Georgia turned to look at her with heavy eyes and pinched eyebrows. "There are just some things you can't forget." She leaned back against the couch, put her palm on her forehead, and moaned. "I'm so tired. I think I need to lie down."

Sharon helped her recline on the couch. After she got her meds and a hot cup of tea, Georgia was soon sound asleep. *I've got to talk to Rudy about this. If he doesn't know, he has to have a chance to talk it over with her.* She considered sending him a text, but then thought better of it. This was a matter for a personal conversation. Besides, he was probably preoccupied right now. She'd talk to him when he got back.

She'd let Georgia sleep for twenty minutes, and then they had to leave for her appointment.

After Rudy got through security at the warehouse, he looked around. "Where's Brooks?"

"He's on his way to the State Hospital with three men in a helicopter. They're going to pull Jody out of there."

"Right now?!"

"Oh, you don't know, do you?"

"Know what?"

"We recorded a phone call to Pierre's phone about the time you called. The psychiatrist called Pierre about Jody. From what was said, they suspect she knows too much, and someone might believe her. She'd be in danger, so we're pulling her out and taking her to a safe house."

Rudy's heart sank. "So, Gary's suspicions were right!" After a brief moment, he gasped. "We have to get Vera out, too! If they think *she* knows whatever Jody knows, they'll off her too! Let me get her out!"

He could tell by Rice's face that he was treading on thin ice. Rudy grabbed Rice's shoulder and asserted, "I *have* to make this phone call now. Then, I'll tell you what's happening."

Knowing Callie was still on the way home from the hospital, he called Gary and told him that even though they still had to iron out a few details, their plan had to be done right now. "Can you do it, and do you have the time?"

"Yes, we're only about ten minutes from there, but you'll have to call Mark. If he can drive the van to the nursing home, we should get there about the same time. I have to make two more phone calls. Callie can let you know when it's over."

When Rudy finished telling Rice what they were going to do, Rice shook his head. "If this doesn't work …."

"Believe me, I understand."

Chapter 27

Gary was nervous and relieved when he saw Mark waiting in the van down the block from the nursing home when Callie dropped him off. Callie showed Mark where to park in the alley while Gary ran for the employees' entrance.

They had already devised a tentative plan, but not having it complete was the tricky part. There was no choice; it had to happen now. The thought that it could fail made him cringe. As Gary hurried inside, he fretted, *I could so get fired … hah, I could go to jail!* He took a deep breath and hurried to Vera's room.

Even with the rush, he was thankful that Marci was willing to help with Vera's escape. However, they had originally planned to enact their plan right after a meal so none of the residents would faint from low blood sugar; but now, it couldn't happen that way. He was glad she was on duty and that he was able to alert her right after the call to Rudy.

If he was seen before it went down, he would claim he'd come in to pick up something he'd forgotten, and then the alarm would go off.

The only tricky part would be if he were seen with Vera.

Reaching her room, he put her in the wheelchair and took her to the therapy room. Closing the door behind them, he wheeled her chair to face the bench. He sat down in front of her to explain what was going to happen and why.

"Remember, how we explained that your room is bugged?"

She nodded.

"Your sister is being watched too. We just found out that she's in danger and had to be rescued – and you're next."

She gasped, which made her wince with pain.

"Also, your doctor is scheduled to examine you tomorrow. You've made good progress, and he'd probably release you. We can't allow you to go back to the Carellis. They're the ones behind the threat. So, we have to get you out of here now. We're going to hide you in a safe location, and we need your cooperation.

"You'll be okay," he reassured her. "A fire alarm is going to go off, and Marci is going to wheel you out the emergency door to a van. Callie's going to sit with you in the back, and her brother is going to drive. I'd go, but I have to help the staff get everyone outside safely. After Marci gets you in the van, she's coming back to help with the rest of the residents. Okay?"

Vera nodded, but her expression was strained.

"Callie will be able to explain it in better detail, but I don't have time right now."

The fire alarm went off in less than a minute. They heard shouting and scuffling noises, and seconds later, Marci rushed in.

"I've got it," she ordered.

After she took Vera outside, an aide saw Gary and asked him to help her evacuate a bed-bound resident. He knew he'd be here for a while.

Marci wheeled Vera out through the side exit without anyone seeing them. They had chosen this door because it wasn't a designated exit for fire drills, and it was handy to reach a vehicle. Thankfully, everyone else was distracted with evacuation at other exits.

Mark was standing with Callie at the open side door of the van. Marci did a double take when she saw his clear hazel eyes staring at her – with interest. She felt an instant connection, but she made herself focus on the task; they couldn't make a mistake now.

Callie waved her over and then leaned towards Vera. "This is Mark, my brother. We're going to take good care of you."

While Callie was talking with Vera, Marci couldn't help staring and smiling at Mark. She was certain he looked at her in the same way, with definite interest.

Callie broke the spell by chiding them, "Come on. You can flirt later, I need help here!"

Mark blushed and lifted Vera into the middle seat while Marci and Callie put the wheelchair into the back. Then Marci rushed back inside, but not before looking over her shoulder for another look at Mark. He was taking a last look too as he paused at the open driver's door.

Mark jumped into the driver's seat and started the engine. Callie put on her seatbelt, and they took off.

Anxious, Vera started to tear up.

Callie offered her a tissue. "Are you going to be okay?"

"What's going on?"

"We were concerned that you might not be safe if you went home. So, we're going to take care of you until everything is sorted out."

"Why wouldn't I be safe?"

Callie patted her hand. "Let's just say we heard from reliable sources that the Carelli family wants you and your sister out of the way." She grimaced. "Gary and I talked with Jody, and she knows something incriminating, and the Carellis don't want it to come out."

"What? What's incriminating?"

"We've been told that we can't say what it is. Not yet."

They drove a circuitous route to make sure nobody was following them, and after forty minutes, they arrived at Bonnie Parker's house. She was one of Sharon's half-sisters that she discovered when she inventoried her mother's estate about three years ago. Bonnie worked from home and would be able to take care of Vera. Plus, she had the room.

Bonnie was waiting for them when they drove up. She had perfect posture as she watched for their arrival. There was no missing her with her excited jiggling and the electric green shirt she wore. Her large green eyes seemed to be laughing, just like Callie's when she was excited. Her wavy brown hair was cut to a perfect, wedge and it bounced with each jiggle. She waved them into the attached double garage when they drove up.

Mark drove in, and Bonnie closed and locked the garage door. She turned around to the back of the van just as Mark jumped out.

Bonnie clapped her hands together as she tittered excitedly, "This is so cool! I can't believe my little girl's room has someone to stay in it again." Although her daughter had moved out years ago, she still called her 'her little girl,' and she had always kept that bedroom ready just in case her daughter needed to come back.

After they got Vera settled, Callie sent Mark to the drugstore with a list of medical supplies that Gary had written out for Vera. They had agreed to have him shop at several drug stores so he wouldn't arouse suspicion.

Roy was almost finished with the report on the last case he investigated when his personal phone vibrated. He closed the door to answer the call. A quick look verified that the blocked caller was on the line.

"This is Roy."

The usual gravelly voice came on, "A woman was kidnapped from the Peace Tree Nursing Home. Her name is Vera Carelli. The police will be notified, so call me with her location when she's found."

"Got it."

Chapter 28

Rudy said to himself, "Well, here goes," as he dialed the number.

"Carelli residence, may I help you?" the husky voice asked with a pleasing vibrato.

"May I talk with Tanisha Brown?"

"This is Tanisha."

"My name is Rodney Calvin. I work for Algers, Tate, and Olney. We are handling the estate of a relative of yours, and we need to speak with you regarding an inheritance. Can you meet with me sometime soon?"

"Oh! Of course. How soon?"

"As soon as possible."

"I get off work at six. I can meet you after that."

"The office is closed then, so we could meet at a coffee shop."

"There's a coffee shop downtown on Fifth Avenue. I'd have to take the bus, so about 7:00?"

"That would be perfect."

She gave him the address, described herself, and told him what she would be wearing.

When Tanisha walked in the door, Rudy stood up and waved her to his table. "Hello, Miss Brown?"

"Yes." She smiled as they shook hands.

She was tall, slim, and had short, curly black hair that nicely framed her chocolate skin. Her broad nose was balanced by large eyes, long lashes, high cheek bones, and full, pouty lips. Rudy thought she would do well as a model.

"Please sit down. I'm sorry to get you here like this."

"Oh, it's no problem. Was it Aunt Betty that passed?"

"I apologize for the deception, but I'm actually investigating the shooting at the Carelli mansion, and I need to know what you saw," he whispered.

She stiffened.

"When did you first know that there was going to be trouble?" He was phishing. Callie had already told him Jody's perspective on what happened, but he wanted to verify that with Tanisha's statement. But he'd have to get her to offer it. He didn't want to be accused of feeding the story to her.

The young woman swallowed hard. "I, uh – I don't think I should be here."

"Why? Will you be in trouble?"

Her eyes widened.

"Don't worry, I have a transmission blocker, no one will be able to hear you. I just need to know what you saw."

She bit her lip, and her eyes darted around, finally looking out the window. She took a deep breath and spoke quietly, "I was dusting in the dining room. I knew something bad was going to happen when Miss Jody ran into the room carrying that shotgun. She started yelling at Mister Brent and aimed it at him. I thought she was really going to let him have it."

"What time was that?"

"Just about nine, Mister Brent and Miss Vera had just started breakfast."

"How are you sure of the time?"

"Because when she came in with that gun, she said she was going to put nine hundred holes in him to match the clock!"

"What happened next?"

"I was *scared!* So, I ran to the corner ... *I* didn't want to get shot. Right then, Mr. Carelli ran in."

"Was that Anthony or Brent?"

"The father. He insists we call him Mr. Carelli."

"Exactly where was everyone standing?"

She thought for a moment. "Like I said, I'd hurried to get out of the way, behind Miss Jody, in the corner to her left. Mister Brent was right in front of me. And since Miss Vera was sitting across the table from him before Miss Jody ran in, the table was still between them."

"So that I understand exactly where everyone was positioned, was the table to the left or right of Brent as you were looking at him?"

"To the right. Then Miss Vera was to the right of the table, on the other side."

"Okay. What happened when Mr. Carelli came in?"

"I only saw him when he grabbed at the gun. That's when the gun went off." Tanisha started to tremble. "I couldn't believe it when Miss Vera fell and hit her head against the dining room table on the way down. I thought for sure she was dead."

"So, did Mr. Carelli run in from Jody's right side or left side?"

"Well, it had to be on her right, because I didn't see him until he grabbed the gun."

"Was he running in?"

"Like I said, I didn't see him until he was right there, so, I don't know."

"What happened after that?"

Tanisha's face dropped, and she swallowed hard. Her thick lips seemed thinner as the corners pressed down. She hesitated. "First, Mr. Carelli wrestled Jody to the floor. Then Mrs. Carelli came in and called 911. I was kind of surprised she was even up. She'd been kind of sick lately."

"The police report says that the neighbors heard the shot at 9:05 p.m."

She nodded. "That sounds right."

"The 911 call was recorded at 9:30. Who did Mrs. Carelli actually call? And what happened in that 25 minutes?"

She caught her breath and quickly looked around the room again.

Rudy leaned forward and whispered, "Are you concerned that someone may be watching you?"

She nodded.

He rubbed his chin. Then he pulled a card out of his pocket, jotted down a note, and handed it to her.

She looked at it and nodded. "Okay. But what do I tell Mr. Carelli since this isn't really about an inheritance."

"Just tell him you have to come to the office to sign papers. You'll be safe there." He pointed to the card. "That's the address."

The next day, Rudy was early. He was thankful that he had retained this connection. He frequently did research for the lawyers here in exchange for using one of their offices as a cover. Even the receptionist was prepared.

He was certain that Tanisha would be followed by one of Frankie's men. He would see the office but not be able to gain access here to listen. To cover the possibility of a bug on her, Rudy brought his transmission blocker and turned it on.

When she arrived, the receptionist buzzed him, "Your appointment is here, Mr. Calvin. I can send her in now. Would you like refreshments?"

He smiled, knowing that was the code they had prepared, meaning that she saw someone in the hall right after Tanisha arrived. "Yes, send her in. But, no thank you on the refreshments," his code for refusing the man's admittance.

Tanisha went in and sat down.

He smiled. "First, don't worry about anyone hearing us. I've blocked any transmissions you may have on you. And I'm going to tape our conversation."

She closed her eyes and seemed to wilt. Then she exhaled with half a smile and nodded. "How did you know?"

"It's my business to know. By the way, my real name is Rudy, Rudy Burke." He reached across the desk to shake her hand. "So, let's get on with it. When we broke off our conversation, I had just asked what happened in that 25 minutes from the shot to the 911 call."

Her voice seemed shaky. "After Vera fell, and Mrs. Carelli made the call, Brent just stood there while everyone else was yelling and running around. It seemed like chaos. So, I ran to Miss Vera to see if she was alive. I was so glad she was, but there was so much blood, and she wouldn't wake up." She shook her head slowly, thinking. "She seemed like the only sane person in the house. She was my friend," she said kindly. But she stiffened when she added, "But Mrs. Carelli, she thought it was 'inappropriate' to mingle with the servants." She used air quotes. "She even threatened my job if I didn't stop letting her talk to me. As if *I* had control over that."

Rudy bit his tongue. He really wanted her to get on with it. He realized that his worry over Georgia made him impatient with others. He had to tell himself to calm down.

Thankfully, she continued, "Anyway, Mr. Carelli was sitting on Miss Jody trying to get the gun from her. Even though Mrs. Carelli was still sick, she was barking orders. Then, things got scary. The gardener, he came in, and he had a syringe! Mr. Carelli already had Miss Jody down on the floor, so he held her while the gardener gave her the shot. Mrs. Carelli, she started telling all of us what we were supposed to tell the police. I couldn't believe they would do that."

"So, nobody told the truth to the police, and the reports are not what really happened?"

Tanisha grimaced and nodded slowly.

"Do you remember what Jody was saying when she first came into the dining room, besides drilling him full of holes?"

"Something about Mister Brent being a pig. She said she wasn't going to stand for it and he was going to pay. That's when she aimed at him."

"Did she say anything else?"

She paused, thinking. "No. But Vera said the strangest thing."

He waited.

Tanisha looked like she was struggling with the right words as she related slowly, "She told Jody not to do it, or she wouldn't tell her where the money was. I don't know *what* she was talking about 'cause she never got an allowance or even a credit card ...."

Gotta figure out what that's about, he told himself as he handed her a tissue.

"... that's when Mr. Carelli grabbed for the gun. Since he was on the other side of her, I could see his face. He was really angry. Thanks for the tissue," she squeaked. She started to sob and put the tissue up to her face.

Rudy wondered, *Was he angry about the gun? Angry about Vera having some money? Enough money to be secretive about?* He gasped. *Could he have thought she took that money from the Switzerland account?* He moaned inside. *If he did, Vera's definitely a target. It's a good thing we got her out of there.*

After a couple of minutes, she wiped her eyes. She looked at Rudy with her brow furrowed. "Miss Jody wasn't what they said, not anymore," she implored.

"What do you mean by 'anymore?'"

Her mouth made an inverted U. "When she first moved in, she was kind of wild. She used marijuana and coke sometimes. But she stopped when they insisted. I know she was clean, for almost a year. So, when they made us say she was high on drugs, I knew that was wrong. I think they set her up with that syringe." She blew her nose and mourned, "Why would they do that? It was obvious she was at fault by bringing in that gun. So, why do *that?*"

"Is there anything else you remember?"

She thought for a moment. "I saw Selena was watching from the door at the kitchen. She's the cook. She looked awful. I knew she was scared. I was scared too, but not like her." She cringed. "I don't think I should tell you this."

He leaned forward. "Is she an illegal alien?"

"How did you know?" she blurted out.

"Educated guess. Continue."

"I could tell she wanted to run away like her cousin."

Rudy picked up his pencil and twirled it between his thumb and index finger. "Her cousin? Who's her cousin? And why did she run away?"

"Her cousin's Angela Pelayo ..."

Rudy stopped breathing. *Bingo.*

"... she was their maid for a while. I don't know all the details, but Selena wanted to avenge what they did to her. Afterwards, we talked. Now she's scared and wants to run, too. She thinks the cops are going to focus on her, and she'll get deported."

"You tell her I know what happened to her cousin, and I'll help."

Tanisha's mouth gaped open. "How?"

"It's my job to know. Just tell her to hang in there. Okay?"

She nodded incredulously.

"I can see that they have her under their thumb. But what holds you there? Why don't you just quit?"

She looked down. "My mom got sick about the time I realized what they were up to. I wanted to quit anyway, so I used the excuse that I needed to take care of her. They tried to talk me out of it, and when I said, 'No, I have to go help her,' they offered to pay for her medical expenses. At first, I just accepted it." She shrugged. "It seemed like the only way to help Mom. Then when she got better, I wanted to quit again. This time, they ... they didn't say so outright, but I understood that Mom and I ..." Her eyes darted to the ceiling and out the window. "... that we'd disappear." Her voice quavered as she continued, "And I had to be silent about anything I heard. So, me telling you *anything* puts us in danger."

"You can't repeat this to anyone, but things are going to happen that should end your nightmare soon."

Her eyebrows pinched together as she jerked to look at him. "How can that be? Everyone that opposes them disappears."

"I can't tell you what's happening, but it'll be soon."

Her lip quivered. "I want to believe you, but ...." She pulled out her tissue and dabbed at a tear. She shook her head. "If only ...."

"One other thing. I'll need Selena's cousin's address. Text it to me and then delete the message."

She sat up rigid and gaped at him in horror. "You're one of them, aren't you?!"

"No!" *These poor women are really terrorized.* "No, I need it in order to help her."

"I don't know if I can trust you." She cringed.

He picked up the phone and made a call. "Hey, Brooks, Rudy here. I've got Tanisha Brown with me; she's the Carellis' maid. She needs verification that I'm not part of the family. Is it okay for her to talk to you? I want to make a deal for her and the cook in exchange for talking." He nodded a little. "Okay, I'll put her on."

He handed her the phone. "He's with the FBI. He'll vouch for me."

She hesitantly took the receiver. "Hello," she said doubtfully. "How do I know what you're saying is true?" She was silent for a while, listening. She sighed. "Okay, I guess. So, you're saying Selena and I will get immunity for helping?" She listened again. "Do you need to talk to ... Mr. Calvin, uh, Mr. Burke again? ... Okay." She handed the phone to Rudy. "I'm still not sure about this."

"Just in case the Carellis need to see something, here are some documents that will make it look like you're in the process of inheriting a few things from your aunt. The supposed reading of the will is several months away to allow for 'settling of the estate.' Any questions?"

"I don't think so."

"Don't act any differently so you don't arouse suspicion. Remember, mum's the word."

A look of horror gripped her. "Are you kidding? Saying something would be suicide!"

"I'll contact you if need be."

"Okay."

They shook hands, and she left. He gathered his equipment, exited via the back, and called the Feds on his way home.

Chapter 29

Rudy had just returned home with Georgia after a chemo session, and it had taken its usual toll on her. The doctor had explained that she would need complete rest after each one. Yes, it always affected her adversely, but lately, her reaction seemed to be even more debilitating. Until they actually started treatments, he never fully comprehended how thoroughly exhausted she would be. Most of the time, she didn't even have the strength to eat, but he managed to coax her to eat some medibles this time. The doctor had prescribed them for her as needed, which she seemed to need more and more often. They didn't remove the symptoms, but at least, she was able to cope. He helped her into bed and kissed her forehead.

He closed the bedroom door, turned on the TV, and put on the local news for a distraction. He sat in the dining room to get his messages. He had just replayed the one from Agent Brooks when the doorbell rang. He cursed to himself at the interruption because he wanted to call Agent Brooks for the complete details. For now, he had to hurry to the door to prevent a second ring from unnecessarily disturbing Georgia.

He was surprised to see Gary and Callie come rushing in as soon as the door opened.

"What's up?"

Callie was usually the vocal one, but it was Gary who blurted out, "I just got off work. Something weird happened this morning. I called Callie right away, and we need to talk to you."

Rudy waved them to sit down on the couch.

Gary looked as if something was crawling under his skin. He rubbed his hands together, looked around repeatedly, and cleared his throat several times. "You won't believe this." His worried eyes flicked around the room, finally landing on Rudy. "Someone came by the nursing home to visit Vera." He spread his hands in dismay. "All this time, no visitors, and the day after we take her out of there, someone comes to visit?"

"You know who it was?"

"He told Marci he was a cousin."

"That's not possible! Callie was with me when we talked to all the relatives. There aren't any cousins that aren't in jail or even remotely interested in her, let alone even know she was *in* the nursing home."

"I know. Callie told me about your interviews. On a hunch, we brought the pictures to Marci. You know, the ones Callie took when she was on surveillance. Marci identified this guy." He handed him the matching photo. "That's when we knew we had to come here."

Rudy looked at it with a poker face, but by Callie's expression, he knew he couldn't downplay it. "So, we know it was him," Rudy needlessly added.

Gary went limp. "So, we got her out just in time."

Just as Rudy nodded, a local newscaster caught their attention from the television:

> "This special bulletin just in. Early this morning at 12:50 A.M., a Sellwood-Moreland resident called 911 and reported that he had found an unknown dead man in his house when he came home from a business trip. Found in the hallway, the dead man had two bullet wounds to the chest, apparently killing him instantly. According to police, he has been identified as Brent Carelli, son of well-known philanthropists, Frank and Phaedra Carelli. The immediate family has been notified, but there is no known reason why Mr. Carelli would be at the home in SE Portland. More information to follow."

As if he'd been stabbed, Gary's mouth dropped open, and he gaped at Rudy.

Callie had blanched and covered her mouth with a shaky hand.

Rudy frowned. "What?"

Callie offered, "Does that report have anything to do with Vera?"

Gary jerked to face her angrily. "Are you suggesting she had something to do with it?"

"Of course not!" she retorted. "I was just wondering if there could be a connection."

Rudy ran his fingers over his short hair several times. "I have to tell you something." He stood up and started to pace. "You can't ever tell anyone what I'm about to tell you. Agreed?"

They both nodded. "Of course."

"The Feds have been listening to Pierre and his phone calls, and they've been keeping me informed. The psychiatrist on Jody's case called Pierre to tell him that the Feds took her from the hospital. That's when I called you to get Vera out. Well, he admitted that he was paid to drug Jody and not because she needed it for treatment."

Gary snapped, "I knew it! She didn't act like she needed it."

"He took her off it before your first visit, but then when he put her on it again, he said the meds didn't work the same after that."

Callie and Gary exchanged a bewildered glance.

"Back to the phone call. When the psychiatrist told Pierre to make sure his name didn't come up in any investigations, Pierre told him to clean up his patient files so there'd be no ties to him." He nodded to them. "Good call on talking with her. We may not have found out until it was too late if you hadn't."

Then he turned to Gary. "I need to know. What's it like at work? What are they doing to find Vera?"

Gary looked down and then up again. "They're asking everyone who went to her room to evacuate her? 'What did you find when you got there? Did anyone see her leave? Did you see anyone or anything suspicious?' Questions like that."

"What did you say when it was your turn to be grilled?"

"I told them that I'd come in to get something I forgot, and the fire alarm went off before leaving. So, I started evacuating residents. I told them I didn't know where she was." He huffed. "So, as of now, they're panicking over losing a resident. They called the police yesterday after talking to everyone and not getting any answers."

"What about Marci? Is she holding up?"

"I haven't been able to talk to her yet. Everyone is being watched."

When Rudy put his hands into his pockets and paced again, Gary and Callie exchanged worried shrugs.

Finally, Rudy stopped pacing, his eyes focused outside the window. "Vera only has amnesia surrounding the shooting, right?"

"Yes. But she remembers everything else," Gary reminded him.

"I think I'll go visit Vera tonight and quiz her about the family dynamics. Maybe there's something we can find out."

"Are you going to tell her about Brent? It wouldn't be fair not to."

Rudy put both hands on his head and let out a deep sigh. "Maybe it would be better for you and Gary to tell her. She knows you. Besides, I've got to take care of Georgia." He looked at them sternly. "But you'll call me right away if you learn anything. Right?"

"Of course. Anything in particular you want to know?"

"No. I usually play it by ear. Generally, an answer will lead to the next question and so on. Kind of like a fishing trip, you never know what you'll pull out. Just don't tell her about Jody yet."

"Why not?" Callie wondered.

"She'll get excited and want to go to her. They have to remain separate, or both their lives could be in danger. Oh, and make sure you aren't followed there."

Callie stood up and gave Rudy a hug. "Georgia's going to get through this." She looked up at him with tears welling up. "And give her a hug for me, okay?"

Even if Rudy wanted to, he wouldn't have been able to pull off his poker face. As stoic as he tried to present himself, it just wasn't going to happen at that moment. Speechless, he nodded.

Gary unsuccessfully tried to swallow the lump in his throat. His voice was a notch higher than usual when he added, "I don't know her as well as everyone else, but from what I've seen, Georgia's a great lady. Would she be offended if I asked you to give her a hug, too? For me?"

Rudy laughed sadly, "No, she'll love it. Look, you guys had better get going," he ordered before he gave in to tears.

They were almost to Bonnie's house before they could bring themselves to talk.

Gary started. "Any idea what we're going to say?"

"I guess we start with the bad news."

Gary hung his head. "Yeah. That ought to go over well."

"I know. Even though their marriage was rocky, I know she cared for him. I could see it in her eyes when she talked about him."

"Right."

She parked, but trying to compose themselves, they waited for a couple of minutes before getting out.

Gary knocked on the front door, and Bonnie answered quickly.

"What are you doing here? I thought we were supposed to pretend no connections."

Callie stepped in. "We have to talk to your guest."

Bonnie shrugged and stepped aside. "Okay."

Bonnie led them to Vera's bedroom and announced cheerily, "You have company. Callie and Gary are here."

Vera looked up with a big smile. "What brings you here?"

Gary picked up a small chair and set it near her to talk face to face. "How are you doing? Are you keeping up with your exercises?"

"Yes," she said with a big smile. "I'm actually getting better balance. Walking with just a cane now."

Gary's heart wasn't in telling her; but not knowing what else to do, he forced a smile for her sake. But not well enough to convince her.

She leaned back a little and squinted. "Is something wrong? Am I supposed to be farther along than that?"

"No. That's not it. You're doing great." He cleared his throat. "But I do have some bad news to tell you."

"Did something happen to Jody?!"

Gary quickly shook his head. "No." He bowed forward, looking at his feet. "Uh ... Brent's dead."

Vera gasped as her eyes popped in horror. "What happened?!"

"We don't know yet, but someone shot him. The police are investigating now."

Callie sat on the bed next to Vera and held her hand.

Bonnie looked at her quizzically. "Who's Brent?"

Callie looked up at her and mouthed, "Later."

Although Vera stayed motionless for several seconds, tears ran down her cheeks. Slowly, she shook her head. She brought her free hand up to cover her quivering mouth. Her eyes filled quickly, overflowing with more tears, and she started to sob.

Callie pulled out two tissues and gave them to her. She cringed a little before continuing, "Do you know who he's been seeing? Maybe where he hangs out?"

Vera shook her head. "He never told me anything, but I'm pretty sure he was chasing women." She looked away. "Even his parents knew about his conquests. Jody and I heard them arguing with him about it several times." She shuddered. "Apparently, there were a lot of women."

Callie put her arm around her shoulder and squeezed. "I'm sorry. I wish the situation was different."

"When did it happen?"

"It was last night." Callie fidgeted some, and Gary saw that Vera noticed.

"What's wrong?" Vera asked, as if she would be afraid of the answer.

"The police are looking for you as a person of interest. I guess they always want to question the spouse."

Vera's mouth dropped open. "Do they think I did it?"

Callie cringed. "It's because you disappeared just before it happened." She hesitated before adding, "There's a witness out there that said they saw you at the scene of the crime." She added quickly, "But we know you didn't do it because you've been here the whole time. Rudy says to stay here and not let anyone know where you are until the investigation is over."

Vera closed her eyes for a moment and then they popped open. "Do they think Jody did it?!"

Callie shrugged.

Gary knew that was a deception, but it had to be. They couldn't let Vera know where Jody might be. As they talked, Gary's heart went out to Vera. He watched as Callie tried to comfort her. He knew what a good heart Callie had and how she always showed empathy for others. He felt so hopeless right now, thinking, *she'll never accept me as anything more than a brother. I might as well give up.* When the ache inside became too much, he stood up nervously. "I have to go get some more supplies. I'll let you two talk. Callie, can I use your car?"

He was surprised when she handed him the keys.

Bonnie escorted him to the door and gave him a hug. It was a struggle to hold in the emotions until he was out of sight, but he managed to wait until he drove off before letting the tears flow. He wasn't sure if it was because he was feeling sorry for Vera, Vera's unexpected visitor at the nursing home, or his carefully guarded feelings for Callie.

What a sap!

Chapter 30

Rudy paced as he waited for Sharon to arrive. He had called the Feds to give them an update on Vera's unsolicited visitor. They, in turn updated him on their latest. They were trying to find out who the anonymous caller was that claimed they saw Vera outside the house where Brent was killed. *I can't believe they're trying to frame her.*

Then there was the guilt that was eating at him. He could always count on Sharon taking care of Georgia whenever he needed to be somewhere, but he hated leaving her like that. Yes, Georgia was asleep and would probably still be asleep when he got home, but not being with her still tormented him. He fretted, thinking that he wasn't doing his best for her. But he felt an obligation to help Vera, too. His mind and emotions were spinning, and he hoped the distractions wouldn't affect his ability to decipher any information he might get about or from Vera. He would definitely have to quit after this case was over.

As he parked in front of Bonnie's house, he tried to think of anything that might be important from what Callie and Gary had gotten from Vera. Nothing came to mind.

He rang the doorbell, and Bonnie opened it with a big smile. "Come on in. Callie said you'd be coming over to see her."

She offered him coffee and cookies.

"Thanks," he accepted the coffee with an obliging smile. Small talk seemed so counterproductive when you have a mission to accomplish. What he'd learned about Bonnie was that she wasn't the brightest bulb on the string, but he had to keep his demeanor low key, for even she might detect his anxiety. He didn't want to explain everything to her right now.

After a few minutes, Bonnie led him upstairs to the large bedroom. Vera was reading a book while slowly rocking in an upholstered rocker. She looked up and smiled.

He introduced himself, "Hi, I'm Callie's uncle Rudy. Glad to meet you." He strolled up to her, bent over, and shook her hand.

A puzzled look came over her face. Her mouth opened a little, and she gasped. "Your cologne!"

He stepped back. "I'm sorry, are you allergic?"

"No, Brent sometimes wears it – wore it." She spoke slowly as if trying to recall a memory. "He wore it at breakfast, but I was angry with him. That must be why he wore it. He knew it was my favorite, and that it always got to me. I guess he wanted to distract me, maybe calm me down." Her hand flew up to her mouth, and her eyes widened with shock.

"What?"

She stared hard at him. "I remember!"

He caught his breath. Then, he asked cautiously, "Remember what?"

Her eyes showed horror. She gasped again and froze.

"What's wrong?"

She moaned.

He grabbed a chair, placed it in front of her, and sat down. "It'll be alright. Just breathe slowly."

"Oh-h-h; I knew she couldn't have."

Bonnie looked confused. "Huh? Callie? What couldn't she do?"

Rudy turned to Bonnie, put his index finger firmly to his lips, and authoritatively shook his head. He returned to Vera, patted her shoulder, and tried to comfort her. "You'll be okay. Are you remembering what happened that morning at breakfast?"

She bent over with her face in her hands. She nodded and moaned again.

"Are you going to be okay?"

She took a deep breath and let it out slowly. "How could he?!"

"He? Who?"

"Mr. Carelli. He did it on purpose!"

"Did what?" He knew what she meant; he just had to let her say it.

She looked up in horror, staring into space. "I *knew* she couldn't have done it!" She shook her head. "Why would he *do* such a thing?"

Rudy put his hand on hers. "Can you start at the beginning?"

She finally looked at him, and her shoulders slumped. Wracked with anguish, she started, "It was never right from the beginning. Even on our honeymoon, he flirted with waitresses, clerks … anyone wearing a skirt. It was awful. He would always apologize and be nice for a while, but it never ended. After a while, he tried to buy me off with expensive gifts, but I didn't want them. I just wanted my husband. The last straw was that awful night."

Groaning in anguish, she rocked back and looked at the ceiling, apparently trying to keep some measure of composure.

Rudy looked back when he heard sounds behind him. Bonnie had moved a chair and sat in it. He noted her sympathetic frown, but he turned back to Vera. "What happened then?"

"It was just after midnight, the night before, when Jody … she came to me crying. I could see how hurt she was. At first, she said *she* was sorry. Then, she said he was too strong. Brent …" She closed her eyes fiercely. "… he *raped* her," she croaked. Vera's face reddened with rage and she glared at Rudy. "I was furious. It was bad enough finding out about all those other women, but Jody? I threw some glassware into the fireplace 'cause I had to break something."

Then she cringed. "Poor Jody, she thought I was mad at *her*. I tried to convince her it was *Brent* I was angry with. I sat with her for a while, holding her and crying with her. Then I helped her get cleaned up. We decided we were going to talk to Mr. and Mrs. Carelli about it. We hoped they would listen; you know with Brent having a thing with women. We hoped they'd finally be on our side.

"When we got to their bedroom door, they were arguing. At first, we couldn't make out what they were saying. Mrs. Carelli had been sick lately, but we could tell she was mad. We picked up a few words here and there, and then we realized Brent was in there too and they were arguing with him about what happened." She bit her lip.

"What did you hear?" He hated making her talk, but it was the only way to hear her story.

She pinched her eyes closed. "She said we were a liability from the start. Then, she said she was tired of all the stupid mistakes he was making. Usually Mr. and Mrs. disagree on most things, but they agreed they had to clean up his dirty laundry again. We knew it would be useless to talk to them, so we went back to our rooms.

"We decided we'd pack up and leave. I was going to tell Brent the next morning at breakfast. I could see Jody was still upset, but I had no idea she was planning on shooting him. If I had known that, I would've left with her that night."

When Rudy was ready to leave, Bonnie walked him to the front door. "I can't believe it. She remembered, just like that."

"Smells will do that."

She turned to him, confused. "Huh? How is the nose connected? Or was it, what do you call it? A short skirt?"

Rudy snorted. "Do you mean a short circuit?"

She brightened, "Yeah! That."

He stifled a chuckle. "Actually, smells are associated with memories. Like flowers can remind you of a date. Or salty air can remind you of a trip to the beach. In the same way, Brent's cologne reminded her of the last time they were together that awful morning."

Confusion reigned, so Bonnie gave the usual response when she really didn't understand something yet didn't want to acknowledge it. "O-kay."

He knew he'd never be able to get her to understand, so he just said, "Thanks for taking care of her."

"Sure. I'm glad to do it." She looked bewildered just before asking, "Are you allergic to me?"

His eyebrows pulled together in confusion. "No. Why do you ask?"

"Well, you made that weird sound. A lot of people do, so I wondered if you were allergic."

"Sound?"

"Yeah. It sounds kind of like a snort, like you're trying to get something out of your nose."

He paused trying to think of a way to sidestep the issue; he certainly didn't want to embarrass her. "No, just allergies."

"Oh. Okay." She mumbled as she closed the door, "I don't get it. How does the nose remember? Weird."

Chapter 31

As Rudy sat behind the one-way mirror, even he thought Brooks was intimidating as he interrogated Jody's psychiatrist. Brooks paced with fists planted on his hips. "Dr. Hanover, when were you first asked to make Jody Perkins' diagnosis a fake?"

"It was the morning of her arrival at the police station. They always do a psychiatric analysis for crimes like hers. And with her history of 'mental issues,' it was required."

"Were you contacted before or after you met with Miss Perkins?"

"Just after. I was actually making out the report when I got the call on my cell. I was told to make her look guilty and crazy. With her testing positive for cocaine and having a history of depression, and since drugs can influence violent behavior, making her look criminally insane was easy and believable. I just added a couple more diagnoses."

"And what did you list as her mental issues?"

"It's in the report."

"I repeat, list them."

Dr. Hanover blanched. "Psychosis with hallucinations triggered by drugs, delusions, drug dependence, aggression, intermittent explosive disorder. It wasn't a stretch to diagnose her criminally insane."

"Did you get paid for that?"

He nodded.

"Answer verbally."

"Yes."

"How much?"

"Ten thousand."

"How'd you get paid?"

"I got paid with cash in an envelope. I don't know who or how it was sent, but it came in the interoffice mail. Somebody else at the hospital could be in on it."

"Why did you go along with this ruse?"

The doctor looked down. "I already had a working relationship."

"What do you mean by that?"

Hanover avoided eye contact when he responded, "There were other cases. I've done fake diagnoses for other patients."

"Who contacted you?"

"I don't know. He didn't tell me, and the number was always blocked."

Brooks stopped in his tracks and spun around to face the doctor down. He crossed his arms and glared at him.

Rudy shook his head as he thought, *I sure could've used those moves. Too bad I've decided to quit when this case is over.*

Brooks' tone of voice even gave Rudy a chill when he bellowed, "We recorded a call you made to your contact. So how did you know what number to call?"

Dr. Hanover blanched again as he flinched. Then, a defeated sigh escaped. "It was for emergencies. I panicked."

"Why was this an emergency?"

"I got scared because she had a visitor. After that first visit, the medication seemed to be less effective. I thought it was a little early for her to develop a resistance to the meds. Patients do, but not usually so quickly. Anyway, on the second visit, one of the guards alerted me to how lucid she seemed. I figured she was pretending to be drugged when I checked her in private because when I came to the visitation room, she was very alert as if I hadn't given her anything. So, I called him."

"So, the guards were in on your deception?"

"No, they were only following my instructions."

The interrogation continued for several hours and revealed how he started, names of other patients he misdiagnosed, what happened to those patients, how he covered up his actions, and why he cooperated.

Chapter 32

Frankie came in with Phaedra's nightcap. He had noted that her health was deteriorating lately, but he hadn't expected her to be curled up in a comforter on the bed rather than sitting in the rocking chair in front of the fire. As usual, he dismissed their private nurse for the evening. When she shut the door, he sat next to Phaedra. She was flushed, perspiration had beaded on her forehead and upper lip, and her breathing was shallow.

He placed her drink on the nightstand as he straightened the lapel on his smoking jacket. He looked down at her and could tell she was very sick. "You must be feeling pretty bad to be in bed so early."

"I just couldn't get up today." Her voice was weak, and she didn't open her eyes.

"Does that mean you don't want your nightcap?"

"You'll have to help me."

He scooted her up against three pillows. "Are you sure you want it?"

"It might help me sleep."

"I'm sure it will," he said with a crooked smile as he picked it up and he held it up to her mouth.

She took a sip. "Would you call the doctor? I think I'm just getting worse."

"He's out of town tonight, so I'll have him come tomorrow."

She groaned.

He held the glass to her lips again. "Come on, you can do it."

She took another sip. "My taste buds must be affected. That tastes strange."

"That's because you're sick. But it'll do the trick."

"When's the big job again?"

"Just a couple more days. We're almost ready." *She's losing her memory. She's asked the same thing every night for the last week. Good timing.*

"What did we decide about the sisters?"

He held up the glass, encouraging her to take a long drink. "You don't need to worry. I'll take care of them."

She looked confused. "I don't remember telling you what to do." Her breathing increased as if she was panting. Her eyes became panicky. "Are you sure the doctor's out of town?"

"That's what I said. What's wrong?"

"I can't seem to catch my breath. Call 911."

He pretended to call. Then he lifted the glass to give her another sip, but she turned her head. He put his hand behind her head and forced her to drink the rest. "There that should do it."

"What? You think a drink is going to help?" Her breathing became more rapid.

"Oh, yes. It will. Oh, and thank you."

"For what?" she wheezed.

"Remember when we were kids, and Eric gave you your nickname, Frankie? I know how you hated it, but I thought it was cute, being the phonetic equivalent of your initials. The kids teased you mercilessly; but kids will be kids, you know. You *do* know why he kept pestering you, don't you? He liked you, but then in high school, you had to get revenge by leading him on and dumping him. But at the prom? In front of everyone? That's when I realized how ruthlessly calculating you are."

"What are you getting at?" She wasn't getting enough air and seemed to be gasping for breath.

"It's because of your history with him that I asked him to be your private doctor."

She glared at him. "And why would you do that? I told you at the time, I didn't want anything to do with him."

"Just be patient, and I'll get to the point. You see, I knew he wanted to get back at you, not just for that high school feud, but because of the sabotage of his internship with John's Hopkins."

"But I didn't do that! You did!" she gasped.

The crooked smile grew on his lips. "I know. I just told him it was you to make sure he'd cooperate."

Fear pinched her face. "Cooperate? What do you mean?" Suddenly, she grabbed at her chest.

He patted her cheek. "It shouldn't be long now."

"What are you talking about?" she gasped for air and from fear. "What did you do?" she wheezed.

"With Eric wanting revenge, he gladly came aboard as your doctor after I told him my plan. He's told everyone you have a failing heart. Of course, that's not true. It's what I wanted everyone to believe. I orchestrated the whole thing."

He put his finger to her lips when she tried to protest. "Shhh. Let me finish. There's a reason your nightcaps have tasted different. It's not because you're sick; they're the *reason* you're sick. You see, I've been giving you very small doses of cyanide in your night caps for the last few months. That's what makes everyone think you have heart trouble, so we won't need an autopsy when you're gone." He shrugged. "And even if there was one, the cause would be difficult to find. And if there was a problem, I'd just buy the medical examiner."

She clutched the comforter tightly and grimaced in horror. She tried to cry out, but he held his hand over her mouth.

"Now, now. I can't let you do that." His crooked smile turned sinister. "Don't worry; everything will go smoothly without you. We've already gotten rid of anyone who might suspect that you, Phaedra Rose Carelli, are actually Frankie. Now that all the men know *me* as Frankie, you're no big loss."

Panic pulled at her face as she stared at him in disbelief.

"One other thing, now that your spoiled brat is gone ...." He paused with a self-satisfied huff. "He caused far too much trouble and drew an intolerable amount of attention from the media. Good riddance."

She gasped in horror. "Don't tell me you had him killed?!"

"I can honestly say no. It was his own doing. He just picked the wrong woman. Her husband didn't much care for that kind of shenanigans." He leaned forward and whispered, "At least, you didn't have to bail him out again." He smirked and sat upright again. "His indiscretions are actually the reason I started this clean sweep – well, mostly. So, when you're gone, nothing will change, nothing, for me, that is." He put on a mournful façade. "We'll mourn you, of course."

She groped for the phone. Bringing it to her lap, she tried to turn it on. Immediately, her hands dropped into her lap, and she sobbed.

"What a shame. I must've forgotten to charge it."

Desperate, she tried to get up, but fell back on the bed. As she went into spasm, he held her down, making sure the last thing she saw was his evil grin. He waited for five minutes, regularly checking her pulse to be sure she was dead. He pushed her down under the covers and straightened them. He made sure the phone was in her hand, turned on the bedside lamp, and turned off the overhead light. "Good night, Frankie," he said as he closed the bedroom door. When he got to his office, he called for Pierre to finalize the plans for the big job.

It was about two in the morning when they heard the scream. They raced upstairs where Tanisha was still screaming in Phaedra's bedroom.

"What's wrong?!" Frankie demanded as he rushed in.

"I think she's dead. She isn't breathing!"

He rushed over to the bedside and realized he hadn't taken the cocktail glass with him to clean it. He pretended to be checking Phaedra for pulse, breath, any sign. "Call 911!" He started CPR.

Tanisha ran out.

"Pierre, call the doctor!" Frankie commanded.

"The phone's right there in her hand." He walked around to pick it up. "Oh, it's dead."

"There's one in the hallway," Frankie barked.

When Pierre ran out, Frankie put the glass into his jacket pocket.

Within minutes, police, paramedics, and her doctor arrived.

Frankie put on a good performance of the grieving widower as the doctor gave the medical history to the police, explaining that they were trying to make her comfortable in the last stages of heart disease.

As the paramedics got ready to take her out on the gurney, Frankie managed tears as he sadly caressed her cheek.

The police stayed for several minutes asking more questions. Satisfied, they left.

Since Tanisha was hysterical, the doctor gave her a tranquilizer and ordered her to go to bed.

Frankie and Pierre headed down to the office after everyone left.

When Frankie closed the door, Pierre asked, nodding at Frankie's coat pocket. "Is that the glass that was in the bedroom?"

Silence.

Pierre frowned. "It was poison, wasn't it?"

Frankie pulled the glass out of his pocket and set it on the desk. "It *may* not have been natural causes." He glared at Pierre. "You need to keep quiet about this." He tapped the edge of the glass.

Pierre nodded. "No problem, boss."

Pierre was the last person in the family who knew the truth – that his real name was Tony Ratone, and Phaedra was actually Frankie, and she called the shots. Pierre knew the history – that she was ready to take the position from her father, a cruel and domineering crime lord, and she had learned his tactics well. But the legacy fell apart when she got pregnant. That's when Tony helped Phaedra and Pierre make and implement their plan. Phaedra manipulated her father to be in position and Tony fired the shot. They had originally planned to dispose of the gun, the body, and any evidence that indicated it ever happened. But circumstances didn't work out as planned and the gun wound up in the evidence locker. That's when he recruited Pierre to make it disappear. Tony promised himself never to handle a gun again. He didn't want anything to incriminate him.

The next step was crucial to their plan. They moved to Portland and although Tony was only Phaedra's cousin, he took her name, Carelli, and pretended to be her husband. Even Brent believed he was Frankie. Although it appeared that he was Brent's father, Phaedra wouldn't allow him to discipline the kid, and Brent grew up thinking he could get away with anything. That was the biggest challenge Tony had: he had no control over the kid. Continually bailing him out had become their biggest expense. His only regret was that he'd never have the chance to make Brent face his consequences. But revenge was insignificant now.

Up to the present, even with the occasional nagging doubt, Tony was always grateful to Pierre and always gave him latitude for his help in implementing the plan to make him the figurehead. Over time, the gang had been slowly culled, and new men were brought on board. Pierre called him Frankie in front of everyone, and eventually all the men believed Tony was the real Frankie. Now, Pierre and Eric were the only ones who knew the truth. Too bad. That occasional nagging doubt had turned to raging certainty. Just *two more loose ends to tie up*. It wouldn't be long now, and Anthony Ratone would forever be Anthony Carelli, AKA Frankie.

When Pierre left, he called Shiv.

"What's up, Frankie?"

He glowered fiercely. "Not only was Doc incompetent, but I believe he was responsible for Phaedra's death." He leaned forward with mock rage. "He's a murderer, and he needs to disappear from the face of the earth."

Shiv's lips became a thin, hard line. "Gladly."

Frankie coldly stood up straight. "And I found out we have a leak – Pierre. It appears that while he was feeding stories to the FBI, he gave them crucial information. He turned traitor. Time is of the essence on both."

With increasing rage, Shiv snarled, "I knew we couldn't trust him. I'll have it done by sunup, boss. Since he ratted, how much do we have to change our plans on the job?"

"We can't change the timing. The shipment arrives as usual. We're going to have to change the route getting to the warehouse."

"Do we have time to do that?"

"We'll have to use plan B." Frankie ran his finger across his neck as he added, "This is important, Doc disappears with no hope of being found. But Pierre goes first, immediately!"

"You've got it." Shiv turned quickly and shut the door quietly as he left.

Frankie looked out the window to see when Shiv left the premises. Then, he locked the door and opened his safe. He pulled out all the evidence he had collected to frame the doctor. He put everything into a briefcase, grabbed some latex gloves, and went out the back way to make sure nobody would see him leave.

Wearing the gloves, he drove casually, going over the steps in his head. He'd park several blocks away so no one could make the connection that he was at Doc's house. He knew Doc would either already be passed out or be in the process of drowning his sorrows.

His affinity for alcohol was another reason Doc was such a perfect choice for this plan. Although Doc had controlled his alcoholism years ago, it was a simple thing to reintroduce the addiction by spiking his drink last year. It was too easy. That, combined with the stress of helping with Phaedra's demise, just pushed him over the edge. Frankie had even given him some expensive brandy and whiskey as a gift in the last few months to make sure. He would just make sure that he stocked Doc's house with a few more bottles. If that didn't prove he was culpable, nothing would.

He smiled thinking how Fingers had taught him several tricks on the computer. Now, he knew enough that he'd easily be able to create a record of the ticket purchase to Argentina, the ticket he actually bought in the doc's name.

It would be easy enough to put several drops of cyanide in the medication the doctor was giving Phaedra. He'd pour it out and place the empty bottle in the trash can to make it look like Doc was trying to get rid of the evidence. The motive would be revenge. Frankie had been careful to select the man who previously had a rocky relationship with Phaedra, one that ended badly. If asked, he'd be able to supply that information.

He'd create several condemning emails to support the motive he created. He would quickly pack a bag with the doc's belongings as if he'd packed for a trip. Of course, he'd have to destroy the bag. He would take the Doc's car to the airport parking, take the bus back to doc's house, and drive home. He hated the bus, but he wasn't going to take a chance that a taxi driver's records could be traced to him. And that disguise in the trunk would guarantee nobody would ID him on the bus. No one could know what he was doing, not even Shiv. When the police discover Doc didn't board the plane, they would likely assume that the ticket was a diversion. It didn't matter whether they believed he was on the plane or not, they'd never find the body.

Chapter 33

Rudy was there when the Feds got the phone call. Everything was already set to record any incoming calls, so Brooks put the call on speaker. "Hello?"

As Pierre spoke, Rudy soon realized there was even more that he didn't know. He listened carefully.

"Pierre here. I haven't got much time, so listen carefully 'cause I'm only going to tell you once. About that box of evidence, you're right, I was holding back. AR is Anthony Ratone, the kingpin. VP is Vic Parsons; he goes by the name Shiv. Back in '97, Phaedra Carelli's father was the kingpin of a gang, and she was going to take over for him. But she got pregnant, and he disowned her. Her cousin is Anthony Ratone. We helped her get rid of her father. She made sure he was home alone, Tony shot him, and I was supposed to get rid of the gun. Things didn't go as planned, and the police got involved. I arranged for someone to get the gun out of the evidence locker at the station, but I kept it for insurance. That's why it's in that box."

He gave a quick explanation how Anthony became Frankie, the kingpin.

"Frankie's planning a diamond heist in two weeks." He explained the details and then continued, with his tale about Anthony. "I'm telling you all this because Anthony Ratone killed Phaedra tonight, and he knows I know. I need protection, so I'm coming …" There was a loud thud, screeching tires, and a solid crunch. About ten seconds later, they heard breaking glass, and the phone went dead.

"Sounds like an accident." Riley commented.

"Where was the last GPS signal?" Brooks asked.

Riley clicked a few buttons and announced, "About five miles from here."

Brooks gathered three men, and they took off leaving Rudy with the rest of the crew.

The CB crackled. "Headed for the last reading. ETA ten minutes."

"Brooks must have had one of the other men drive since he's on the CB."

Rudy asked if they could replay the phone call.

Riley set it up in another room for him and an agent to listen to it. "What are you listening for?" Riley asked.

"The sounds on that accident, I want to hear them again. Something doesn't sound right." He listened to the call twice. By the time he came out of the room, Brooks was talking, "… found the car in a ditch off highway 30 in the industrial district. It's pretty badly damaged. The driver's window is smashed, probably the glass we heard breaking. No sign of Pierre *any*where."

Rudy's eyebrows went up. "Hey, Brooks, I listened to the phone call again. That breaking glass was after the crash. What do you think that means?" He had a hunch, but wanted to hear what Brooks had to say.

"The door is jammed and the glass is definitely inside the car as if someone smashed it in from the outside. So, it's possible Pierre was right. It looks like someone came after him and removed his body and his phone."

Riley shook his head. "At least we got the scoop on that gun. And who's really who."

A week later, a family had been hiking at Oaks Bottom when they discovered a body partially buried in mud amongst thick sedges and blackberry bushes. The Feds brought Rudy with them to the morgue to see if he could identify the body. Although the body had been made unrecognizable, Rudy knew it was Pierre. There were two small moles, one on his left earlobe and the other behind his right elbow. They didn't release the information; they didn't want Frankie to know they identified the body.

Chapter 34

Callie stopped in at a family-owned, convenience store on her way to Georgia and Rudy's house. She looked around and asked the young clerk where the barbeque sauce was. He directed her to the third aisle. She found it about halfway between the back and front of the store and squatted down to reach the bottom shelf. She heard the bell ring from the front door opening. Out of curiosity, she leaned to see who came in. A muscular customer, about 5'5", was wearing a hoodie that was pulled over his head and pulled down to a big pair of sunglasses. *Something's not right,* she told herself. *A hoodie in this weather?*

Creeping to the end of the aisle, she peeked around the end of it just as he put his hand in his pocket and pointed a gun-shaped bulge towards the clerk. He spoke with a deep raspy growl, "Collection time. And count it out."

She sneaked back to get two cans of chili. The shelves were metal, so she was careful not to make a sound as she picked them up. Stooped over, she tiptoed to the aisle near the front of the store. Keeping out of his line of sight, she made sure she had a straight shot. With furious control, she threw the first can. Before she could throw the second one, the first one struck the back of his head, sending him forward into a face plant on the counter. He slumped to the floor in a crumpled pile on his back.

Callie ran towards him and slammed her foot onto the wrist of the hand in his pocket. "Do you have a rag or something?" she demanded from the stunned clerk. "Hey! A rag!"

"Uh – yeah, okay." He reached under the counter and handed her the dusting rag.

She grabbed it and pulled the robber's hand from his pocket. Then she used the rag to pull out the gun. "Well, are you going to call the police?"

Reaching for the phone with a shaky hand, he stammered, "R-right. Got it."

When she pulled the broken sunglasses off his face, she caught her breath. She recognized him as a regular at the mob's mansion. "You got some twine or zip ties?" she called out to the clerk. She studied his description as the clerk, still on the phone, ran to another aisle, grabbed something from a shelf, and tossed her a roll of duct tape.

When she took her foot off his wrist, she saw the tattoo on his right hand. It was just like the one Rudy had drawn last year, the same one she asked the tattoo artist about and the same as the one she'd photographed on the other man at the mansion. A chill ran down her spine. After a brief shudder, she shook off the adrenalin rush and did a thorough job in hogtying him. *Thanks Georgia – just like a calf at the rodeo.*

She made sure to stay out of his line of sight until the police arrived.

She was finally able to leave after giving her statement to the responding officers. About halfway to Georgia's house, she realized she'd forgotten the barbeque sauce and had to turn around to pick it up. Although she was late for dinner, she was still proud of herself.

She walked to the back yard with a self-satisfied grin.

Sharon was making the preparations while Georgia sat, unwillingly, at the picnic table. Rudy had insisted. Although the surgery went well, she was now receiving the next phase of treatment, radiation. It was difficult for her to move around, so everyone else pitched in, and Sharon had been promoted to director.

Sharon had just brought out the last bowl when Callie came around the corner of the house with that unmistakable expression on her face. Sharon knew something was up, but she decided to wait until everyone was settled before asking her about it. Just a couple of years ago, Callie would be prattling a hundred miles per hour, announcing whatever news had excited her. But having worked with Rudy and Georgia this last year, Callie had learned some restraint. Although Sharon missed Callie's unbridled enthusiasm, she knew it was for the best that she exercise some self-control.

Callie sat down but didn't say anything except to apologize for being late.

Sharon sat down as she set the bowl on the table and looked at Georgia sitting across from her. She was sad to see her look so tired. The surgery and radiation were taking their toll. Of course, everyone expected that, but to see her actually weakened like that was difficult. Everyone wondered if she should be inside, perhaps resting more, but Georgia insisted on being included.

She noticed Rudy studying Callie. It wouldn't be long now, unless Callie's news was something that had to be discussed in private. That was happening more often, now. If that was the case, she might not even hear about it. Although she knew her daughter had to grow up, the adjustment was a challenge.

"Okay, I can't hold it in any longer." Callie's face lit up even more. "I've got to tell you something *really* amazing!"

Oh, good. I'll get to hear what it is. Sharon leaned in to hear every word.

"I stopped by a convenience store to pick up some barbeque sauce – sorry I didn't get it here in time for you to use it. Anyway, a robber came in, and I clocked him with a can of chili! Got him right at the back of his head, and he dropped like a stone! I had to stay and talk to the police. That's why I was late, so … sorry about that part."

Sharon groaned inside, trying not to think about what could've happened.

Gary's mouth hung open in shock.

Mark slapped her arm. "What were you thinking? You're not some super hero you know."

Jack just shook his head.

Rudy frowned sternly. "You know that was *dangerous*, don't you?"

"I know. But the opportunity was there, and I took it. I made sure he didn't see me."

When Sharon saw the tear run down Georgia's cheek, she caught her breath. "Are you okay, Georgia?"

Everyone looked at her, and she cringed a little. "When I started training you, I knew it was possible, but I didn't really think there would be danger." She looked straight at Callie when she added, "You have a lot more to learn. Yes, you're strong, smart, and savvy, but you still have *so* much to learn. Please, always discuss things with Rudy. He has a lot of experience, and he knows when it isn't safe to move forward." The apprehension on top of her illness seemed to etch ten years on her face.

Callie's face dropped as she absorbed Georgia's admonition. "I'm sorry." She looked at Rudy, "Can we talk some more afterwards?"

"Of course."

Well, here's the part I may never hear about.

It took about an hour to get Georgia ready for bed after everyone left for the night. Then, Rudy led Callie to his office and he directed her to sit in the 'electric chair.' He knew it made her squirm, but he needed the edge. When she sat down, he remained standing. "I could tell you were holding back something. What is it?"

"That robber was one of the men that I photographed at the mob's place. And he's the same guy that came to the nursing home claiming he was Vera's cousin. And he had that tattoo on his hand."

This case was getting close to home. He didn't know if anger, worry, or fear hit him the hardest. He realized he'd neglected his poker face when she reacted. "Did he see your face?"

"No. I made sure to keep out of his line of sight. Even when the police questioned me, it was outside. Oh, something else. I don't think it was an ordinary robbery 'cause he said it was collection time."

He asked her to check on Georgia while he made a call. Making sure the door was closed, he looked at his watch as he pressed one of the numbers on his phone. "This is Rudy. About three hours ago, the police picked up a hood in the act of robbing a convenience store. I'm pretty sure he was there to collect protection money. Get to the station and make sure he doesn't get out. He's one of our targets ... yes, that's what I said. Find some way to put one of your men on his interrogation. He could be a key player and get someone to watch over that convenience store, too." After more discussion on how the Feds would handle the situation, Rudy exhaled with relief.

When he let Callie back into his office, she asked, "What now?"

"Don't know. Depends on a lot of things. Let's hope for the best."

"What's the worst that could happen?" She grimaced.

"Let's just hope he doesn't figure out who you are."

She sank down, but her shoulders tightened even more. She knew she had a dozen questions, but she couldn't think of a single one right now.

"So, we wait and see. Then we go from there."

On the way home, she started worrying about Georgia and wondering what Rudy's phone call was about. He wouldn't discuss it, and that concerned her. She started to wonder if the thrill of being a detective/private investigator was worth the danger. Was she getting in over her head? Yes, it was exciting, it challenged her, and it made her feel alive. But for how long? She could die. This was serious.

Chapter 35

Roy shuddered. The clear night air had a chilly edge, but what could you expect? It was almost the middle of October, too close to November, the anniversary from when he proposed to Callie. He wondered if the chill was more related to his emotional state than to the weather. He sat on the log, the river glittering in front of him, but he refused to reminisce. Too painful. So, he waited, rubbing his temples, with his elbows resting on his knees.

The phone call woke him just after one, giving him so little time to get here that he had just made it. His heart pounded from nerves. This was it.

When footsteps on the gravel alerted him that his contact had arrived, he sat upright. The disguised voice came from behind. "Don't turn around. When you get to the station, call me with the number of officers on duty today. Here's the map showing the route. There will be several diversions in other parts of town. Make sure the cops are busy with them so they don't get in the way."

"Do you have everything I asked for?"

"It's all in the envelope with the map."

"I want to check it out before you leave."

"I'd expect it."

Roy heard the envelope slap onto the log next to him. He picked it up and pulled everything out. He held his flashlight in his teeth as he counted the money and checked all the rest. After taking the flashlight out of his mouth, he said, "Looks good. When is it going down?"

"Three hours and ten minutes. Don't forget to burn the map."

The gravel crunched as the man walked away, fading to silence until he heard the car door shut quietly and then tires driving away on distant pavement. He waited the required ten minutes and left. *Three hours to go, but I have a lot to do.*

When the diversions started, he knew he'd get a call to check in.

Rudy rushed into the warehouse. Yes, Sharon had come to be with Georgia, but waiting for her had delayed his departure by twenty minutes. Special Agent Brooks waved him over to the table where everyone was collaborating.

He filled Rudy in on the details that Roy had given them, showing him where the diversions were as they had been reported so far, a warehouse fire and a bomb threat. Several swat teams had already left to be ready to catch the mob members with the goods.

Rudy was allowed to go along, as long as he remained in the surveillance van. Even though he wouldn't be near the gunfire, he still needed protection, so he grabbed the gear and put them on en route.

Chapter 36

Frankie's good mood was a rare commodity. He was cocky with smug anticipation, and that encouraged everyone; this operation would be a shoe-in. The planned diamond heist was going to go down just as planned. Yes, they would garner a huge amount of money from selling the stolen diamonds, but the icing on the cake was the fact that they had completely outsmarted not only the police force, but the FBI as well.

Frankie and Pierre had counted on the FBI bugging Pierre's phone, and it worked out just as planned. Using that phone, they purposely fed them false information to lead the cops and the Feds to a warehouse at the opposite end of town. And with all the diversions they had set up, the law would never catch on.

There was only one hitch. Since Pierre was dead now, Frankie had to lead team Rhino, blowing the safe and coordinating everyone by phone. He really didn't like being hands-on, but there was nobody else to do it. The upside was that he wouldn't have to share the money with Pierre. They were in the clear, so he was confident. Thus, his good mood.

Frankie arrived early with team Rhino, the safe cracking team, to check out the warehouse for the umpteenth time. Again, he wanted to make sure the structure was going to do the job. Pyro, the safe cracking leader, gave Frankie a final walk-through. They walked around a multi-level frame that would contain the blast and prevent any damage to others. They had hung 2x4s from the ceiling and attached ballistic-quality canvases from the boards all the way to the floor. This construction would provide a strong but flexible makeshift room with 'walls' that, when the door or other parts of the safe flew into them, would absorb the blast. They would place the safe in the center, cut a hole in the top of it with a cutting torch, fill the safe with water, and place dynamite into the hole. The door was expected to blow right off, and with the diamonds being impervious to damage, it would simply be a matter of sweeping them up.

Frankie had assigned Knuckles and Ringo to man the police band for the last week. They listened for any outright statements or even hints that there was a change in plans or that they had caught on. But all they heard was chatter off and on that they were getting set up to take down the supposed electronics heist – at the wrong location.

The banter between these two occasionally drowned out the radio itself. They indulged in laughter, high-fives, and jokes about the 'fools on the goose chase.' They didn't care about missing small parts of the audio because they were having such a good time poking fun at the incompetence of the police force and the FBI.

The transmission crackled: "Detective Rollins reporting in. Haggarty and I are sitting outside the warehouse on the North side. No activity to report. Are you sure we're in the right place?"

"Keep the chatter down. We've been collecting intel on this job for weeks. *That's* the place, and it *is* happening."

Knuckles called Frankie on the phone. "We're good boss. The Feds are all over that fake warehouse."

The police were busy coping with all the diversions that the mob had created. In addition to the warehouse fire and the bomb threat, a sniper was shooting into a downtown apartment building, a max train had derailed causing a traffic jam, and a multi-car accident piled up on the Sunset Highway. With all on-duty police officers handling all that, only two officers could do surveillance in their squad car outside of the Best Buy warehouse. They occasionally broke radio silence to question whether they should be there or out helping their fellow officers since nothing seemed to be happening.

The Feds were split into several swat teams around the warehouse. Special Agent Brooks was in radio contact, directing them into position for the take-down. He had several agents posted along the transport route, ready to capture the members of Team Shepherd after the truck went by.

Frankie texted the team leaders to give them the go-ahead for the biggest night of their criminal lives. Each of the three sent out a group text to their teams to get into position and wait for further instructions.

The time finally came, and Frankie gave the go-ahead. Part of team Python was already parked in a long box truck behind the jewelry store with a forklift hidden in the back to move the safe. A minivan drove up, spilling three men at the back of the building. Fingers disarmed the alarm, picked the lock, and they rushed in.

They didn't have to worry about alerting anyone with any noise they made, for demolition by one of Frankie's contractors in the next block was making enough earth-shattering ruckus to camouflage any noise they'd make. The men set two explosives, one to open a space large enough to let the forklift in from the alley-side wall and the other to free the safe. They communicated by phone to coordinate the timing of the blasts with the demolition crew.

As the forklift driver drove out of the truck, the other men scrambled to remove the rubble so the forklift could maneuver. The driver went in through the blown wall to where the safe had been released. He simply picked up the safe with the forklift, drove it out to the truck, and placed it into the back. Two men jumped into the back with the safe, one of them pulled the back door down, locked it, and jumped in the seat next to the driver, who took off. It was just over ten minutes from arrival to departure. The truck backed into the open door of the warehouse and up to the structure they had built to open the safe. The exterior door was shut.

Each member of team Shepherd called in to let Frankie know the truck had passed the checkpoint without a hitch. Frankie chuckled. After the truck passed each one, the driver ended his phone call and started his engine to head for the warehouse by a different route to make sure there was no suspicion aroused from too many cars parading through the streets. In each case, as soon as the driver put his car in gear, another car slammed into the front fender. As each driver angrily got out, including Brick, he was cuffed and arrested, and unable to communicate to Frankie about their capture.

As each arresting pair checked in letting Brooks know they had captured another one of the check-points, Brooks smiled. Putting the GPS and bug on Brick's phone had paid off big time. Since Brick was on Team Shepherd, the Feds immediately knew where he'd be stationed; and with the chatter among the mob, the rest of the locations had been determined quickly.

Now to take down the warehouse. A swat team was waiting outside at every entry point. With all the off-site thugs caught, they were certain to get the rest of them. Brooks smiled like a cat ready to pounce on an unsuspecting mouse. He always had an adrenalin rush with these take-downs. Of course, he knew Best Buy was a smoke screen.

He glanced over at the small building where Rudy's nephew had opened his garage and thought, *what a stroke of luck getting that surveillance footage from Rudy. We got the plate number, ID'd the driver and passenger and the exact location of their destination. The Feds' own surveillance confirmed it all. And then, catching that robber! Bugging his phone, arranging for his release, and tracking him was priceless. They won't suspect a thing until we storm the place. Collaborating with Rudy was a lot more useful than I thought it would be.* However, he wondered why Rudy took so long to correct Pierre's early statement when he said Andre was the kingpin.

Another small detail bothered Brooks. Roy hadn't checked in after alerting them of the time of the heist, but they were still monitoring the GPS signal on his phone. He was apparently assigned to one of the diversions. He shook off the concern because he had to focus on the task at hand and be prepared for the worst, that the mob wouldn't go down without a fight.

Brooks was determined to prosecute Frankie to the fullest extent of the law. With Pierre's last phone call, there would be no question that Frankie would go to prison for the rest of his life – if they took him alive. Rudy had brought in a picture of Frankie, but he never admitted to how he got it. He wondered about that too. At least, they knew who to look for.

Adrenalin shot through him – the truck was here. He alerted everyone, and they were all ready for the go-ahead. Every possible entry point had been covered.

Rudy had been allowed to stay in the equipment van as long as he didn't leave it. He could watch as the federal agents manned the equipment: monitors displaying the heat-radiating bodies in the warehouse, images of the agents surrounding the warehouse, and the microphone chatter as Brooks gave instructions. Rudy was impressed that they were able to put up all the cameras without suspicion. Apparently, the Feds impersonated linemen working on power lines in the area.

Although the images from the heat-sensitive cameras were not nearly as clear as film, it was good enough to see where the men were. After the truck entered the warehouse, men repositioned themselves to shut the exterior door, unload the truck, move materials, and stand near exits. Several of them hovered around a large, block-shaped image as it exited the back of the truck. The three men walked with the image into what seemed to be a square cleared area surrounded by what looked like a large empty square. Puzzled, Rudy wondered what that was. They stopped in the center of the empty space, and after about a minute, one of the men left the area, leaving the rest who seemed to be working on something in the middle of the space. After about ten minutes, they exited.

As men moved around inside the warehouse, Brooks repositioned his men so that when they stormed the building, they would have at least a four-to-one advantage as they entered. Rudy watched anxiously, knowing that Brooks was waiting for the right moment. They had to catch them in the act.

BOOM!!

The equipment van shook with the explosion, and Rudy almost lost his balance. The video display flickered several times and then came back on. Brooks' men were storming the place and he could already hear the gunfire.

When the explosion blew off the safe door, the power was cut off from the building putting it in total darkness. At the same time, Brooks gave the signal to send in several smoke bombs through the windows of the warehouse. With night goggles and gas masks secured, the swat teams stormed the building. Inside, they heard the mobsters coughing from the smoke of the explosion and from the smoke bombs. Several of the mobsters had been nabbed before the rest of them realized what was happening. Amid the shouting, many started shooting aimlessly into the smoky darkness. A few unsuccessfully tried to escape the building.

Water that had filled the safe and then blown through the door covered the floor. The door had shot straight out with more force than expected. Although the canvas was ballistic quality, it wasn't attached well to the framework, and the canvas and several of the boards broke away, allowing water and debris to fly beyond the intended contained space. The mangled door, along with the diamonds and other materials from inside the safe, were scattered everywhere. Although the Feds stumbled over the rubble occasionally, it wasn't difficult to capture all the mobsters, some with minor injuries ranging up to several dead. The lights were turned back on when the melee was over.

Although Brooks wanted to catch Frankie, a bullet from one of his men hit the mob boss in the chest, and he had fallen face down, breathing hard, occasionally coughing up blood.

When the gang had all been subdued and cuffed, Rudy was allowed to leave the equipment van. He ran in just in time to see Brooks reading Frankie his rights. Even though he had been rolled over onto his back, it was apparent that he had been critically injured.

When Brooks was done, Rudy glared at Frankie and demanded, "You're going to die soon, so you might as well confess. How did you shoot Vera?!"

Frankie stared at him but remained silent. He clutched his chest with blood soaking his shirt, draining down his side, and mingling with the water on the floor. Reluctant at first, and interspersed with choking on his own blood, he eventually answered all of Rudy's questions, telling all; pulling on the shotgun to shoot Vera, injecting Jody with cocaine, arranging her misdiagnoses, trying to frame Vera for shooting Brent. He explained how he, Phaedra, and Pierre did away with her father, and he had just started to tell about Phaedra's demise when he stopped breathing.

Chapter 37

It was finally over. Guilt still nagged at him, but now he could give his full attention to Georgia. She'd gone through radiation and surgery and was currently in chemo again. Thankfully, yesterday was the latest treatment. The day after was always the worst, but today was especially hard. Being weak and nauseous, she wanted only to sleep on the couch.

The light noises that Rudy made while cooking or cleaning in the background seemed to jar her nerves today, so he decided to reread some of the files he had gotten from the Feds, just to keep informed. Just because he wasn't going out in the field anymore, didn't mean he wasn't still interested.

He sat across the room to give her space to relax. It was cold outside, so Lucky was in the house, and he was annoying her. Even though she loved the mutt, his persistent nuzzling apparently irritated her. There was no way she could relax. She looked like she was just about at the end of her tolerance, so Rudy decided to put him into one of the bedrooms. Just as he stood up, Lucky bumped the end table next to Georgia and tipped it over, dumping everything onto the floor with a crash. Tissues, hand lotion, medications, and breakfast dishes had spilled everywhere. She put her hand over her eyes, apparently trying not to cry.

Rudy came over to pick up everything from the floor. He groaned, and Georgia murmured, "Don't worry about the broken lamp."

"It's not that," he moaned apologetically.

She opened her eyes. He had her mother's picture in his hand as he tried to put the broken frame back together.

This seemed to be the last straw. Struggling to sit up, she reached out for it as she tried to hold back the tears.

"I'm sorry. I don't think it can be repaired," Rudy apologized. Then he looked confused. "Wait a minute there's another picture … and some paper behind the picture." He handed everything to her.

Confused, she took them. "I've never seen this before." She separated everything and saw that the paper was a letter. Feeling very weak, her hands dropped to her lap. "Would you read it please?" Her head drifted to the back of the couch.

He sat down next to her and took the letter to read it.

Dearest Ian,

Please forgive me for hiding your picture like this. Mick insisted I get rid of everything about you, but I just couldn't. I think it may have been a mistake marrying him. But I was desperate, and the girls needed a dad. I'll always love you and miss you, my dear Ian. I wish it was different.

Love, Olive.

Georgia's eyes sprung open as she sat upright. "What?" She reached for the letter and the pictures. "This is my dad, Rudy!" She stroked his picture as her tears flowed.

Rudy sat next to her and held her close as she sobbed. Eventually, she fell asleep with her dad's picture held tightly against her chest.

The next day was a little better. At least, she could function. She spent most of the day gazing at her father's picture. He understood that she wanted to have that image deeply imprinted so she could always envision it. In the picture, her father was standing in front of an old Hudson holding an infant that Georgia assumed was Alice. She drew her finger around his features: the slim face, his hollow cheeks, light eyes that she assumed were blue, and his curly hair. She wondered if he had red, dark blonde, or mousy brown hair. She smiled at his long ears and narrow nose that gave him a gaunt appearance. But his cheerful eyes drew her in. Rudy had commented that Georgia had the same happy eyes. That had to be what her mother found endearing. It certainly was the first feature that attracted Rudy to Georgia.

Rudy watched her from across the room. He smiled gratefully, knowing she finally had some peace.

"Rudy?" she asked weakly. By the sound of her voice, he wondered if she had something awful to say.

He put down the files and sat next to her. "What is it, Sweet Cheeks?"

"Can you take me to her, the other stepdaughter?"

"What on earth for?!" He instantly regretted speaking so sharply and said so.

Her sad eyes were at half-mast as she looked up at him. "I need to assure her that he didn't get to abuse any more girls after Alice and me."

He was astounded at the courage and grit of this amazing woman in his arms. For her to be so sick and still want to help someone, it amazed him. "Shouldn't we wait until you feel better?"

"We can't wait. She's got to be older than I am. I don't want to take the chance that she … she might not make it to hear what I have to say. Can we go tomorrow?"

He knew he wouldn't be able to dissuade her, and he wouldn't want to. Holding her back would do more damage to her recovery than the doctor-prescribed rest could help. "Okay, but we're going to take it easy, okay?"

She nodded gratefully. "Thank you," she whispered.

The drive took longer than the two hours he'd driven the first time. He was in no hurry to do this task. He wasn't even sure the woman would open the door to them. He had done everything he could think of to make the ride comfortable. He reclined her seat so she could rest her head easily, brought all her meds, including pain control, put soft music on the CD player, provided plenty of liquids, and, hopefully, pleasant conversation. He pointed out interesting sights as they drove by, held her hand often, and laughed at her familiar jokes.

Too soon, they pulled up to the farmhouse. Mounds of clutter filled the area, lumpy tarp-covered shapes, old furniture, and bags of trash marred the yard. The house and barn were in disrepair, and the fence had fallen down. He shook his head thinking how much worse it was now than when he was here last time.

Remembering what happened the last time, he hoped she wouldn't turn them away. He squeezed her hand. "Sweet Cheeks. I'll go to the door first. If she opens up, then I'll come get you."

"No, I want to go now."

"But I don't want you to use all that energy if she doesn't answer or isn't home."

"I'll be able to convince her."

He relented and helped her to the door. Several rings of the doorbell were fruitless, and three knocks on the door resulted in the same.

"Martha Harrison, I know you're home. Please open the door. I talked with you over a year ago, and my wife wants to talk with you, too. Please?"

More silence.

Georgia knocked. "Martha, my name is Georgia Burke. My mother married Mick Johnsen. I have to tell you something important about him."

A few minutes later, Martha opened the door just enough that she could see out. Although Rudy recognized her from before, she looked much older. The shoulder that he could see was in a tight shrug; he assumed it was from tension at seeing them. Her lips were pressed into a thin, curved line that turned downward. Her eyelids drooped down on her brown eyes, giving her a weary look. Before Rudy could say anything, Georgia stepped forward.

"Mrs. Harrison. This is my husband Rudy. I believe you spoke with him before?"

She gave one nod.

"I have something very important to tell you about Mick. I don't suppose we could come in?"

Martha looked behind her and shook her head. "No, you can't come in."

Rudy's heart sank. Previously, when he'd investigated her, he'd discovered that the neighbors had many complaints about her being a hoarder. He hoped that her being embarrassed wouldn't prevent her from talking. "Please, Georgia's sick and she really can't stand for long. And I'm pretty sure you'll want to hear what she has to say. Maybe we can sit on the front porch?"

The woman paused a moment. Then, she opened the screen door, came out, and quickly shut the door. She pointed to the porch swing and rocker at the end of the porch. "We'll sit over there." Coming outside made her pale skin look even more sickly.

He helped Georgia to the porch swing and sat down next to her.

When Mrs. Harrison sat in the rocker, Georgia started. "Mick Johnsen married my mother when my sister and I were only eleven and twelve. She was older than me."

"Your husband told me that last time. I'm sorry for you."

Georgia squeezed his hand. "I'm not here to get your sympathy. From what my husband explained about your conversation, I'm pretty sure Mick was abusive to you too. I don't expect you to acknowledge that, but the rest of what I have to say is very important. I'm not proud of what I did, but you can be sure that he never abused another child again after us."

Mrs. Harrison seemed to boil with hate as she blurted out, "You can't *make* someone like that just *stop!* He was *evil!*"

"Believe me, I know." Georgia seemed to struggle with the rest. "My mother worked two jobs, and he was supposed to take care of us to save babysitting costs."

Mrs. Harrison huffed as her gaze wandered out to the driveway. "I'll bet."

When she mumbled, Rudy thought she said, 'Sounds familiar.'

He was sure Georgia heard it too because she grimaced. "Exactly. But we were afraid of telling our mother because we figured she loved him, and we didn't want to hurt her." Rudy felt her shudder and squeezed her hand.

"He had diabetes, so we researched the library to find out ...." He was surprised when she closed her eyes and vice-gripped his hand. He didn't think she was capable of that much strength right now. "... to find out how to kill him."

The woman's unseeing gaze instantly focused on Georgia.

"We talked it over and after dinner, we put sleeping pills in his coffee and waited until he was asleep. Then she injected him with large doses of insulin. It only took a few minutes." Georgia stopped to swallow hard. "The coroner said it was an accidental overdose." She sighed. "I just wanted you to know that no other girls suffered. I would've wanted to know, so I figured you would, too."

Mrs. Harrison's shoulders slowly dropped down as she stared out to the road. A peaceful calm seemed to descend on her as she started to rock. Her mouth relaxed and softened, and a tear ran down her cheek. She nodded and without looking at them said quietly, "Thank you." She continued to rock and stare for several minutes.

After a while, Georgia looked up at Rudy and whispered in his ear, "I knew it. She finally has closure."

The ride home was uneventful. He was pleasantly surprised at how peaceful Georgia looked after this taxing mission. She was right, and he should have known better. The body isn't the only part involved in healing. Just as important is the mind and emotions. He was amazed at how much he'd learned from Georgia. She was more than smart; she had a solid grip on life. He actually caught a glimpse of himself in the mirror, smiling. Things were going to get better.

Chapter 38

Gary had never guessed he would ever feel like this. Funny how life changes, and how it changes you. Most of the animosity was gone, and he actually had some hope for him and his dad – just a little. He didn't want to be disappointed again, probably because it would hurt even more this time. But it truly seemed like Billy had changed. Having a positive relationship with his dad was new territory, and he really didn't know what to expect or how to handle it.

Thank goodness, he had the Coopers to help him with his attitude. As he dwelled on their help through the years, that familiar warm, comfortable, and safe feeling wrapped around him. He was so thankful they had been there for him, and that they still were. Hoping for a measure of that closeness with his dad, he had decided to pay it forward; maybe he could help his dad adjust his attitude too. Although, Sharon's comment about Billy not being able to connect emotionally made him question the degree of success on that.

The house had been repaired with everyone's help. Gary had used practically all of his paychecks to pay for the materials, but it looked better now. More importantly, it was safe for them to live here. He shuddered to think about all those years of neglect, and how fortunate it was that someone hadn't been injured sooner or more seriously.

But that was in the past, and he looked around the house with pride. He stopped to think how that was a new feeling. He'd never felt that here before, and it felt good. He smiled. It was time to pick up his dad.

He climbed into the Coopers' borrowed van. He got teary thinking about the scene where literally every member of their family offered to go with him and then about all the love they'd given him through the years, accepting him as one of their own.

He declined their offers to go with him, knowing he had to try to connect with his dad alone. If any of them were there, that couldn't happen. He realized now how private a person his dad really was. He would never express his feelings with someone else there, even if he could.

A sudden pang of guilt hit when he realized it was only recently that he was able to express thanks to the Coopers for all they did for him. Yes, he'd written a note of thanks a few years ago, but he felt the sentiment more deeply now, and he'd responded by expressing it profusely. Too bad he had to live with all that anger for so many years. He shuddered to think that without the Coopers' help, he might've turned out like the dad he hated in the past.

Knowing he was different now, he shook off his regrets. How thankful he was for that. Even with this new resolve, he still worried how things would go for him and his dad.

His heart rate quickened when he pulled into the parking lot of the nursing home. No matter how much he wanted to reconnect, he knew it was possible that nothing would change between them. Still, he held onto that glimmer of hope.

When he came to Billy's room, Marci was helping him get ready for release. "Well, Billy, it looks like the canary is almost freed from his cage."

Gary was surprised when he saw his dad look up at her and start singing *You Are My Sunshine*. He came in slowly, watching them interact and wondering what could have brought him to the point of singing. He couldn't remember his dad singing at *any* time in the past. Although he sang it out of tune, he was actually engaged, and Gary's face softened as he nodded with approval. He waited until Billy was almost done before he asked, "You ready to fly the coop?"

Startled, Billy stopped instantly and looked at him.

"I'm sorry, I didn't mean to interrupt. You go ahead and finish."

Flushed, Billy shook his head.

I'll bet Mom's right. He's probably as anxious as I am on how this is going to go. I guess I've been just as much at fault as him for our disconnect.

Marci helped Billy get into the wheelchair. "There. I'm sorry to see you go."

Billy smiled. "Me too. Well, not about going, about not seeing you every day."

She bent over and gave him a hug. Gary had a twinge of guilt when Billy hugged back.

"His bags ready?"

Pointing to the closet, she said, "Right over there." Marci started to push the wheelchair out, and Gary followed with the bags.

Gary was so consumed with nagging doubts, worry, guilt, and anxiety that he tuned out Marci's small talk on the way to the lobby. He wiped a wet eye with his sleeve just before they approached the front desk.

"I believe all the paperwork is ready for your signature, Billy." Marci picked up the clipboard and a pen and handed them to him.

As Billy signed the papers, Gary shook Marci's hand. "Thanks for everything." He leaned over to whisper into her ear, "And thanks for bringing him out of his shell."

"It was my pleasure. You still have someone to stay with him while you're at work?"

"Sure do. Mom and Dad. You know, my other parents."

She chuckled. "Yes, I remember when you told me about them."

He blushed.

The drive home was uneventful and uncomfortable. Gary struggled to make conversation. *Why should this be so difficult?* he kept asking himself. So, he decided to act as if he didn't really know him. He berated himself when he admitted that was actually true. Out of the blue, he thought about his dad singing to Marci, and he wondered what had brought it on. He tried small talk again.

"Dad, Sharon or Jack will be with you while I'm at work. Do you have something to keep you busy?"

"What do you mean?"

"Oh, like a hobby. Some people do crosswords, crafts, collect things. What interests you?" He glanced over at his dad and became concerned when Billy looked stumped. "Maybe we can start something for you. How about we start a garden?"

Billy grimaced. "In my condition?"

"We can start slow. First, we can draw out a plan, where to plant it, how big, what to plant. That should take a while, just until you get up to speed. If we like it, we can enlarge it."

"I guess. Never done that before." He seemed to think about the possibility.

That question about his singing still nagged at him. He decided to follow Jack's training, 'It doesn't hurt to ask.' He gathered up his gumption and spit it out, "Dad?"

"Yeah?"

"I really liked hearing you sing to Marci. I was wondering, how come you never sang before?" He glanced over at him and was concerned to see a pained expression. "Dad, what's wrong?"

When Billy's lip quivered, he felt alarm. "What is it? Did I say something wrong?"

Billy inhaled quickly, turned red, and looked out the passenger window.

Gary pulled to the curb, put his hand on his father's shoulder, and looked at him tenderly. When Billy turned back to him, there was a tear in his eye.

"You can tell me. I'll understand."

Billy wiped the tear away and looked down, ashamed. "That Marci, she reminds me of your mom."

Gary was ten when she died, but she'd been sick for the last few years with cancer. He didn't truly remember what she was like before she got sick, only a few pictures to look at. He thought about what his dad had said for a moment and realized Marci did resemble her. Mom didn't have Marci's bronze skin, but the shape of her laughing eyes, her pixie haircut, and the way her smile invited you in did remind him of her. It all made sense now. He wondered if that resemblance was why he didn't see her as a potential girlfriend. It would be weird to have romantic feelings towards a mother figure.

Billy interrupted his reverie. Billy hung his head and his voice seemed tight with emotion, "When Marci laughed, I felt like your mom was there. We used to sing together ..." Billy started to smile. "... and she would always tease me how I couldn't carry a tune in a bucket. But we had fun singing because her laugh made it okay."

Gary was overwhelmed seeing this side of his dad. He listened intently.

"We'd put on the radio and sing along while we did the dishes or when she'd help me with the yard." Billy coughed to clear the catch in his voice. "Even when she got sick, we'd sing while you were at school. I didn't feel much like it, but she insisted." He put both hands over his face and started to sob, his shoulders convulsing.

"It's okay, Dad. Let it out." He used his sleeve to wipe his own tears.

When Billy gained some composure, Gary rubbed his dad's shoulder. He took a deep breath and asked, "So, why didn't you tell me before? I would've loved knowing that."

Billy shook his head. "It hurt too much, to talk or even think about it." He slowly looked at Gary, guilt and sorrow weighing him down. "I'm sorry. I just couldn't. I just buried all the pain. And I guess I kept everything else down with it. When I went to AA, they told me what I already knew, that I was self-medicating with the bottle." He let out a sigh. "I'm so ashamed. That wasn't fair to you. You have every right to hate me."

Gary swallowed hard. "Hey, we have a fresh start now, and we have all the time we need to talk." Gary squeezed his arm. "I don't hate you, and even though you didn't ask, I forgive you." Gary bit his lip. "Can you forgive me for checking out? I treated you pretty badly, too."

Billy's lips pushed into a firm but quivering line as he nodded. He reached out for Gary's hand. "I had it coming, I don't blame you one bit."

"So, you were actually going to get on that airplane?"

He chuckled. "Yeah. I guess it didn't turn out like I planned."

"I'm touched that you tried. That means a lot to me. But now we can go forward, maybe try to make up for lost time."

Billy nodded and Gary pulled him over. They hugged for a long moment as both of them let the tears flow.

"Oh, by the way, we're invited for dinner at Jack and Sharon's tonight."

Billy looked down at his hands and fretted.

"Something wrong with that?"

"I don't feel like I deserve their pity."

"Dad. It isn't pity. They're just being neighborly. And they're family. You'll enjoy yourself."

Chapter 39

Rudy looked at the New Year as a new beginning. The three months since the mob was taken down had passed quickly. He'd been able to focus on Georgia, and she had really needed it. He still struggled with the guilt of not being entirely available before then.

He held the door open for her while balancing the cake plate. She wore a red scarf over her bare head. She had shaved it to equalize the bald spots that had overtaken her scalp. Besides, the freezing weather made her feel colder than everyone else.

"We're here!" he called out.

Callie came running to help them. "I'll take that cake off your hands."

"I'll bet you will," Georgia teased.

Callie put her hand on her hip and teased back, "Then I guess you'd better fight me for it!"

Georgia laughed. "Maybe later when the boys can cheer you on."

"No thanks, I don't want to lose face in front of them."

Georgia waved her hand as if swatting a fly. "Pssh. As weak as I am, there'd be no contest."

Callie gave her a hug and then carried the cake through the kitchen to the back yard, waving them on. "Everyone is on the patio."

When they got to the newly enclosed patio, everyone was busy setting putting food on the table and placing chairs. Sharon came out with the last of the food, a macaroni salad.

Jack was at the barbeque tending the chicken and ribs. He looked up and joked, "Leaving the cooking to me, huh? And here I thought you were going to be the new grill guru."

"Nah. You're doing just fine." Rudy chuckled and he gave Georgia a squeeze.

The picnic table was finally loaded with food, and a card table had been added at one end to accommodate all the family, including Gary and his dad.

It was almost back to normal, multiple noisy conversations, laughter, and passing dishes of food.

Rudy smiled contentedly, tapped his fork on his glass, and announced, "We just got the results today. Georgia's numbers are acceptable, and the chemo is over."

Everyone clapped and cheered, with Mark and Gary hooting as if at a game.

"There's more good news, although not as good or personal." He knew he had their attention when all of them became quiet. "Georgia and I talked, and I'm going to open a center for low-income and at-risk kids. Something like a Boys and Girls Club. That means I really am going to quit being a P.I."

Georgia chuckled. "I'll believe it when I see it."

Rudy looked hurt. "No, really. And to prove it, I'm going to set Callie up in her own office with all my equipment." He turned red and shrugged, "And if my equipment is out of date, I'll update it."

"No way!" Callie stood half-way up and leaned over the table with both hands on the edge. "Are you *kidding*?!"

"No joke. You pick the office, within reason, and I'll pay for the rent until you get some clients."

She laughed hysterically. "Wow. I can't believe this. Thank you, so much."

"Don't worry about it," he reassured her. "Of course, I'll still consult when you need it."

Everyone congratulated her on her new business.

Looking at Gary, Rudy added, "About that center, I've seen what personal attention can do for a kid …"

Gary's ears turned red.

"… and I want to have a part in that for other kids. I'm setting up a charitable foundation to fund it, and I've already located an empty store to convert."

Mark frowned. "Can you afford that?"

"I've already started fundraising. Plus, after all my years as a detective, I've got some money stashed away, but it's going into the pot anonymously."

Rudy saw Georgia's subtle reaction, recognizing that she knew exactly where the money was coming from. He continued as if nothing happened, "I figure the building will be ready in four months." He turned to Mark and said, "I'd like to offer the position of director to you."

Mark's fork stopped halfway to his mouth, and he stared cautiously at Rudy. "Seriously?"

"Of course. I know you haven't got a job yet, and you have that degree in business management, so I figured you'd be a prime candidate." Rudy stammered, "*If* you want the job."

"Are you kidding?! That would be awesome!" Mark broke out in a huge grin. "And I didn't even have to interview for it."

After everyone congratulated them, Rudy hesitated. "We're going to need a nurse to be on duty too. Know anyone?" Although he knew exactly who Mark wanted, he played dumb.

Mark laughed. "Funny you should ask. Marci's graduating in May. I'm sure she'd love to jump on board."

Jack grinned knowingly. "I don't suppose you're suggesting her because of any other reason?"

Mark chuckled. "So, you could tell, huh?"

"Mark, Mark. Although you weren't even a glimmer in my eye, I was a young man once myself ..." He cocked an eyebrow when he added, "... centuries ago. Don't you think I'd know the signs?"

"Okay. I guess I wasn't very subtle. Yes, we're dating. And yes, it would be nice to work with her, but we still have to ask her."

"Of course. We wouldn't want it any other way. Have her call me."

Still wearing a big grin, Mark said, "You got it," and dug into a chicken thigh.

Callie nudged her brother. "Why didn't you tell me you were dating? I think it's pretty cool, you and her. I guess I should've picked up on it when I saw you two meet the first time. I was worried we'd never get Vera out of there in time with you googly-eyeing her."

"Googly-eyed? Come on, Sis," he said with a mouthful.

"Hey, if you saw yourself, that's what you'd say. 'Nough said." She nodded triumphantly.

Sharon smiled. "What happened to Heidi, your treasure hunt partner? I thought for sure you and she were going to pick it up again."

Mark shrugged. "We've both changed. Being in the car for two hours helped us realize there wasn't a spark anymore."

Callie had a glint in her eye when she asked, "So is that why you didn't have very many pictures?" She waggled a single eyebrow.

He rolled his eyes. "No! Nothing happened. We just talked and discovered we have different priorities now." He stopped and eyed his mother. "Wait! How'd you manage to get us on the same team?"

Sharon blushed. "I had Rudy's help. He figured out a way to pull certain names, so it was easy."

Rudy held up a defensive hand. "She asked me to do it, so don't let her off the hook." He saw Gary's face flush a little. *So, you figured it out, huh. I won't say anything if you don't, but apparently, setting you up as partners for the scavenger hunt didn't work for you two, either. Too bad. I thought for sure you had a connection.*

Mark laughed. "Thanks for doing that, though. I wondered how I'd feel. Now there's no guilt, so I can proceed with Marci."

When Mark turned to Callie, Rudy thought the jig was up. "We're going bowling next Thursday. Why don't you and Gary come along? It'll be fun."

Rudy saw Gary's eyes widen. At the same time, he detected an urgent look in Mark's eyes, but no one else seemed to notice.

Callie shrugged. "Okay with me. How about you, Gary?"

His ears were red as he said, "Sure, I'll go."

"Does anyone know ..." Sharon looked concerned as she ventured, "... what happened to Vera and Jody?"

Rudy took a breath before telling all. "You heard all the news reports about how the crime syndicate was taken down."

Everyone nodded.

Then, he looked at Jack, "That's why I insisted you not go to the garage that day. It was too close to where everything was going to happen."

Alarmed, Sharon jerked her head to Jack. "What?! How close?"

Jack took her hand. "The shootout was a block away."

She wilted with dread.

"Remember when Rudy came to check out my security system, he saw one of the hoods drive by on the security display. Later, he heard more as he worked with the Feds, and he just figured it out. Then when he told me to stay home, and he made me promise not to tell you until it was over."

Sharon squeezed her eyes shut in a tight grimace.

"It's okay," Rudy reassured them. "We're all safe now. The heads of the crime family are all dead, and what's left of their minions are in jail."

Mumbling inaudibly, Sharon covered her face in relief.

Rudy made an effort not to look at Callie as he continued, "What helped us most was that Roy was acting undercover with the Feds. Since he'd taken that bribe a few years ago …"

Sharon's hands dropped, and she sat up with a start. "What?! He took a bribe?"

She grabbed Callie's arm and looked her in the eye. "Is that why you two broke up?!"

Callie nodded.

"Oh honey, I'm so sorry. Can I ask what happened?"

Rudy interrupted, saying softly, "I'll tell you later." He cleared his throat to continue, "Anyway, since the mob figured Roy was overlooked in the sweep of the station, they thought he'd be easy to buy because he had taken a bribe before. They contacted him to get him on board. The Feds knew all that and put a GPS on his car and a tap on his phone. The mob paid him to find out how many officers were on duty, where everyone was located, and make sure the escape route was clear." He paused. "But there was a hitch."

Sharon frowned. "What do you mean by a hitch?"

"Everything didn't go as we thought. The Feds were tracking him with the GPS. It looked like he was busy at one of the diversions, but, apparently, he left his phone in a squad car and ran off with the money the mob paid him. Nobody knows where he is."

Rudy watched Callie stare at her plate.

Sharon started to rub her shoulder. She whispered, "It's okay to cry, honey."

Then he noticed a hopeless sadness in Gary's face as he watched Callie shrug.

Trying to change the subject, Mark asked, "So, what happened to Vera and Jody? You never answered Mom."

Happy for the distraction, Rudy put on a smile. "Jody was cleared of all charges around the shooting. It turns out that her father-in-law was responsible for shooting Vera. In the struggle, he pulled on the gun to aim at Vera and forced Jody to pull the trigger. It all happened so fast that Jody didn't realize it until thinking about it later. Oh, one more thing about Jody, the crime boss hired the psychiatrist to write a false diagnosis and to keep her drugged so the story wouldn't come out. He's in jail now, by the way."

"Oh, Gary, you wondered why Jody was so lucid on your second visit with her. It turns out she cheeked the drug they were giving her so it wouldn't affect her."

Gary slapped the table, startling everyone. "I *knew* something wasn't right!"

Billy's mouth dropped. "*You* were in on it?"

Gary blushed. "Yes, but Callie did most of it."

"And *you* suspected that drug thing?"

He nodded.

Astonishing everyone, he grabbed his son and gave him a mighty hug.

Gary sat stunned.

"I'm so proud of you, son."

Slowly, Gary snapped out of his shock and hugged him back. "Thanks," he said with a catch in his voice.

Rudy waited for the moment to pass before continuing, "Not to interrupt, but as for Vera and Jody, they were cleared of suspicion in Brent's death. As it turned out, the husband of one of his conquests had caught Brent with his wife and shot him. As you heard on the news, with Vera being the spouse, she was the prime suspect and Jody the next, especially with both of them apparently missing. The mob tried to frame Vera by calling in an anonymous report about seeing her at the scene. But it would never have worked because we had Vera hidden at Bonnie's house. And Jody was being sequestered by the FBI. Besides, Vera wasn't in any condition to hunt down anyone.

"Since Brent and Vera's in-laws are all dead, she's going to inherit everything. The girls have been reunited and are currently living at a hotel. The mansion is being inventoried, and then the estate has to be settled before they can go in there, after the Feds search the place for evidence in the trial for the remaining henchmen, that is."

Sharon shook her head. "I feel so sorry for them. All they wanted was a family that cared." She looked expectantly at Jack.

Jack chuckled. "Yes, you can invite them over."

She gave him a hug.

Rudy slapped his forehead. "Oh, one other thing. You know that article about Brent supposedly raping that maid? Well, the cook is her cousin, and she told me where to find her. Brent really did do it, and Vera wants to help her with raising the baby that resulted from it. Vera's going to give her a job as a maid, and she can live with her and Jody. Actually, it'll be more of a friend position."

Sharon got a little misty. "I'm glad things are finally going well for them."

It was starting to get dark, and everyone said their good-byes. Rudy and Georgia drove home quietly.

She looked over at him and placed her hand on his between them. "I've been a little out of it lately."

"You don't need to apologize. I understand."

"Actually, I just wanted to clear up something."

He frowned with worry. "Did I do something?"

"Oh, no. I just want you to explain something about those girls."

Relieved, he said, "Shoot."

"I think I heard you say something about Vera's family thinking she took the money out of their account in Switzerland. What made them think that?"

"Apparently, Brent took her on a vacation the same week we were there. Then, just before Jody, actually her father-in-law, fired the gun, Vera said, 'Don't do it, or I won't tell you where the money is.' Well, nobody knew *I* took that money, so they assumed *Vera* took it."

"Then, what money was Vera talking about?"

"That's a good question. I don't know."

After everyone cleaned up the back yard, Mark pulled Gary aside and said, "Have you told her yet?"

Gary rolled his eyes. "No. Not yet."

"It's been six months since we got home. What are you waiting for? This is ridiculous! If you don't, I will."

"Don't you dare. I'm not a little kid that needs his hand held."

"Then *act* like it."

Gary looked past him at nothing in particular. "Right."

"Do it before Thursday, okay?"

Gary sighed. "Believe me, I've been trying."

It's now or never. Gary decided to ask Callie to carry the leftover chips and dip while he helped his dad get home. *We can talk over there.*

There was small talk as they slowly went next door. Gary helped his dad into the recliner, handed him the TV remote, and went into the kitchen. Still unable to bring up the subject, he said, "So, what do you think of Rudy's offer to get you going as a P.I.?"

"I'm shocked and a little scared. It's really going to happen."

"You've already got some experience under your belt. What's so scary?"

"*You're* asking that?"

He huffed, "Yeah, well. You know I wasn't planning on that field of work, so it took me by surprise. Yes, I was scared. But you – *you* were prepared and wanted it." He put the leftover dips into the fridge.

"Rudy said that if you stop being afraid, then you get careless. I guess being afraid has to go with the territory." She shrugged.

"You want some tea or coffee?"

"Sure. Tea, please." She leaned towards the living room, "Hey, Billy, you want some tea or coffee?"

"Yeah, coffee with cream, thanks," he called back.

Gary filled both the coffeemaker and teapot with water. His pulse rate increased, and he started to sweat. "What did you think of what Rudy said about Roy?" He set the teapot on the stove to make sure to be facing away from her so she wouldn't see him stressing.

She didn't answer right away.

Oh great. She's thinking of a way to say it that won't hurt my feelings.

Finally, she said, "I can't believe it. He said he always wanted to be a policeman. Well, that's not going to happen. I'm shocked."

He put some beans in the grinder. "But how do *you* feel?"

"I don't know what you mean? Didn't I already tell you?"

He took a deep breath as he put the filter and coffee into the coffeemaker and pushed the start button. He sat down across the table from her and realized she'd see his red ears. "What I mean is do you still have feelings for him?"

"Well, he'll always have a place in my heart."

Gary felt like his breath dropped out from the bottoms of his feet. But he had to ask, "Romantically?"

She frowned. "I guess I just feel sorry for him. He's a nice – *was* a nice – person. I guess I was right not to trust him, not to put my faith in him."

He watched as she looked up. He was sure she was looking at the perspiration on his forehead. Although she didn't mention it, he knew she saw it.

"Why do you ask?" she said strangely.

Unable to decipher her tone, he studied his hands, which were intertwined on the tabletop.

"It's true, then?"

He looked up quickly. "What's true?"

"What Vera said."

He cocked his head and squinted. "Why, what'd she say?"

Callie's face turned red, and her mouth opened as if to say something. Then she paused. "Just tell me if it's true. When we were at Bonnie's house, and you left to get some supplies for Vera, she told me, 'I wish Brent had looked at me the way Gary looks at you.' When I asked her what she meant, she said you were in love with me. Is that true?"

He felt his ears and face get hot. *Just great. Dead giveaway.* He tried to swallow the large lump in his throat, but it wouldn't move, so he nodded.

She sat frozen, just staring at him.

He thought he saw tears welling up, but he wasn't sure. It's hard to tell when you really don't take a good look. Finally, the lump went away, mostly, and he croaked, "So, what now?"

She bit her lip and fidgeted.

He bent his head down as he mumbled, "I knew it. You don't feel the same way."

"I don't know. I've thought about what she said, and I'm flattered."

Well that's a clincher. Trying to save my feelings. "So, you're saying you aren't interested."

"I didn't say that. What I meant is, I don't know if I'm ready to move on. I like you a lot. You're a great friend, and I'd hate to lose that."

"Please. Stop. You're just making it worse."

"I'm trying to say that I haven't ruled out the idea of us being a couple. I just don't know … yet." She moaned. "Look, I want to keep you as a friend, and eventually, that friendship might grow into something more. Please don't be mad."

He shook his head. "No. I'm not mad." He sighed. *It's hopeless.*

She reached out to hold his hand.

"Don't do that. It's just torture."

She grimaced. "I'm sorry."

The silence seemed excruciatingly long and overbearing.

She pressed her eyes shut and finally asked, "Can we keep going as we have? It'll give me time to adjust."

He shrugged.

"Does that mean yes?"

He looked up sadly. "You just don't give up, do you?"

"Does that mean *you* want to give up?"

The pained expression on his face made her wince with regret for saying that. "That's not what I was thinking. No, it's okay."

"Does that mean we're still on for bowling?"

He shrugged again. "Sure. Why not?"

Chapter 40

"This feels weird," Jody murmured.

"What does?" Vera said as she looked at her sister in the driver's seat.

"This car. It makes me uncomfortable."

"Why? Because it was Brent's?"

"Well, that too. But, it just seems kind of out of our league, too fancy."

"I could get used to it."

Jody shrugged. "Maybe."

"We're almost there."

"It's been a long time."

"Actually," said Vera, "I've been here a few more times than you."

"Why didn't you say something? I would've loved coming along."

"I'll tell you later." The hint of a smile flickered across Vera's face.

Jody parked the car at the edge of the lane. "I'll get the tool box from the trunk. You lock the doors."

Vera laughed. "Really? All you have to do is press a button. Big job, there."

Jody chuckled. "Oh, right. I keep forgetting about that. Fancy car, electric locks."

Jody looked at the flowers in the box as they walked up the grassy hill. "I like the Snowdrops. We'll have to get some colorful flowers when spring gets here."

"Jody?"

"Yeah?"

"Did you do it?"

Jody looked at her sideways. "Do what?"

"Did you kill Brent?"

"You were there. Mr. Carelli had his mitts all over that shotgun. After you went down, well, everyone told you what happened after that. So, I didn't get the chance."

"No. I mean did you *kill* him? You know, when he actually died."

"If I had been free, then I probably would have. But I was in custody, so there was no way."

Vera nodded. "I just needed to know."

Heavy remorse weighed on Jody's face. "I'm really sorry you were shot, but Mr. Carelli was so strong."

Vera put her arm around Jody's shoulder and hugged her tightly. "I know."

When she finally let go, Jody raised an eyebrow. "Where'd that come from?"

Puzzled for a moment, Vera frowned. Then she smiled as she asked, "The hug?" She thought about it and shrugged. "I guess I picked it up from the Coopers. Feels nice, huh?"

"Yeah, I noticed that. At first, I thought they were all fake."

"So did I. But I can see they really mean it, and I like it."

Vera put her arm around Jody's as they walked up the hill.

As they approached the grave marker, they paused again.

"I wish we could've afforded a nice headstone for Mom," Jody bemoaned. "We should do that after the estate is settled."

"Perhaps sooner."

Jody frowned, wondering what she meant.

"At least the flowers will make a nice frame for the marker."

Jody set the box down next to the marker, and they both knelt down.

When Vera started to dig, Jody grabbed the trowel. "Here, let me do that. You're probably still pretty sore and weak."

Vera shrugged. "Okay, but make sure to dig deep."

"Why? You're not supposed to put these in very deep."

"I have my reasons," she purred.

Jody looked at her sister suspiciously, but dug anyway.

With Vera's instructions, she dug a wide hole, six inches deep. When the trowel hit metal, Jody leaned in to see. "What? What *is* that?"

With a sly smile, Vera urged, "Well, pull it out."

Jody sat back on her haunches and glared at her sister. "O-kay." Then she dug out more dirt, loosened a metal box, pulled it out, and asked again, "What is this?"

Vera dusted the dirt off the metal box after Jody placed it on the grass. "Remember all the times I caught Brent cheating on me?"

Jody's fierce snarl almost matched the tone of her voice, "What of it?"

"Remember how I always made him pay for it with expensive gifts and then I sold them?"

Jody's eyes lit up. "Is this where you put the money you got?"

She nodded with a smug "Yup. I never told you where it was because I didn't want you to let it slip."

"I always resented you for not telling me, but I guess it could've happened."

"At first, I saved this so we could escape. But now, we'll use it to live on until we get my inheritance and sell the mansion." She rolled her eyes. "Some people want to make sure we don't take anything before it's been inventoried." Then she shrugged. "And then there's the fact that the police are all over the place collecting evidence. That'll probably take a while."

"So why did they release the car so soon?"

Making air quotes, she said sarcastically, "They searched it to see if I was involved with the 'family business.' Since there wasn't anything in there, and I needed transportation, they let me have it." Then she smiled, "You didn't know this, but after one of Brent's escapades, I made him transfer my name to the title. Besides, how could they say no to a victim?"

Jody shook her head with a sly grin. "You're pretty good at that."

"At what?"

"Using use your looks to get what you want."

"Well, it got me a rich husband."

"Yeah, right. Look where *that* got us."

Vera shrugged in defeat. "I guess that didn't work out so well." She looked up with a sad face. "Maybe we should rethink this con stuff?"

Jody studied her for a moment. "Seriously? You want to do that?"

After several seconds of reflection, Vera laughed and answered with a mighty, "*No!*"

Jody gave her a shove, "You had me worried there for a second. So how much do you have?"

"Over six hundred thousand."

Jody's eyes popped. "Whoa!"

"We can start looking for a nice four-bedroom house. Then we can send for Angela and her son. Did you know that Selena, the cook, is her cousin?"

"No way! But why'd she take the job as a cook? She *had* to know what happened." Jody slowly started filling in the hole to accommodate the flowers.

"Selena told Rudy where Angela lives, and it turns out she isn't in Mexico after all. He said she wanted to find some evidence, maybe get someone to tell the truth so Angela could be avenged. I've already been talking with her, and she'd love to stay with us." Vera sighed. "What do you think of giving her son half the inheritance? After all, he is Brent's son."

Jody looked at her suspiciously. "Wait. Are the Coopers rubbing off on you?"

"I don't know, but I feel drawn to them. I like how I feel when I'm with them." She looked over Jody's shoulder at nothing in particular. "Do you think they're for real? Not just scamming us to get some of our money?"

"I don't know. I've never known anyone to care before."

"Tell me about it!" Vera put her head down. "We should probably keep our guard up." Then she rolled her eyes. "Guess what."

"What?"

"We should have expected it, but when the news got out about me inheriting everything, guess who's been calling."

Jody sneered. "Don't tell me... the creeps who dropped us when they couldn't get paid from the state anymore?"

"You got it. "I had to get a new phone with an unlisted number, but I expect they'll be knocking on the door when the estate clears."

Her sister pointed her finger at her angrily. "They're not getting a dime." After a moment of thought, she added suspiciously, "Do you suppose the Coopers are worming their way in to get a piece of it?"

"I don't know. But they did help both of us. And they never said anything about getting something in return."

Jody squinted. "I don't believe it."

"Let's wait and see. Of course, we'll keep up our guard, but I think we should test them out." She shrugged and then brightened. "Oh, did you hear, Gary and Callie have gone out on their first date."

Jody looked puzzled. "Wait a minute! First date? When they came to see me, she said he was her fiancé. What gives?"

Vera chuckled. "They just said that so the hospital would let him in to see you, too."

"I'm beginning to feel like an outsider. What else don't I know?"

"You can ask them yourself. We're invited to dinner this Saturday."

Jody's jaw dropped.

"I know. I couldn't believe it either. Even after all the drama is over, they still want to see us. It'll be a good way to check them out. You know, to see what they're really like. Find out if they have an agenda." Vera shrugged. "Who knows, we could actually belong somewhere. Like a family?"

When Jody's face reddened, Vera leaned over to give her a big hug. "Let's hope not everyone is like the Carellis or our relatives."

Jody's face dropped as she leaned back. "Or like us."

Vera looked strangely contrite. "Do you think we could change?"

"You always said we could do anything we put our minds to."

Vera gave a knowing nod as she gazed at her sister. After a few moments, she took a cleansing breath. "Okay, let's get these flowers planted. You fill in the hole a little more, and I'll put in the plants."

Just then, Jody let out a joyous laugh and fell back on the grass with her arms stretched out.

Vera smiled at seeing her little sister so happy.

When they finished planting the flowers, they put the metal box inside the tool box so no one else at the cemetery would notice their treasure. With satisfied smiles, they walked casually back to the car and drove away.

List of Characters

(Be aware that there are some aliases in this story, so there is some overlap of characters)

Rudy Burke

Georgia Burke

Detective Roy Jackson

Callie Cooper

Special Agent Brooks (FBI agent)

Todd Maxwell

Pierre Martine

Agent Juarez (FBI agent)

Alice Frainey (Sharon's mother)

Sharon Cooper (Callie's mother)

Jack Cooper (Callie's father)

Bonnie Parker (Sharon's half-sister)

Charlotte Knapp (Sharon's half-sister)

Arlene Rand (Sharon's half-sister)

Mark Cooper (Callie's brother)

Gary Rawlins

Billy Rawlins

Bertie (Nursing home resident)

Mr. Townsend (Nursing home resident)

Inez (Nursing home resident)

UNWANTED FAMILY

Vera Carelli

Lucky (Georgia's dog)

Heidi (Mark's old girlfriend)

Marci Collins (Aide at nursing home)

Roger (Nursing home resident)

Elaine (Nursing home resident)

Agent Riley (FBI agent)

Frankie (mob boss)

Shiv (mob thug)

Jody Perkins (Vera's sister)

Brent Carelli (Vera's husband)

Phaedra Carelli (Brent's mother)

Tanisha Brown (Carelli's maid)

Carlos Hernandez (new police Captain)

Ralph and Cora Cooper (Jack's parents)

Tina (Aide at nursing home)

Anthony Carelli (Phaedra's husband)

Angela Pelayo (Carelli's past maid)

Patrick Hughes (Director at nursing home)

Harriet (worker at Oregon State Hospital)

Fingers (tech guy for mob)

Dr. Mercer (Georgia's doctor)

Mick Johnsen (Georgia's step-father)

Lissy (Alice's nick-name)

Don (Sharon's father)

Selena Cortez (Carelli's cook)

Vic Parsons (Carelli's gardener)

Uncle Fergus (Vera's and Jody's uncle)

Jeff (guard at Oregon State Hospital)

Rodney Calvin (Rudy's alias)

Aunt Betty (Tanisha Brown's aunt)

UNWANTED FAMILY

Dr. Hanover (psychiatrist at Oregon State Hospital)

Eric Arnico (Phaedra Carelli's doctor)

Brick (mob thug)

Pyro (mob thug)

Knuckles (mob thug)

Ringo (mob thug)

Detective Rollins

Detective Haggarty

Ian (Georgia's father)

Olive (Georgia's mother)

Martha Harrison (one of Mick's step-daughters)

UNWANTED FAMILY

About the Authors

Sandra Denbo and her daughter, Tamarine Vilar, live in Portland, Oregon, which is the setting for their stories. Sandra has five children, Tamarine being the youngest. Sandra has had a wealth of experiences and has met a wide variety of personalities, each with their own idiosyncrasies. This fertile bed is the source of ideas for creating the characters you will learn to love and hate. Sandra has always had the ability to clearly describe ideas and feelings.

Tamarine Vilar has one son and also lives in Portland. She has a Bachelor's degree in English with a minor in writing from Portland State University. Because Sandra loved to read, she read to Tamarine from infancy. As a result, reading became her favorite way to relax. Professors and fellow students alike have enjoyed her natural ability to evoke emotion, even tears, with her writing, and have encouraged her to continue writing.

UNWANTED FAMILY